Gallows
Iron

B J MEARS

The Dream Loft

First published in Great Britain in 2014 by The Dream Loft
www.thedreamloft.co.uk

ISBN 13: 978-0-9574124-6-0
ISBN 10: 0-9574124-6-0

Dedicated to my grandfather,
Frederick Elias Mears.

*

Special thanks
to Joy for your support and for help with the blurb
to my ever-diligent editor, Edward Field
and to all the friends who have
helped along the way.

'All that is necessary for the triumph of evil is that good men do nothing.'

Edmund Burke

'Never, never, never give up.'

Winston Churchill

Contents

Prologue

Chapters

1. The Thames
2. Angel
3. The Tombs of Chacarita
4. Eucrates Onuris IV
5. The Parchment
6. Extraction
7. The Power of Ghosts
8. Alfric Crane
9. Gallows Iron
10. The Spear
11. The Source
12. Knife's Edge
13. Blades of the Sturmabteilung
14. Ghost Squad
15. Albert's Death
16. Estancia la Candelaria
17. The Haunted Forest
18. Mulungu
19. Crossing Over
20. The Heart
21. The Rite
22. Caged
23. Ghost Finder
24. Old Magic
25. Night & Fog
26. Hunting
27. Control
28. The Inventory
29. Banjul

30. The Mariana

31. Vault 65

32. The Ring

33. The Casket

34. Sheol

Acknowledgments

Prologue

São Paulo, Brazil: 0100 Hrs.

Crickets chirped their soft symphony as motion-sensing lamps blinked to life. Halogen light shimmered though a shifting entity. The General entered the regal, stone house, leaving the temperate night air to glide effortlessly through lavishly adorned walls and across glossy, marble flooring.

The General was one of the more powerful entities among those recently reinstated to the Reich, and strong enough to move some objects of the physical world. As a ghost he could vanish before humans at will, but he remained visible, choosing to climb the stairs like a living human. He searched for other ghosts as he ascended, knowing that ghosts could not hide from one another unless concealed by something of the physical world.

He knew that the house belonged to the Vice President of Brazil. He also knew that, tonight, he would find the Vice President unattended, and he found him so, asleep. The General paused at the foot of the bed. He looked down, checking his own appearance: Nazi officer uniform all in good order. He waved a hand playfully through the head of the sleeper, who twitched and rolled over. The General glided to a handsome dresser, collected a handgun from the second drawer down and checked it for bullets before returning to the bed with the gun poised at his hip. He cleared his throat. With mild irritation at the sleeper's indifference, the General reached down to give the bed sheets a firm tug. The exertion of carrying the physical gun and moving the bedding was a drain on his power, but it did the job. The Vice President stirred, turned over and was drifting back to sleep when he realised he was not alone. He looked up, face paling at the presence, and recoiled in his bed, backing up into silken pillows and an unyielding, teak headboard. Groping beneath his pillows he dragged out a gun and emptied its magazine into and through the General, startling the still of the night. Across the room bullets lodged harmlessly in wall plaster as the General laughed.

Terror contorted the Vice President's face and, for a moment, the General feared that the man might die of fright before mission completion, but he continued with the plan as his training dictated, gesturing with the gun.

"Who are you?" muttered the Vice President.

"That's not important. Move."

Hands raised in submission, the Vice President nodded and backed his way around the room to the open door. He traversed the hall as the ghost followed, aiming at the man's head for added incentive. The General smiled. He would not need to use the gun. Fear alone held enough power for his task.

The Vice President backed his way through the house, pausing at the front door to fumble with the locks. He staggered out into the night, breathless with panic, where an arc of armed men and more ghosts awaited.

The Thames

Central London

Tyler May viewed the scene before her with trepidation: the bench where he had sat to look out over the broad stretch of the Thames in the shadow of Westminster Bridge. The sound of the lapping river sent a shiver through her as she ran her eye down the stone steps leading to the submerged bank; steps she had once used in flight. The water level was higher than it had been that unforgettable night. Sunlight glinted on every crest of the rippling surface. She would submerge before long and it would be cold, even with the thick, protective layer of her figure-hugging neoprene wetsuit.

A copy of The Times lay folded on the bench. Tyler grabbed it to scan the front page.

GHOSTS: A FACT OF LIFE

It's official! Following recent, remarkable events, ghosts have become an undisputed, recognised field of science. Parapsychologists are studying phantoms and have bona fide, documented, scientific proof of their existence. Although they continue to be illusive and uncooperative ...

"Tell me about it." She ditched the paper.

Old news...

She glanced across the bridge recalling the site packed with thousands of ghosts from the contrap, four years before. She sensed ghosts drifting along the street around her, and knew none of them were showing an unhealthy interest in her presence. They came and went, leaving her with no sinister feelings. It was different when a malicious entity was nearby. Then the hackles of her neck would rise involuntarily. The ghost of Albert Goodwin was there, as always, watching over her every move. He remained invisible, hiding his soot-stained shirt, waistcoat and shorts, his bare feet, grubby boyish face and curly hair, but she sensed him as tangibly as she had felt the newspaper in her hands.

Oak leaves floated by. Autumn's early reaping.

Tyler was also aware of the pedestrians gawping. What did they see that was so intriguing? An athletic girl of eighteen in a wetsuit with diving fins and mask. She felt ridiculous and wished they would all move on, wished she had taken the trouble to have police cordon off the area for the investigation. She was MI6, after all. It would not have been beyond her powers.

Oh well, better get on with it. We've already delayed the moment for months because Mojo wanted to be here when we did this.

"Is this gonna take long?" asked Lucy Denby, glaring through her heavy goth makeup. "Only, I've ordered two thousand TAAN hoodies and baseball caps and I have to go check a sample at the printers."

"Know what? You can be *so* annoying."

"What colours are you getting?" asked Melissa Watts. She held a towel and fretted while Lucy dumped scuba gear on the pavement and stalked up and down behind the bench like a possessed Hell bird.

"Black, of course."

Melissa shrugged. "Right."

Tyler hefted the dive tank on and strapped it in place, tested the air flow and checked the gas gauge, ready to dive. She drew out the ghost machine from the neck of her wetsuit to study the small heart symbol incised on its smooth, silver casing, wishing she knew its meaning; the last of the ten symbols to be understood. She did not have the faintest clue as to its function although she had tried everything she could think of to trigger it.

She set the contrap's switch to the *Past Eye*, focused on the bridge and drew back the lever where the chain met the silvered edge. She watched time reverse through the contrap's crystal lens. She was experienced with the strange, silver device; had used it many times to look back in time. It took her less than five minutes to zip back four years and locate the exact moment that Leopold Bagshot-Mcguire paused, mid-bridge, to take out his newly acquired contrap. Her contrap. Tyler watched as he examined it and spoke to someone on the other side of the *Ghost Portal*, knowing it was Travis, the Norman knight, the ghost who had tricked Bagshot into the portal.

She watched it all happen again, there on the bridge; A flash of neon blue as Bagshot's spirit bolted into the crystal lens; saw the contrap leave his hands to roll from the edge of the balustrade and plummet into the Thames below as another figure, her younger self, made a grab for it, missing it by inches. It disappeared into the water, lost.

She turned her attention to the bench at her side, drawing the lever further round the contrap's edge to make time fast-forward several minutes, slowing when the gloved ghost of Mengele rested his meddling backside on the narrow, wooden slats.

Josef Mengele. Joseph Meddler, more like.

The thought of that name shook her physically and she reached out to the bench for support. There he was; Christmas Eve, deep into the night. She watched him take his place and gaze at a certain spot on the surface of the Thames, the collar of his long coat turned up, the brim of his trilby shadowing his eyes. He took out a golden pill box from his pocket and turned it over in his hands. She glimpsed a motif on the small box: an imperial eagle carrying an encircled swastika. She heard him mutter and she drew the lever back to listen again, hoping to discern more. The words did not come as a surprise, but rather as confirmation. It *was* as they had feared: Mengele had indeed set out to rescue the ghost of Adolf Hitler from the *Ghost Portal*. She replayed it again to be sure she had heard correctly.

"I'm coming for you, mein Führer."

Tyler fast-forwarded through the next couple of hours watching Mengele remain statue-like on the seat, peering at the water where the contrap had entered. She let the film-like images play at real time when he left the bench and walked down the steps to the small gravel bank and all the while he eyed the water. She stood and took a few paces forward to follow his progress. He removed his shoes and his coat. He folded the coat neatly, placing it over the shoes before dropping his trilby neatly on top of the pile. Tyler descended the steps, tracking him through the *Past Eye* as he walked into the water. He waded out until he was deep enough to swim to the exact place below the bridge where the contrap had fallen, and dived beneath. Tyler shadowed him the whole way and pulled her diving goggles over her eyes to dive. Murky water clouded her view and she lost him immediately, but she floated face down and adjusted the contrap's lever until she glimpsed him submerging again so that she could follow, diving one handed, aided by the drive from her fins.

Mengele seemed to have no problem sinking to the river bed. Nor did he struggle to find the contrap in the slick ooze. His hands plunged into the mud and came out grasping it. Tyler glimpsed a chink of its silver in the gloom. He adjusted the contrap's switch and took something from his trouser pocket. He spoke, releasing precious streams of bubbles and Tyler could not hear, but knew exactly the words he said.

Phasmatis licentia.

She saw the golden pill box, Hitler's pill box, held against the contrap and the depths were at once illuminated with an explosive, blue light as Hitler's ghost shot from the portal into Mengele's form. She glimpsed Hitler's sullen, ghostly face. Mengele adjusted the contrap again, this time setting it to the *Safeguarding Skull* and walked along the river bed and out of the river, strolling as though in a park.

Tyler abandoned her pursuit allowing the contrap to fall on its chain at her neck, and swam to the bank. She didn't need to watch him leave the river to be confronted by her younger self with a canister of Mace UV Defence Spray. She remembered it all as if it was yesterday. Four years ago, Mengele had possessed the contrap for a matter of minutes and yet, in that small space of time, had succeeded in bringing Hitler back from beyond. She dragged herself out of the water, slipping off her fins to walk up the steps back to Melissa and Lucy. She noticed Chapman had arrived while she had been busy.

"Well that confirms it. Mengele is also Hitler. Two ghosts. One gloved body. I saw Mengele summon Hitler's ghost from the portal."

"Makes sense of the weird mood swings you witnessed," said Melissa. "One minute Mengele's in charge, the next, Hitler surfaces. Sounds like they're fighting for control."

"Must be a real party in there," muttered Lucy.

Melissa looked thoughtful.

"And I'm guessing the physical body has retained Mengele's form as he was the initial ghost to be gloved."

"It's just as well we know where we stand," said Chapman, as Tyler ditched the scuba gear, wrapping herself in the towel that Melissa offered.

"We're going to need another Hitler artefact for sure if we're to stand a chance of summoning his ghost into the portal. If we use one for Mengele at the same time, maybe it will work this time." Tyler eyed the three bullet-like capsules strung on a chain around Lucy's neck, each containing a summoning artefact for the remaining gloves. Now Hitler had resurfaced they were one short.

"I'm on it," said Chapman. "I'm sure Melissa will

want to do some research, also. Between us we'll come up with something." He turned to Lucy. "How's the leg?"

"Getting there. I'm giving it a pretty intensive physio every day. High calcium diet. Give me a few more weeks and I'll be as good as new."

"Good. I've a feeling we'll be sending you back out very soon, maybe chasing one more artefact."

"Living for the day, Sir."

Chapman nodded. "The good news is we do have a possible lead on Mengele, or Hitler, as we now know."

"We're calling him the oppressor," said Lucy. "It's less confusing."

"All right, the oppressor. Anyway, we found something. It won't surprise you to learn it's in Argentina, but I don't want to say any more yet. Don't want to get your hopes too high. As soon as we know more..."

"We'll be ready," said Lucy.

*

Albert watched Tyler pace her room, edging the long, lead casket, back and forth. Inside the closed casket, six Mordecia chains laid folded, ready for use against the gloves. Tyler's problem was that no one knew where the gloves were, even though it was becoming globally obvious what they were doing. They were stirring a war.

Why is Chapman being so secretive about the new lead?

Tyler wasn't the only one feeling it. Lucy, previously laid up for months with a broken femur, was slowly going crazy and Melissa was worrying herself to death. Tyler feared if the three of them were not set loose on a mission soon, they would all be the worse for their confinement.

"Any ideas, Albert?" asked Tyler, ignoring the chime

of her mobile as it registered a message.

"Relax, Missy. Just give 'im a few days. I'm sure 'e's doin' all 'e can."

"Relax? Easier said than done."

"Aye."

Lucy stuck her head into the room.

"That was Chapman. Get your coat."

*

Tyler, Melissa and Lucy were surprised to find the ghost of Zebedee Lieberman in Chapman's office along with several heads of departments, of whom the girls had only a vague knowledge. Tyler recognised the Director General of MI6 among them. *Must be serious!* The girls greeted those they knew and Chapman introduced them to the others.

Zebedee removed his top hat and inclined his head in greeting.

"So this is why you wanted to be released," said Tyler, running an eye down his black, tailed suit with waistcoat and pocket watch, and pausing on his highly polished shoes. "You're looking very dapper. Albert, you might as well come out. Seems ghosts are welcome today."

"You're very welcome, Albert," said Chapman. "We presumed you'd tag along in any case."

"Quite a gathering," said Tyler, eying Chapman with suspicion as Albert materialised at her side and doffed his sooty cap to Chapman and the other officials.

"Isn't it just?" said Zebedee with glee. Chapman cleared his throat.

Just exactly what is going down here?

"You've been called to this meeting because each of you has a part to play in this. Please, take a seat. Yash, take us through what you have, if you will."

Yash, a Sikh wearing a sharp, charcoal suit and a black turban, worked a large, transparent touchscreen at the head of the room. They watched images of maps of São Paulo and images of its bustling hot streets as he talked. Recent photographs of Mengele's gloved ghost flashed up, strobing; him getting into a car; leaving a shop; drinking coffee and smoking cigarettes at a side street café, cleanly shaven and dark hair slicked back.

"Josef Mengele, AKA the Angel of Death. He escaped the allies and retribution for his war crimes in World War II, and lived out his life moving around South America using a host of fake names until he died in 1979. As you all know, he has returned from the grave and is once more in hiding."

Lucy chipped in.

"His ghost was located and brought back into our realm by a man named Leopold Bagshot-Mcguire and his team of Nazi scientists. They created the GAUNT machine and used it to glove his ghost to the body of a living human: an innocent boy called Steven Lewis. We've just confirmed that Hitler's ghost is also in that body. So Mengele is also Hitler. We also know of two other surviving gloves created by the same process; Reinhard Heydrich and Adolf Eichmann, also both extremist Nazis, guilty of mass war crimes."

Yash nodded his thanks and swiped through more images of Mengele on the control laptop while glancing with fascination at the ghosts in the room.

"Last week INCI, that's the International Nazi Conspiracy Investigation for the benefit of our newcomers, hit a payoff. We had to wait for corroboration, but earlier today it arrived, a confirmed sighting of Josef Mengele in Buenos Aires, Argentina." A series of stills showed Mengele in a trilby and shades leaving a doorway, walking to a car and driving away. "Not a prior address as far as we know, but a place on the outskirts of the city." Yash zoomed in through a crowded shot onto Mengele's figure and paused on a blurred but recognisable close-up of his face. "We know very little about the location, I mean, whether or not he's renting or borrowing it from a sympathiser. We suspect he simply murdered the owner and moved in. Agents are following up on this as we speak and we'll update you as we learn more. In the meantime we need to act swiftly. Get a team out there. Take him out. Pull a *Mossad*, as it were. We're calling it Operation Angel. While our agents are observing and mapping Mengele's daily schedule from afar, we need to prepare to go in for the extraction. Over to you, Sir." Yash took a seat as Chapman stood.

"Operation Angel. It has to be quick and it has to be quiet. No mess. We'll ascertain the best time, the best place. When we're ready we'll go in hard and fast, but first I want you three girls to get in close and scope him out. Recon the place. Once you're there, you can debrief and take over from the others. Learn his daily routines, where he likes to eat, who he meets. I want to know what time he brushes his teeth. Understand? I want details.

"From here on in we'll refer to the mark as Angel. I can't stress enough the degree of discretion required here. This whole case is as politically sensitive as it gets, so no cock-ups. We already suspect a political infiltration of Nazi sympathisers within the USA and we're pretty damned sure they're already taking over South America, so this entire thing is like a bomb waiting to blow. I'm sending you three girls because you can slip under the net where other agents can't. Nobody will suspect you. You don't look like agents and you're too young to be agents. Play your advantages. Use the contrap. Use your feminine charms. Use whatever you have."

"Ah-hmmm." Melissa nudged Tyler and whispered. "You should tell him..."

"What?" asked Tyler.

"...about the *sensing ghosts* thing."

"Something you'd like to share, Agent Ghost?" asked Chapman.

"Well, yeah. I guess." Tyler shot Melissa a dark look. "I'm pretty sure I can sense ghosts." Several of the officials eyed her doubtfully. "Ever since I came out of the chasm, I can sense them. Something must · have happened to change me. I figured it's because I was a ghost for so long. It's left me with an ability I didn't have before."

Silence.

"Well, use it," said Chapman at length. "It could come in handy, which leads me to your second objective. I'm increasingly convinced *they* are using ghosts to spy and to help infiltrate. It's another good reason for me to send you.

"Learn what you can. Find out how the NVF are using ghost spies. Your report on the Urubici castle spoke of a ghost army in training. Our investigations have also proved the existence of some industry there, though it seems to be nothing too sinister and certainly nothing criminal, just hand-forged metalwork, candlesticks, gates, fire irons and the like. All this by an international company named Hobson and Crane Industries. We need to know exactly what they're planning and how they're recruiting the ghosts. Zebedee and Albert will go with you, if they're agreeable."

"You try and stop us!" chirped Zebedee.

"I'm goin' wherever Tyler goes," said Albert.

"That's settled, then. Zebedee and Albert can assist in any way they can. Use them."

"What about the artefacts, Sir?" asked Melissa. "I couldn't locate anything on the web. Not one. Every museum or private collector that had something of Hitler's has experienced a recent theft or disaster. Uncanny, isn't it?"

"I admit, initial reports are discouraging, but we can't hang around. Hitler artefacts have become scarce. Angel has clearly been busy, collecting them to prevent us from acquiring them, and he's done a thorough job. So far my other researchers also failed to locate a single target."

"But you're sending us anyway," said Melissa, concerned.

"It's better than twiddling our thumbs here," said Lucy.

"It doesn't matter," said Tyler. "If I get the chance to use the contrap and put Angel into the chasm, I'm going to take it. I know we don't have an artefact, but if he was unconscious or something..."

"No. I'm sorry. I know that is *your* priority, but in the light of us having no available artefact to give you an edge, we want him taken alive, ghosts and all. We want to question him. I'm asking you to prioritize this mission over your own agenda. Can you do that?"

Tyler didn't like what she was hearing. "I'm not sure, Sir."

"I'm ordering you to do so. I give you my word, as soon as we're done interrogating, you may use the contrap on him.

"One last thing. Last night, the Vice President of Brazil vanished without trace from his house in São Paulo. Police found several bullets embedded in the end wall of his bedroom but no blood. No bodies. His abduction is not the first and it's concerning because he was a stabilizing factor in the Brazilian government, one of the good guys. I'm sending Weaver and Pratt to Brazil to look into it. You're heading to Argentina, but my point is, keep your eyes open while you're out there and don't take any unnecessary risks. We don't really know how far this thing has gone. Be in no doubt a war is coming and you don't want to go down in history as the ones who triggered it."

"No pressure, then," said Melissa.

"So basically, watch Angel and extract him, keeping him alive. Find out what the Nazis are doing with their ghost army and find out what's happened to the Vice President of Brazil. And do it all with total secrecy."

"Something like that. Are you complaining, Miss Denby?"

"No, Sir."

Angel

Crows Nest
(MI6 black site airfield and communications centre)
0600 hours

Tyler looked down the page. It was, beyond doubt, the most intimidating list she had ever contemplated.

Extract Angel from Buenos Aires
Locate and recover the Vice President of Brazil
Find out how the NVF are recruiting their ghosts
Find out what the ghost spies are doing
Put Reinhard Heydrich and Adolf Eichmann into the
chasm

She memorised the words before borrowing a lighter from a passing mechanic and burning the list. Flames greedily consumed the paper until nothing remained but ash.

Too risky, even to leave in my back pocket.

Tyler, Melissa and Lucy watched as agents hefted the long, lead casket from a grey Land Rover to stow it in the fuselage of the private jet. Other gear that would not pass airport customs' inspections followed in two black, armoured cases. Amongst other MI6 innovations, the cases contained a set of NanoSect spy drones; the latest in remote, robotic, drone surveillance technology. The plane left the hanger, taxied out onto the runway and took off, scheduled to land in an MI6 black site near Buenos Aires in a few hours, ahead of the girls' arrival.

"What's our cover?" asked Lucy.

"Apparently we're a group of friends on vacation," said Melissa.

Lucy pulled shades from the top of her head onto the bridge of her nose.

"I can handle that. Buenos Aires here we come."

Tyler was not in the holiday spirit.

"Just hope it doesn't turn into a *permanent* vacation."

*

Angel checked his watch in the shade of a low palm on the café's street front. He crossed his legs and read a newspaper while drinking coffee and sitting back.

"It's cappuccino," said Melissa, repositioning herself for a better view from the car window.

"No way. Americano," countered Lucy. "There's not enough froth."

"Does it matter?" asked Tyler, snatching the binoculars from Lucy and focusing on Angel. "I don't know how he has the nerve to sit there like that."

"It could be important. You never know. I'm putting Americano." Melissa jotted notes in her field-book. "Of course, we could use the contrap to find out what he drinks."

"Too risky and it's *not* important. At this proximity he'd sense the contrap the second I unboxed it. We'll have to stick with the old-fashioned methods for now, but I'm putting them into the chasm the first chance I get."

"You can't!" said Melissa. "Chapman wants Angel brought in. He gave you an order."

"An order I never agreed to."

"Doesn't matter. You still have to do it. Tell her, Lucy."

"Whatever *she* said," said Lucy, tracking Angel's every move.

Tyler watched the golden glow of the sun slowly sink beneath the city's dusky horizon.

An hour later when the sky had fully darkened and the city lights glowed with a warm plume overhead, Lucy started the engine. "The café's closing. Angel's on the move." Angel left his table and hailed a cab. Lucy piped MCR's *Welcome to the Black Parade* into the car's stereo and tailed him behind three other cars through town.

"Where's he going?" asked Melissa, over the music, studying the satnav on the dash. "His house is on the outskirts of town in the opposite direction."

Lucy glanced at the small screen.

"Looks like he's heading for Agronomia. Wherever *that* is. No. Wait he's turning off."

Angel's cab took several more turns before pulling in to the curb outside a vast entrance arena of creamy stone. The building resembled a classical temple, with down-lit Romanesque columns and, above, a stone relief depicting figures and cherubim. On the apex of the roof, a sculpted, stone angel with outstretched wings pointed across the city. Angel left his cab as the girls drove by to park a short way further down the street. Tyler kept him in sight as he took keys from his pocket and unlocked the black, iron gates fronting the entrance.

"It's the Chacarita Cemetery," said Melissa, reading information from the web on her phone. "The biggest cemetery in Buenos Aires. It's locked every night. How did he get the keys?"

"And why?" asked Tyler. "What's he doing here?"

"Guess that's what we're here to find out," said Lucy, slapping a 'Policia' sign on the windscreen to deter interest in their illegally parked vehicle. They left the rental on the curb and, from a distance, watched Angel lock the iron gates behind him and disappear in to the vast cemetery, slipping between its tall pillars. Tyler waited until he was out of sight before speaking.

"Albert, follow him. Zebedee, stay with us."

Albert materialised, gave a nod, and passed through the wall and the gates, tailing Angel into the cemetery while the girls ran to the iron railings. Tyler paused at the gates.

"It's too tall," said Melissa, gazing up at the vicious spikes that topped the rails. "We can't climb over."

"It's not that. I don't like what I'm feeling. There're too many ghosts here. So many I can't tell where they are. It's kind of freaking me out."

"I'm not exactly getting a good vibe, either. It's okay with me if we leave. It's dark and the oppressor is leading us into a massive graveyard. There could be anything waiting for us on the other side of those pillars."

"Wait, wait, wait. We're not going to turn back now, are we?" asked Lucy, drawing level with the others beneath the vast palms that sided the gates. "This is what we've been waiting for! We've waited years to get here. Gone through hell."

Tyler checked up and down the street before taking her lock picking tools from her jacket pocket. The area was quiet. Other pedestrians were far enough away to be oblivious to what she was about to do.

"No. We're going in." She picked the lock with ease and they entered, pulling the gates shut behind them to maintain a locked appearance.

"I could stay here. Keep an eye on the car."

"You're coming with us," said Lucy.

"We might need you," confirmed Tyler. Melissa shrugged and, with resignation, climbed the steps with the others. They stopped at the end of the wall where the columns ended before a set of descending steps, to gaze over thousands of grey mausoleums in tree-lined blocks.

"Wow. That's a lot of dead people," said Lucy, surveying crosses, statues and the various doors and rooftops of tombs. Some were built from a darker marble and were larger and taller. Others were simple, granite boxes with black, closed doors. The more intricate among them resembled miniature mosques with ornate, domed roofs. All looked weathered and old. Nothing stirred.

"It's a necropolis," said Melissa. "A city built for the dead."

"We've lost him." Tyler descended steps to dart across the open courtyard and peer around the corner of a tomb at a long, dim road. Lucy and Melissa split up and searched other roads. Albert appeared, standing at a junction a few paces from Tyler.

"Pssst! This way!" He waved the girls over and they joined him, peering into the murky reaches of another shrine-edged road, where the pale blue of Angel's unnatural skin gleamed softly as he walked. During daylight the heavy make-up he wore concealed the glow, giving him a believable, human appearance, but not so in this darkness, which revealed his true nature. The girls followed, knowing their black clothes would not give them away so easily. Albert vanished again.

Angel turned left into a cobbled street; more shrines of marble, all drab shades in the seemingly-endless, unlit cemetery. They tailed the bobbing, blue shimmer deeper in through several more streets until the mausoleums gave way to an open area of simpler graves, these marked with modest wooden and stone crosses. Narrow paths crisscrossed this graveyard and large trees dominated its edge. The girls clung to the last of the tombs and watched Angel take a footpath crossing the centre.

They waited, blinking at movements in the dark. A figure with a glowing face and hands left the cover of the trees on the opposite side and walked out towards Angel.

"Another glove!" hissed Lucy.

"We have to get closer or we won't be able to hear what they're saying when they meet." Tyler spied a Mausoleum further around the side that was closer to the meeting point. "Albert check that out, will you?"

A moment later Albert returned.

"All clear. No one there, Missy."

"Thanks, Albert." Tyler gestured for Melissa and Lucy to follow, and flitted across a breach between tombs, hoping to pass unobserved. They reached the mausoleum, hugging its wall. Tyler found the tomb in a state of decay, its wrought-iron grill door rusting and open, its old padlock hanging loose. She brushed cobwebs aside and slipped inside, followed by Melissa and Lucy. Broken glass that once backed the iron grill doors lay shattered, cracking underfoot as they entered. At the centre of the small room a dusty, stone sarcophagus concealed the interred and, on the back wall, a large, cobwebbed cross presided over all. The entire place was dusted with cobwebs and the filth of neglected years. Tyler ducked low at one of the three gothic windows set in the side wall and glimpsed the two gloves as they met with a handshake. They were talking but nothing more than a murmur reached the girls in the tomb.

"We're still not close enough," whispered Lucy, coming to Tyler's side. "Who's the newcomer?"

"I can't quite tell. It can only be Eichmann or Heydrich."

"The Lord of the Reveries."

"That would be bad news considering our current situation. Reveries *suck the life from your bones*. Basically depress you to the point of death. Isn't that what Albert said?"

"That's what I was thinking. I wish we could hear what they're saying. This could be really important." Tyler took a small box from her pocket and opened its hinged lid to reveal a NanoSect, this one an intricately designed and built, remote controlled mosquito, carrying a miniature camera and microphone. She gave the girls a nod and they each inserted receiver earpieces. Tyler launched the miniscule, metallic bug and it buzzed quietly out of the tomb window to be quickly swallowed by the night. They followed its progress on the small screen that was set into the lid of the box as Tyler guided the bug using a delicate joystick set into the control unit in the base. Through the bug's eyes, they closed on Angel and his companion. Voices reached the girls as the mosquito entered audible range of the gloves.

"They're talking German," said Melissa, straining to hear details.

"Now for the tricky part," said Tyler, guiding the bug onto the sleeve of Angel's long coat. The image shifted as they watched. Angel was moving his arm. They caught a glimpse of his companion as the bug's view drifted up towards the companion's face. As it approached the figure's neck, a dark shape came down with an audible thump making the girls jump, and the screen filled with static.

"No way! He swatted it! It's dead!" said Tyler, listening to the hiss and crackle as her earpiece relayed a broken signal.

"So much for technology," said Lucy. "What now?"

"I'll go. I'm the only one fluent enough to understand German," said Melissa.

"Go where?"

"Closer. We need to hear them. Right?"

"We could wait and come back tomorrow with the contrap. You could use the *Past Eye* to watch and listen-in safely on what was said."

Melissa shook her head, although she paled and her widening eyes betrayed her jangling nerves.

"You said it yourself. This could be too important to wait until then. We need to know now. I didn't hear much before the bug died, but Angel said something about a political strategy and then he talked about finding a ghost. At least, I think that's what he said." She glanced at the door. "Okay, okay. You can do this." She took a deep breath, turned, and squeezed through the open door, heading back out into the cemetery.

"Melissa! No!" hissed Tyler, but Melissa left the tomb. "No, no, no, no, no! This isn't good. I'm feeling something. There's too many of them but they're moving. It feels... It feels like they're closing on us. I feel cold. Is it cold in here?"

"What are you talking about?"

"The ghosts," said Tyler, frantically glancing around the graveyard through the window. She felt for the lead box in her coat pocket, sorely tempted to take it out and use the contrap, but resisted, knowing it would do them no good.

Out in the darkness, the two gloves continued to talk. From a window, Tyler searched for Melissa off to the side of the open graveyard and watched her progress; a shadow dipping along the edge of a block of Mausoleums.

"There she is." She pointed.

"She's exposed," whispered Lucy.

"I know. Let's hope the gloves don't turn around."

Tyler looked back at the gloves. Angel handed something to his companion: an envelope or a document. It was too dark to tell. The other glove, in return, handed a similar object to Angel.

Zebedee appeared by Tyler to point across the graveyard.

"Girls, I do believe someone else is heading our way."

"Who's that?"

Tyler saw it, too: a grey figure emerging from the deep night of the tree line. She squinted at it and then at the figure standing with Angel.

"Lucy, I think I know who that is. It's Heydrich, the Lord of the..." Tyler pointed to the approaching transparent, grey, figure as others emerged either side.

"...Reveries!"

"We gotta warn Melissa."

"I'll go!" said Zebedee.

"Okay, but come straight back or they might get you, too."

"We gotta get out of here!" Lucy hissed.

Beyond their tomb, a shrill scream pierced the night.

The Tombs of Chacarita

Vacant, soul-hungry ghosts ambled out of the shadows all around the graveyard. Tyler sensed them, like a vast cloud of icy vapour invading her mind.

Outside, Melissa screamed again.

"Heydrich is controlling them," said Tyler. "I could use the contrap. Get Heydrich."

She and Lucy turned for the doors but stopped to stare when a narrow dagger floated into view beyond the curling iron grills. Before the girls could reach them, the doors closed as though of their own accord, and the old padlock jostled, clicking shut as they grasped and tugged, trying to break free. Albert appeared, dashing forward as the ghost on the other side became visible; an unshaven man in a trench coat, shimmering in the night and leering in at the trapped girls. He jammed the dagger into the keyhole and gave it a twist, released the lock and backed away, laughing as Albert lunged at him through the doors. The ghost cast Albert aside, spitting several German words as Tyler and Lucy rattled the doors in desperation, and he vanished into the darkness. Albert recovered and, clambering to his feet, brushed himself down.

"Sorry, girls. 'E were too quick. There's a strange fear in the air. I feels it."

"The windows!" suggested Lucy, but however they tried, she and Tyler failed to squeeze through any of the narrow frames. Lucy launched her body against a stone window pillar only to bruise her shoulder. Tyler fled back to the doors and began awkwardly picking the rusty lock from the inside of the grills.

"Where's Mel?" she asked.

Beyond the windows, reveries were massing, their moans rising in anticipation of fresh, young life-force. Melissa fled one way and then another as ghouls lumbered in to block her path.

"She's trapped!" shouted Lucy. "You gotta use the contrap!"

"It's no good. He jammed the mechanism."

"They're on her! They have Melissa!" Lucy turned away from the window. "DO SOMETHING!"

"HELP ME!"

Tyler gave up on the lock and backed up, preparing to stamp at the doors. Hoping to bend the iron and wreck the lock, she ran at the doors to stamp against them. Lucy joined her as Tyler counted down and they tried again.

"Three, two, one..." They hammered in together and the doors groaned and gave an inch. They stamped once more, bending the ornate, old iron. With the following blow the lock broke. The doors buckled, bursting open, and the girls ran out. Tyler grabbed the lead box from her pocket and took out the contrap as they rounded the mausoleum, but they jogged to a halt. Tyler replaced the contrap and closed the lead lid. The graveyard before them was empty and quiet. Not a ghost in sight.

"Well, that went well," said Lucy, as they both looked around.

"They're gone. And they have Melissa."

"Where? Maybe we can follow them."

Tyler and Lucy searched the grounds separately, but Tyler soon called Lucy over.

"It's no good. They could be miles away. I can sense it." Tyler felt unsettled and struggled to pinpoint why. Beyond the obvious reasons, something else nagged.

"Use the contrap! Use the *Past Eye!*"

"Yes, of course." Tyler lifted the lid of the contrap's box again but stopped. "I'm not sure. We could follow but they'd know we were coming. They'd sense *this* stupid thing. We'd be sitting ducks." She raised the lead box, planning to dash it on the ground in frustration but stopped herself. If she broke the box she's have no way of hiding the contrap and concealing their position. "All right. We'll try, but first sign of the gloves or any reveries and we back off. Right?"

"Right."

Tyler took the contrap and set its little switch to the *Past Eye*. She turned it over and looked into the dark lens aiming it at the exact spot she had last seen Melissa. She drew the small lever around the contrap's edge as the darkness retreated, watching figures move in the graveyard. The *Past Eye* showed her the events that had taken place on that exact spot, only moments before. She found Melissa and paused the lever, allowing the replay to move in real time within the crystal. She watched Melissa creep along the edge of a mausoleum, stalking round towards a shrub from where she would be able to spy on the two gloves talking. Tyler shifted view with the contrap and watched the reveries emerge from the trees again. She skipped back onto Melissa, who noticed the reveries and retreated, hoping to escape. More ghosts arrived behind Melissa and she was left with nowhere to go. She panicked and screamed. Tyler turned again to glimpse Lucy trying to break through the pillar of the mausoleum window, only this time she viewed it from the outside. Turning round, she watched Angel and Heydrich. They had given up on their charade now and were watching with glee as the reveries enclosed Melissa in a tightening circle. Melissa screamed again and passed out, dropping to the ground as reveries reached her. They swarmed around until Heydrich strode in from the open ground and the reveries parted before him. Heydrich stooped to hoist Melissa onto his shoulder like a rag doll and he marched away into the necropolis, followed by all the reveries. Tyler turned back towards Angel in time to see him slip away between mausoleums on the other side.

"Come on, Mojo. We'll follow Heydrich. He has Melissa. Angel went the other way."

Lucy kept pace with Tyler as she tracked Heydrich between streets of tombs. Tyler hesitated, realising what had been bothering her. She no longer sensed Albert's or Zebedee's presence.

"Albert? Are you there?" Fear constricted her throat. *He's gone!* "No, not again!"

"Albert?" Lucy called. The night was quiet; the only

reply the occasional chirps from crickets and the startled screech of an owl.

"Zebedee?" Tyler looked at Lucy, alarmed.

"Guess we're alone out here. You want to call it a night? We can come back tomorrow with reinforcements."

"We can't. Melissa needs us now." Tyler looked into the contrap's lens again to see reveries departing and fading into the night. Heydrich had gained ground while she had delayed. "He went this way." She set off again. "Do me a favour. Call Chapman and tell him what's happened."

Lucy made the call as they walked briskly to keep pace with Heydrich's progress in the crystal.

"Pointer calling home. Agent down. Things have gone pair-shaped here. The enemy has Cog."

Tyler tracked Heydrich between ostentatious mausoleums and vast statues of angels, and wondered where he was heading. She was surprised when he opened the doors of a grand mausoleum, larger than the others, and carried Melissa inside.

"Wait. I'll call you back." Lucy ended the call. "Stop. I can see reveries up ahead!"

Tyler lowered the contrap and looked at the large tomb further down the street where Heydrich had entered. She shivered. Two reveries guarded the doors. Tyler boxed the contrap, needing to think. A lowered voice from the darkness off to her left made her jump.

"You took your time!" Zebedee beckoned them and they joined him behind a tomb.

"Where's Albert?" whispered Tyler.

"If he's not with you, I don't know. I followed them. Heydrich took Melissa in there with a handful of reveries." Zebedee pointed down the street where the guards waited. "We may have been spotted."

"What should we do, Zebedee?" asked Tyler. "We have artefacts to summon Heydrich but he's always surrounded by reveries.

"I'll distract the guards while you steal round behind the tomb. Get as close as you can without them seeing you. Take out the contrap and put the reverie guards into the portal. Heydrich will sense the contrap, of course, but I fear he's already aware it's here, which means he will try to claim it and the oppressor may return for it. Tyler, if we enter here it could be a colossal mistake. You don't have an artefact to summon the oppressor and the Mordecai chains are back at the hotel."

"We could go and fetch them," said Lucy.

"Not enough time," countered Tyler. "It could be too late for Melissa by then."

"So we're going in?"

"I don't know what else to do. Mel needs us."

"I understand," said Zebedee. "Once you've taken out the guards we'll need to move fast. Heydrich will most likely be expecting us. Lucy and I will try to draw off the reveries. Use the artefacts. Put Heydrich into the chasm the first chance you get."

"He'll be armed," said Lucy.

"And you have your gun. If he draws his, shoot him."

Lucy gave a nod.

"Then you'll be killing an innocent girl called Susan Ellis," Tyler objected. "Tasers only."

"Ah, yes! Of course," said Zebedee. "Use your Taser thingymebobs."

"Okay." Lucy drew her Taser and checked it was loaded.

"And don't aim for the chest. It can induce heart failure," added Tyler, checking her own Taser.

"You do have an artefact with which to summon Heydrich?" asked Zebedee. Tyler took a plastic evidence bag from her coat pocket and held it up to show Zebedee the finger bone inside.

"All right! Can we get on with it?"

"Ready, Zebedee?"

"Ready, Miss May."

Grasping the lead box, Tyler crept around the back of the block with Lucy as Zebedee became invisible again. They skirted Mausoleums until they approached the one guarded by reveries. Tyler took out the contrap and set it to the *Ghost Portal*. Zebedee walked into the street, stopping before the two reveries to doff his top hat.

"Good day to you, Sirs. Fine weather we're having for this time of year."

The reveries slowly turned to him and began to approach, leering.

Tyler rounded on the ghosts.

"Phasmatis licentia!"

Zebedee nimbly stepped aside, out of the contrap's reach. The reveries gawped as the portal hungrily sucked at their essence before swallowing them entirely. Tyler switched to the fire symbol and guided the lever full-circle until it clicked back into its original position

"Vorago expositus," she said, opening the *Brimstone Chasm*. She caught the all-too-familiar sulphurous stink as the contrap's crystal emanated a fluctuating orange light, and her stomach turned. She caught Lucy's eye and nodded as Zebedee crossed to the doors. *Time to enter.*

Lucy kicked in the doors and charged into the tomb with Tyler close behind, both fully expecting to be greeted by a wall of reveries protecting Heydrich. They came to sudden halt inside. Five horizontal coffins filled one wall, and concrete steps led down to a crypt where more dusty coffins were stacked.

"No reveries," said Tyler, peering suspiciously down the stairs. She smelled damp, musty air and gazed at closed coffins, dreading the moment they would burst open. They remained closed as the girls listened, unnerved by the still silence. Tyler tentatively stepped down, ducking beneath an arch and entering the crypt. A passage ran on from the chamber, its details a secret of the deepening pitch.

Lucy took out her Maglite and aimed it down the tunnel hand over hand with her Taser.

"Better check this out."

Tyler aimed the contrap ahead and together they walked into the retreating darkness.

"Are you there, Zebedee?" whispered Tyler, her ghost sense still reeling.

"Right here," he replied from her side.

"I can't tell if there are ghosts down there. Too many ghosts are around. What about you? Is there anything bad down here?"

"Not that I'm aware of. Wait here. I'll check."

Tyler and Lucy waited, claustrophobia mounting. Tyler studied dank concrete as a distant dripping reverberated. Moments later, Zebedee materialised ahead of them and called out.

"This way. I've found her. Bring the chasm! She is in the clutches of the reveries, but I'm pretty sure Heydrich has fled."

As they chased him, Lucy checked behind with her torch and glimpsed an empty tunnel of wavering shadows. Zebedee's voice echoed from further down the tunnel.

"Just a little further, girls!"

The passage ended and they spilled out into a large, damp chamber where water dripped and a dark figure lay curled up in a corner surrounded by grey, hunkering reveries, who pawed and moaned, jostling to feed. Beyond, concrete stairs ascended. Lucy turned her beam onto Melissa, who failed to respond even to the sudden, blinding light as Tyler aimed the contrap at the reveries. They sensed the chasm and hissed, fleeing into the walls of the chamber.

"She's still alive," said Zebedee. "But the reveries have drained her. Her spirit is thinned to a sprig! She's barely conscious."

Tyler ran to Melissa's side to cradle her.

"Can you stand?" Melissa did not respond, but gazed into the corner, unfocused. "Up you get." Lucy and Tyler helped shoulder Melissa's weight and they lifted her to her feet.

"Where do those steps lead?" asked Lucy. Zebedee flew up the stairs, returning a moment later.

"Outside. No sign of Heydrich or the reveries. All clear!"

Tyler closed the chasm and balanced the contrap.

"Vorago termino. Compenso pondera."

The girls half-carried Melissa up the steps and out into the night and back through the cemetery to the car, where they laid her limp body on the back seat.

Zebedee appeared by the open car door.

"Get her to a hospital as soon as possible. There may be something they can do for her. Keep her warm. Talk to her even if you don't think she can hear you. She needs words of comfort and encouragement. For now, they are the most powerful medicine." He lent into the car and whisper to Melissa. "You've done well, brave girl. You're in good hands. You'll be all right now."

"What's that?" asked Lucy, pointing to a corner of white paper protruding from one of Melissa's coat pockets. Tyler plucked the paper out and flattened it, meeting Lucy's gaze over the image.

"A photograph. That's odd."

Eucrates Onuris IV

Tyler struggled to explain what had happened to Melissa without telling her entire, unbelievable story from day one. *She's been zombified by a gang of soul-sucking ghosts under the control of a dead Nazi SS General who is trying to take over the world with the gloved ghost of Adolf Hitler. No, that's not going to cut it.*

"She's had a bit of a shock," she said, in the end. "She, er, thought she saw a ghost and she passed out for a while. When she came round she was like this. She hasn't said a word since."

"Okay," said Dr Morales, an astute, intense Brazilian with kind eyes. "There doesn't really seem to be anything physically wrong with her. Her body temperature is on the low side and she's mildly anaemic, but apart from that..." He took a form from his desk and jotted some notes before handing it to Tyler. "I'm prescribing these.

Make sure she takes them twice a day until she's back to normal. Beyond that, there's really nothing I can do, but they should help. If she doesn't recover in the next day or two, take her to her local doctor back home and he will refer her to a specialist."

Tyler thanked him and between her and Lucy they collected the prescription and coaxed Melissa out of the hospital.

*

Back at their hotel, Lucy helped Tyler persuade Melissa out of her clothes and into a nightshirt. They cajoled her into swallowing a pill and Melissa slept, curled up like a wounded animal in her bed. Tyler watched her and felt defeated.

"Poor Mel. What have we done to you? We really blew it this time, Mojo. Angel knows we're on to him. He'll vanish and war will come and we'll be powerless to prevent it."

"Hey, you're stealing my thunder. I'm the doomsayer in this outfit." Lucy grinned at her and Tyler gave her a half-smile.

"I guess." Tyler picked up the odd photograph to study it. *Is this what Angel gave to Heydrich out in the graveyard?* She photographed it with her phone and messaged the image it to Chapman.

Found this photo in Cog's pocket when we reclaimed her. We think she may have taken it from Heydrich.

A minute later he phoned.

"It's the Spear of Destiny," he said. "Supposedly the tip of the very spear that pierced Christ's side as he hung on the cross."

"Yes, we worked that out, but why would Heydrich be carrying a photo of the Spear of Destiny? Presumably, Cog took it from his coat pocket before she was overcome.   Pointer and I've been over it and we can't come up with any reason why Cog would've had the picture on her when we set out. It *must* have come from Heydrich." Tyler stared at the image; a close-up of a long, iron spearhead, encased at its midpoint in a sheath of gold and set upon a red velvet plinth in what appeared to be a glass display case. Judging by the silver wire wound meticulously around and crisscrossing the blades, she decided it might well have been several separate sections of iron, bound together to form one object.

"Yes. Pity we can't get anything out of Cog. Her being out of the equation means you're down one interpreter amongst other things.   I'm bringing in a temporary replacement from our Berlin office. He'll be arriving in the morning. You'll remember Klaus."

"YES!" said Tyler, a little too keenly. "I mean, yes. I remember Klaus."

"You approve then?"

"He'll do."

Oh well, it's not all bad.

She left Chapman mulling over the pertinence of the photograph and turned to Lucy.

"Do you think we should go back? Track Heydrich with the contrap. That's the first sighting of him since Berlin and it would be a shame to lose him."

"We should but who's going to look after Mel while we go? I don't mean to be cold but, right now, she's just holding us back, and she needs proper care."

*

At Aeroparque Jorge Newbery, Buenos Aires' most central

airport, Tyler handed Melissa over to two MI6 agents who had come to return her to London for care and recovery. Tyler fought back tears, torn by what she was doing.

"These people are going to take you home. You can recover there without worrying about anything. I'm sorry, Mel. Get well soon. Goodbye."

Melissa gazed vacantly at the airport hustle and bustle. When the agents had escorted her away, Tyler found a café and drank hot chocolate and then coffee, waiting for the flight from Berlin to arrive. She visited the ladies room, fixed her make-up and checked her hair.

Seeing Klaus' rugged face and military-style, blond hair amongst the crowds departing passport control lifted Tyler's spirits. He collected his bags and broke protocol by hugging her, grinning all the while.

"How you doing?" asked Tyler.

"I'm great."

Yes. Yes, you are. She'd forgotten just how manly he was.

"How are you?" he asked.

"So so. Mel's not well, though. She's on a plane to Heathrow."

"I heard."

"She's being looked after. We'd best get back. Lots to do."

Tyler drove Klaus to the hotel and he took a room on the floor above the girls. Tyler, Lucy and Klaus finished lunch together and were in an otherwise unoccupied lift, returning to their rooms, when Albert appeared.

"Wotcher."

"Albert! Are you okay? What happened?"

"I saw Heydrich take Mel, an' I saw Zebedee follow 'em, so I fought I'd best go after Angel."

"You know where he is right now?" asked Lucy.

"Aye. I can show ya, but we'd best be quick!"

*

Angel appeared at the window, a small figure, three levels up in the tall office block, and looked out at the city, unaware of his observers. Klaus focused his field binoculars on Angel across the two roads and the narrow block of buildings between.

"After 'e left the cemetery, he went home, packed all 'is stuff an' moved out. 'E ain't goin' back. He drove out to an 'ouse in the country. He murdered the owner and some men came to take away the body. It were 'orrible and there weren't nofin' I could do. 'E took over the 'ouse. Then 'e came 'ere."

"Well done, Albert," said Tyler, sensing his closeness. "So you can lead us to this house?"

"Yeah. I can show ya'."

"Do you think he'll sense the contrap from here?" asked Lucy.

"I think he might be aware of it but we're too far away for him to get a firm fix. From what I can tell, they need to be quite close for that." Tyler recalled a time when she was sitting a few tables from Hitler's gloved ghost in the coffee shop in Watford, and he had turned to look directly at her. "It's like the closer they are the more they sense it. In any case we're about to find out." She opened the lead box and removed the contrap.

"He senses it," Klaus confirmed. "He's quite lost his smile."

The multi storey car park, although crammed with parked cars, afforded an excellent, elevated view of Angel's latest position. Tyler, Lucy and Klaus leaned on the concrete balustrade, spying.

"What do you think he's up to?" asked Lucy.

Tyler used the *Present Eye* to telescope into the building.

"Seems he's rented an office for some reason." She watched Angel leave the window and sit at a desk. A woman came into his office to deliver coffee in a cardboard cup. Angel thanked her, flashing her a smile. The woman nodded and left.

"He has a secretary," said Tyler.

"I guess wars don't happen without a little admin," said Lucy.

Tyler watched him sorting letters and reading documents, listened in on one side of a phone call he made, and took out her notebook.

"Yes, its me."

...

"Yes, tomorrow. If not, there will be consequences."

...

"Four hundred. This should be enough."

...

"Goodbye."

It didn't tell her much but she wrote it down anyway. *Four hundred what? Enough for what?*

She tried to get a better look at the papers on his desk as Angel stubbed out a cigarette, but the angle was all wrong. She considered flying onto the roof of the office block and peering down through the floors. That would work, but it would be time consuming and limiting. If she did it at night, which would be safest, the office lights would be off and she'd be squinting into a dark room through the contrap's little lens.

"I need to get in there," she told the others. "I want to see what he's up to, before we bring him in."

"It's risky," said Klaus.

Why, Klaus, I never knew you cared.

"Are you sure that's wise?" asked Zebedee.

"We should clear it with Chapman," Lucy suggested.

"Nonsense. It's perfectly within our brief: Learn everything we can about his movements with a view to planning and executing a clean extraction. I'm going in tonight. Albert can come with me. You three can keep track of Angel while we're busy."

*

Tyler waited in the lamp lit street, dressed in a sharp, navy blue suit and glossy heels. She checked her watch: just gone zero one hundred hours. Many resident companies of the block had closed up for the night but a few remained to work shifts through the small hours and so a believable cover was necessary, should she meet anyone along the way.

The third level of the block was a blackout except for one office on the opposite side to Angel's. Tonight Tyler was a Personal Assistant with a set of keys jangling from her belt, running errands around the building from office to office. A little research had taught her the front desk was never unattended.

She would not use a single key but would need to pick any locks that came between her and her goal. She put on a radio headset, one made to resemble a regular Bluetooth earpiece, with which to maintain contact with the rest of the team for the duration of the mission. The contrap nestled in its lead box at the bottom of her leather briefcase.

She sensed Albert approach.

"All clear, Missy. The receptionist's in the loo. I'd say you 'ave a couple o' minutes."

Nerves fluttered her stomach.

"Wish me luck," she said, picking up the case and walking into the ground level of the building.

"People like you don't need luck," she heard Klaus reply, and she smiled to herself. "It's all raw talent." She knew he was grinning and she imagined Lucy rolling her eyes. Reception was open plan and minimalist. Her high heels seemed loud as she tapped across the polished, marble floor.

She took the stairs, not wanting to hang around for the lift where the receptionist might see her upon return. Instead, Tyler called the lift on the first floor and rode it to the second floor where they'd seen Angel at work. The lift opened and she stepped out into an atrium, glad to find the lights on in the opposite corridor. She walked half its length, stopping at a door she calculated to be Angel's office, and read the name on the door.

Hobson & Crane Industries

"Albert?" she whispered.

Albert appeared next to her.

"Keep an eye on the stairs and the lift. Anyone comes this way I need to know."

"Right you are." He drifted away towards the lift but stopped and turned. "Wait, Missy!"

Tyler felt it, too. They exchanged looks. There was another ghost nearby.

"What now?" she whispered. "It's a guard, somewhere in his room. If they run they'll alert the gloves. Give me up. We can't afford for that to happen.

Does the guard know you're here?"

"Aye. They'll know by now. I'll lead them away."

"No wait. I'll trap it." Tyler unboxed the contrap and set it to the *Ghost Portal*. She closed her eyes and walked past the door. She could feel the ghost's presence growing stronger on the other side of the wall as she approached and she backtracked to be sure she had found the closest position before aiming the crystal at the unseen entity through the wall.

"Phasmatis licentia."

A shriek echoed down the passage as the blinding, blue light of the morphing ghost reeled through bricks and mortar into the portal. Tyler equalised the contrap's increased power with the balancing spell. "Compenso pondera." She boxed the contrap, took out her lock-picking tools and broke into the office, easing the door closed behind her.

"I'm in," she reported, looking around at the office. The furnishings were sparse. A simple, wooden desk and a black office chair were arranged near to the large expanse of windows fronting the building. Three filing cabinets stood against a wall.

"No computers." She thought back to what she had seen of the office through the *Present Eye*. "He was using a laptop, but it's not here."

"He's taken it with him. Have fun," said Lucy, through her earpiece. "We're on the move."

"What do you mean?"

"Angel's taking a midnight trip into town. We're not sure why. He's carrying a case that could contain a laptop."

"Keep me posted. There's a lot of paperwork to go through here."

"Roger that."

Tyler set about photographing documents from Angel's desk: letters, invoices, business projections and stock reports. It didn't mean much to her, but money was changing hands and the pages would show it. Ten minutes later she tried opening a filing cabinet and the drawers to the desk. *Locked.* She considered picking their miniscule locks but stopped, noticing a discoloured document on the floor, one she figured must have fallen out from the pile she had searched through on the desk. A voice in her ear startled her: Lucy.

"I don't mean to alarm you, Ghost, but Angel just turned into your road. We think he's about to visit his office."

"In the middle of the night?"

"Not sure where else he could be going. He's not in a hurry. Don't think he knows you're there."

"Okay. I'm heading out. Thanks for the heads up." Tyler put the desk papers back as she had found them and picked up the stray page from the carpet. She was about to photograph it when the content of the page made her hesitate. It was not a regular size and felt different to the touch, heavier and more leathery than normal paper. She viewed it closely. *Not paper, but parchment!* It looked old and the writing on it was faint and hand written in brown ink with great flourishes and sweeping lines. She bent closer to read it in the beam of her Maglite, but the language was not English or French. Only a single name in the bottom right hand corner was legible to her.

Eucrates Onuris IV

"He's just entered the building," warned Lucy. "Get out now."

Tyler's pulse quickened. She stuffed the parchment into her pocket, grabbed her case and left the office, pausing only to lock the door with one of her tools.

As she neared the lift, its red light blinked brightly and its doors slid open with a *ding*. Tyler eyed her case where the contrap nestled in its lead box. Albert appeared briefly.

"Missy, Angel's comin'!"

The Parchment

Tyler looked up as Angel strolled out from the lift, in conversation on his cell phone. She did her best to ignore him, but couldn't help pick up her pace as sweat beaded at her temple. She did not understand anything he said into his phone except for one word: a name that jogged a memory.

Streicher.

Tyler slipped past Angel and was relieved when the lift doors finally closed. She contemplated taking the contrap and going back to try to capture Angel's ghosts, knowing the *Ghost Portal* would still work on them. She stopped herself. Without the correct summoning artefacts to draw him, Angel would be free to run, draw a gun, or deploy any number of defences before she could get close enough to trap his ghosts.

"That were close, Missy."

"Too close."

She left the building, ignoring the barrage of questions firing from the receptionist as she passed, and called-in, to update the others. Leaving Zebedee to stakeout Angel through the night she headed back to the hotel with Albert, Klaus, and Lucy. They gathered in the girls' room sipping chilled beers that Lucy had passed around.

"Anything interesting?" she asked.

Tyler showed them the parchment.

"A couple of things. Can anyone read this?"

"Only the name," said Klaus.

"Same here."

"Me too. I'm pretty sure it came from his desk, though I found it on the floor. Seemed a bit odd, so I took it. But there's something else. Eucrates Onuris the fourth. I know that name. He's one of the contrap's previous owners. Look." Tyler searched in her case and drew out a black notebook. She opened it at the first page, where she had written a title: History of the Contrap. She turned the page, pointed and read aloud.

"My dear Ramla, please keep this trinket safe until my return. If anybody comes looking for me, you must deny all knowledge of me for your own sake. Eucrates Onuris IV." She turned another page and pointed out part of the timeline she had created.

Circa 1650   *Eucrates Onuris IV*
↓
Ramla
↓
Hemmings
(Zebedee's great uncle, unwitting owner)
↓

Circa 1880   ***Zebedee Lieberman***

↓

Circa 1900   ***Orealia Stephensen***
                        (Zebedee's housekeeper)

↓

"So Eucrates had the contrap sometime before it passed to Zebedee," said Lucy.

Tyler grabbed her iPhone to photograph the parchment.

"Yes. And Angel had *this* parchment, written by Eucrates. It's of the utmost importance that we get it translated immediately."

"Let me see that again," said Klaus, taking the page. He studied it more closely before looking up. "I think I can translate this. It looks like ancient Latin. If this Eucrates was around in the seventeenth century as your notes suggest, he must have been quite a scholar."

Tyler buzzed with excitement.

"*You* can read Latin?"

"German, French, English, Polish, Dutch, a little Greek and, yes, Latin."

"Do it! Do it, now!"

"Okay, okay. Give me a moment," Klaus laughed. "It is not that easy. I'll need to check some references. It's been a while. You'll have to be patient if you want an accurate translation."

Tyler paced, wondering what secrets the Latin words concealed as Klaus pawed over the parchment for what felt like an age. She checked the time: 0235 hours. Twenty minutes later he was ready with the translation. She read Klaus' precise freehand script, noting his alternative interpretations for various words and phrases in brackets.

Regarding my investigations into the contraption, I believe I have found a way (solution). Upon the meeting of the four symbols (or when the four symbols come together), the pacts (could mean oaths or arrangements/agreements) will reverse (turn in on themselves, or inverse) and spirit will be released.

Where the heart is concerned, one can only muse (deliberate). Perhaps this was selected as a substitute image because the more accurate (truthful) device was already engaged (in use).

On another matter, today, I learned of a myth that told of the spirits succumbing to the lordship of he who wears a ring of gallows iron. Have you ever heard such a thing? A ring of gallows iron worn and wielded by my namesake, nonetheless! It is surely make-believe.

"That's it, more or less," said Klaus, looking over her shoulder at his handiwork as Lucy also came to look. "It's the best I can do, in any case. There is this one anomaly. The word contraption was written in English. I thought that strange. What do you think?"

"You're not as dumb as you look, Klaus," said Lucy.

"I think you're a genius. That's what I think." Tyler surprised him with a peck on the cheek. "And you don't look dumb, either. Thank you."

"It's weird," said Lucy. "I'm not sure it helps us much, but maybe that's how Heydrich is controlling the reveries: a ring of gallows iron. Whatever *that* is."

"I'm going to bed now," Klaus said, grinning. "Goodnight all. Good luck with your riddles."

"Goodnight."

When Klaus had gone and Lucy was sound asleep, Tyler read and reread the translation, wondering what it was and what it meant. *Is it a letter to someone, or part of a letter? It could be about the contrap. And it mentions the heart symbol! Clearly, Angel has been doing some research of his own.*

Albert appeared by the room's only window, his back to Tyler.

"Hey, Albert, you seen this?"

He didn't answer but stared through the gap in the curtains, out into the night.

"Albert?"

"What?"

"The parchment. Have you seen it? What do you think it means?"

"Don't know." He continued to stare.

"Are you all right?"

"Fine." He gazed for a few more seconds before walking slowly to look at the parchment. "When the four symbols meet? The contrap 'as ten symbols, not four. It don't make sense."

"That's what I was thinking. Maybe he's talking about four of the ten symbols, or I guess he might not be talking about the contrap at all. But then, how would the symbols meet? They're carved into the silver casing."

"Interesting what 'e says about the heart, but it don't mean much to me." He returned to his nightly vigil at the window, arms folded.

What's bugging him?

Tyler took out her laptop. As it booted up she considered where to start her research and felt overwhelmed. The small parchment contained three separate pieces of information and all seemed to be of startling relevance to her. She reread the first paragraph of Klaus' translation.

Regarding my investigations into the contraption, I believe I have found a way (solution). Upon the meeting of the four symbols (or when the four symbols come together), the pacts (could mean oaths or arrangements/agreements) will reverse (turn in on themselves, or inverse) and spirit will be released.

Is it about the contrap? She could not be entirely sure. She recalled Albert telling her about the contrap years ago. *'...it were called a con-trap, I fink. Yeah, that were it – as in con-trap-shun. It were called that 'cause to make it work you first 'ave to con ghosts into the trap, see?'*

Contraption. Is that where the word came from? Did Eucrates decide the contrap was evil and should therefore be destroyed? And did he have the same problem with it; how to destroy it? What would happen to all the ghosts inside, if it was destroyed? How would that affect the different realms it carried? What are the four symbols he refers to?

Tyler took out her notebook and unfolded an old page she had tucked inside, for now at least, presuming the note *was* about the contrap.

THE CONTRAP

BACK

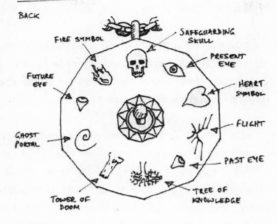

SYMBOLS

- SAFEGUARDING SKULL — SAVES FROM DEATH
- PRESENT EYE — LOOK THROUGH WALLS, ETC (TELESCOPIC).
- HEART SYMBOL — ?
- FLIGHT — MAKES YOU FLY!
- PAST EYE — LOOK INTO THE PAST!
- TREE OF KNOWLEDGE — ASK IT A QUESTION & IT ANSWERS
- TOWER OF DOOM — ACHIEVEMENT INDICATOR
- GHOST PORTAL — IT'S A GHOST PORTAL!
- FUTURE EYE — LOOK INTO THE FUTURE
- FIRE SYMBOL — ?

FRONT

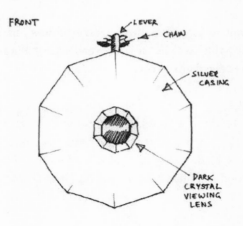

She looked again at the only remaining unexplained symbol, the heart, which lead her to Eucrates next point.

Where the heart is concerned, one can only muse (deliberate). Perhaps this was selected as a substitute image because the more accurate (truthful) device was already engaged (in use).

So the heart symbol is somehow misleading? Was that what Eucrates was trying to say? If it doesn't mean 'heart', what does it mean? And why had the truer symbol already been used? She glanced at each of the other symbols in turn, wondering which of them Eucrates was referring to, and was left baffled. She moved on to the third paragraph, wishing Melissa was with her.

On another matter I learned of a myth this day that told of the spirits succumbing to the lordship of he who wears a ring of gallows iron. Have you ever heard such a thing? A ring of gallows iron worn and wielded by my namesake, nonetheless! It is surely make-believe.

Tyler googled 'ring of gallows iron' and was amazed when one of the search results read 'The Ring of Eucrates'. She stared at the screen.

Unbelievable!

She clicked through to the resulting webpage and read comments about a Greek writer named Lucian who had lived in the second century AD. She read extracts from something he'd written entitled The Liar, in which a character named Eucrates told of his ring of gallows iron, given to him by an Arab, who also imparted an incantation. The ring bore a magical seal and, with it, Eucrates had supposedly controlled an apparition, sending it into a vast, mysterious chasm. After further research she learned Lucian's fictional character, Eucrates, was merely a humorous parody. *So much for his info on the ring. It's all invented nonsense meant to poke fun at those who believe in such claptrap...*

...or is it? Perhaps Lucian was paraphrasing someone he had heard talking, or something he had read, and was mocking them directly. If this was the case, there could be some element of truth in his tale, although he would not have been aware of it!

For a while she waded through pages of associated, yet uninteresting, information and learned that *gallows iron* was iron taken from a gallows or a cross, from a coffin, or was any iron associated with the dead or graveyards. This gallows iron, usually in the form of drawn nails, could be hammered and worked to form finger rings, said to have magical powers over spirits. She googled 'coffin nails' and read snippets from some creepy websites. Coffin nails, it seemed, were widely understood to have magical value and were used as protective talismans, for hexes and curses, in numerous countries around the world. Archaeological search results also backed up this theory as singular, long nails, placed purposefully in many ancient and medieval graves, were thought to have been deposited as protective charms. She speed-read a long article debating the recipient of this suggested protection, but the essay lacked any firm conclusions. The nails were placed in the graves to stop the dead from rising and therefore to protect the living, or they were there to keep malevolent spirits and powers away from the grave thereby protecting the dead. Either

t seemed that, in antiquity, nails were also
ıdered to be powerful in some way.

Tyler shivered and went to bed with her head
spinning, unnerved by her findings.

Extraction

Tyler stirred with a sense that she'd forgotten something as morning light glowed from Albert's gap in the curtains. The feeling irritated her for the duration of breakfast which, today, was in a café a few blocks from their hotel, late morning. She finally remembered the issue as Lucy drew a skull smiley on the table with her fingertip in spilt coffee.

"Streicher!" She phoned Chapman, speaking quietly enough for no one beyond their table to overhear.

"Ghost?"

"Yes. I need a copy of the report I made to the police after the Christmas Eve Incident. Can you email it through?"

"Anything else?"

"No."

"It'll be with you shortly."

"Thanks." Tyler pocketed her phone.

"What was all *that* about?" asked Lucy, pulling on her jacket. Tyler leant in close to the others.

"When I passed Angel in the hallway he was talking on the phone. I didn't understand anything he said because he was speaking German, but I did recognise a name; Streicher. I knew I'd heard it somewhere before. I just realised where, but I need to check. I think Streicher was one of the men who helped create the GAUNT machine. It'll all be in the statement I gave to the police four years ago."

"The GAUNT machine? Was that the machine that brought back the six Nazi ghosts?" asked Klaus.

"Precisely. So, if I'm right, it's not great to hear this Streicher is still around."

"Not great at all," said Lucy. "Listen, we'd best get back to Zebedee and get an update on Angel. He'll be wondering where we are."

They found Zebedee, as they had left him, watching Angel from the multi-storey car park across the street from his office.

"He seems considerably vexed," Zebedee reported as they joined him. "I do believe he's noticed something is missing."

Tyler told Zebedee everything she had discovered and learned about the parchment from Angel's office.

"Can you put it back without him seeing you?" Lucy asked him.

"I could try, but he's likely to sense my presence. It would be risky."

"We don't want to rattle him," said Klaus. "He might bolt again and we could lose him."

"No. Don't put the parchment back. We're going in

to take him. Tonight," said Tyler.

"What?" asked Lucy.

"We've waited long enough. We've observed him. We've noted his movements. We know he likes to be home by twenty-hundred hours. That's where he will be tonight. In his new pad. We'll take him before he enters the house. It's time."

*

Street lamps ended half a mile from Angel's latest residence, a reclusive country house overshadowed by high trees to the rear and to the side. It was easy to see why he had chosen the property. It was remote and yet not too far from the city. Out here no one would hear a scream as he violently removed the occupants and assumed ownership. *Who was slain during the takeover? Where are the bodies?* It did have one minor flaw: The fields all around it were crisscrossed with small tracks and lanes. Close by, in one of these, Tyler, Lucy, Klaus and Albert waited in the car as the sky darkened to an Egyptian blue; cloudless and star-peppered. Lights at the end of the lane sparked a jolt of nerves in Tyler's gut, each time a car passed.

Lucy checked out the old house through the night-vision scope of her LM7 sharp shooter's rifle. She had already loaded it with a dart carrying enough tranquiliser to knock out two men.

Through the *Present Eye*, Tyler scanned the unoccupied house and its surrounding farmland for other gloves or reveries but found only cattle grazing peaceably. A comprehensive, physical search of the property could wait until after the capture. She wondered how far away the nearest graveyard was. *I hope Heydrich is not planning to visit Angel tonight.* She boxed the contrap and wound her window down further. Beyond the glass, insects hummed in the darkness. She fixed her view on a black van, parked down another lane on the other side of the house and glimpsed Weaver and Freddy Carter, or Agent Pratt, as he was codenamed. Chapman had brought in the boys for Angel's extraction, and Tyler was glad of the backup.

The plan was smart and simple. All the same, Tyler went over and over it in her head. At around twenty-hundred hours, Angel would return to the house, driving in his grey, stolen Audi. He would park the Audi in the same parking space he had been previously observed using, in front of the house. His walk from the car to the front door was a matter of ten metres. Lucy would hit him with the tranquiliser, two if he didn't go down quickly. Angel would drop and Tyler would make a call. The boys would drive in and collect Angel in the van. Tyler liked that. She would not need to go anywhere near Angel. She didn't want to. Didn't want to touch him, or even go close. Not unless it was to suck his ghosts into the chasm. The boys would carry Angel, incapacitated, into the back of the van where Albert and Zebedee would be waiting with Mordecai chains at the ready. Angel, tranquilised and bound, would be transported to the MI6 black site airport and flown to London. He would be coffined and carried from the plane directly into the MI6 secure facility without seeing a single streak of daylight.

Simple. Right? What can possibly go wrong? So why is my stomach a sack of snakes?

1930 hours. No sign of Angel.

Tyler boxed the contrap. He should be arriving soon and she did not want him to sense it and bolt. From here on in, the contrap would need to stay concealed. Tyler waited. Twenty hundred hours came and went.

Lucy rubbed her temples, bristling for action.

"Maybe he's not going to show."

"He'll show. Just sit tight."

An hour and fifty-two minutes later, Albert appeared outside Tyler's window.

"Angel's on 'is way. Get ready!" He vanished, going to join Zebedee in the van.

A moment later, car lights swept into the road leading to the house, illuminating the tall grass and willowy trees at the verge. Tyler used field glasses to follow its progress. *All well and good. Angel has finally made an appearance.* But a second car pulled into the road, following Angel's Audi. *Not part of the plan. Angel has brought some friends home. Albert, why didn't you warn me?*

Tyler's mobile buzzed. She checked the caller ID: Chapman.

"I see Angel has company."

"Yes, Sir." Tyler tried to see how many were in the second car and thought she made out three figures.

"Do you want to abort?"

Silence. Tyler thought desperately, reluctant to abandon the chance of grabbing Angel. The team in the van would hear her response via their in-ear comms.

"No. We'll sit tight. Wait it out. See what happens. His friends will have to leave sometime. When they do, we'll take Angel."

"Very well. Good luck, Ghost."

"You think we should put a tracer on the car? Track these guys?" asked Lucy, as Tyler pocketed her mobile.

"No," said Tyler. "It's a nice idea but I don't want anything to jeopardize our primary objective."

*

Klaus nudged Lucy awake. Across the grounds, the front door of Angel's house was opening.

"Rise and shine, Mojo," hissed Tyler. "They're leaving."

Lucy stretched before focusing on the door with her LM7's crosshairs. She scrutinised the slight rustle of the wind in the trees, compensating her aim accordingly to account for drift.

"He's coming out with them."

"Get ready," said Tyler. "Soon as they drive away, take Angel down. Boys, you ready?" She heard Weaver's steady reply via her comms.

"Affirmative."

Tyler used field glasses while chewing her fingernail. The three visitors left the doorway in a span of escaping warm light, and crossed the gravel to their car. Angel accompanied them and shook their hands in turn. The visitors climbed in and drove away leaving Angel to return to the house and, reaching the end of the driveway the car turned the corner and was lost to sight. Angel was still several paces from his door.

"Green light."

Lucy pulled the trigger, the silenced shot making Tyler jump, even though she'd expected it. Out on the porch steps, Angel stiffened as the dart impacted. He pulled it from his shoulder and stared at it, stumbling into the doorway as the interior light went out.

"Damn it. I can't see a thing!" said Tyler, squinting for a sign of Angel through her binoculars. She switched back to night-vision. "Where did he go?"

"I lost him as soon as he dropped," said Lucy, reloading. "The car's in the way."

"Extract!" said Tyler. "We think he's down. He took a hit."

"Roger that."

The rumble of an engine reached them across the short distance as Weaver brought the black van into the driveway, lights off. As he pulled up at the front of the house a fiery explosion rocked the air, blowing the back of the house into the night with a vast plume of flames and smoke. Weaver and Freddy sprinted from the van amidst raining debris.

"What was that?" asked Lucy.

"Who knows?"

"He's detonated a little safety precaution," said Klaus, watching flames through his binoculars. "Seems we'll not be investigating the property, after all."

"Guess he had something to hide in there. Weaver, Freddy, do you have visual?"

"Negative."

"We're coming in." Tyler gave a nod and she, Lucy and Klaus rushed out from car to cross the farmland between the road and the driveway.

"Spread out," said Klaus. "He could be anywhere!" They separated, sweeping torches around the stubbly grass before reaching the driveway to fight through a low hedge and a ditch bordering its length. Finding no sign of Angel, they hurried to the porch where Freddy waited in the flickering glow of the burning house.

"Weaver's searching for him. We found this." He handed Lucy Angel's discarded dart. She held it up in the fire light.

"He may have only received half a dose," she said. "He pulled the dart free quickly. It needs a second or two to fully inject."

"You're saying he might not be fully knocked out?"

"That's exactly what I'm saying. I couldn't get a second shot in because he dropped out of view. I'm gonna take a look around." Lucy headed out into the gardens, searching the shadows through her night-vision rifle scope.

The timbers groaned and a section at the side of the building collapsed. A cascade of burning cinders ascended as fire rose, gaining momentum. Weaver ran around from the side of the house to shout over the roar of the hungry flames.

"We should get out of here! There could be gas. The whole place could blow any minute."

Tyler hesitated.

"What about Angel? He could still be inside!"

"It doesn't matter," bellowed Weaver. "Leave him!"

"And wonder forevermore if he was in there? No. I need to know! You can search the grounds. I'm going in." Tyler charged through the open doorway, as yet untouched by the fire. She felt the heated air even in the porch, and slowed to walk the length of the hall, checking unoccupied rooms along the way. Windows shattered with heat as she worked towards the inferno at the rear and she quickly decided Angel had not re-entered the house. *Why would he when he was going to blow it up?* She backtracked and fled out into the night as more of the structure gave way and rooms folded. She stopped a few metres from the house to squint into the dark grounds. To her left, Weaver worked his way along an unkempt hedge line, checking for Angel. Freddy was nowhere to be seen. She located Lucy at the edge of the garden as Lucy shouted and a muffled shot sounded.

"Lucy!" Tyler bolted across the lawn as Lucy fell, her

rifle released to land in the grass. A second figure was there, sprawled on the ground. Tyler neared and saw it was Angel. Lucy moaned and heaved herself up, nursing her bruised eye.

"Lucy! Are you okay?" asked Tyler, as Weaver reached them. Freddy approached at a jog.

"I found him lurking in the ditch," Lucy explained. "He tried to shoot me but I knocked the gun out of his hand before he could fire. That's when he punched me in the eye."

"But I heard a gunshot!" said Tyler before noticing the tranquiliser dart protruding from Angel's chest. "Oh. Thank goodness."

Freddy arrived to gawp around at them all.

"You got him. We did it!"

Tyler nodded, enjoying a moment of self-congratulation. She looked around at the others with a half-smile.

"We have Angel."

The Power of Ghosts

Behind them, the last standing remnants of the house creaked. Lucy climbed into the van's passenger seat to check her black eye in the vanity mirror. Across the garden the others stood over their prize. Albert carried a Mordecai chain over and launched it at Angel.

"Mordecai obligo." The phantom chain wrapped itself around Angel like a constrictor enfolding its dinner.

"Next time *you* wake up you'll be in London," said Freddy.

"The fire department will be here soon. This blaze must be visible for miles." Weaver glanced at the road with concern. "We better move out."

"You two bring the van closer," said Tyler to Weaver and Freddy. "Klaus, get the car." They left her guarding Angel. She waited until Weaver and Freddy had reached the van before taking the contrap from its box and setting its switch to the *Brimstone Chasm*. She drew the lever full circle until it clicked back into its original position, and muttered the words.

"Vorago expositus." The chasm opened, shedding a fiery glow over Angel and issuing its stink. She sensed a movement off to her left, in her peripheral vision.

"Phasmatis..."

Albert appeared, warning her.

"Look out!"

Weaver reached her, tackling her to the ground and sending the contrap tumbling from her hands. Tyler yelped and kicked him off.

"What do you think you're doing?" she demanded.

"I could ask you the same," said Weaver getting to his feet. "We've orders to bring him in. Not dispose of him! Chapman wants to question him. You can't put him into that thing. Not yet, anyway."

Tyler retrieved the contrap, checking it for damage. Finding none, she closed the chasm and put it safely back into its box before glaring at Weaver.

"Well, you can't blame a girl for trying. Guess I'll have to wait a day or two."

*

Rain welcomed them home. London, grey and solemn, received Angel, bound, boxed, and in secrecy. Tyler personally oversaw the coffin's short journey from Crows Nest to The Roost. She copied her list from memory and ticked off the first item.

Extract Angel from Buenos Aires √
Locate and recover the Vice President of Brazil
Find out how the NVF are recruiting their ghosts
Find out what the ghost spies are doing

Put Reinhard Heydrich and Adolf Eichmann into the chasm

She burned the list as Klaus frowned at her.

"What...?"

"Don't ask."

"Will he stay in The Roost, or is Chapman taking him somewhere else?" asked Klaus, as agents carried the coffin into a prison-like cell.

"He's here for the duration."

A small screen in the control room relayed live video of room twenty-seven. The agents lowered the coffin onto the floor and unbolted its lid with power tools. They removed the lid and recoiled at the sight of the unearthly chain binding Angel. He lay rigid and unmoving as the agents backed away. Tyler hit *talk* and lent close to the console microphone.

"Don't worry. It won't hurt you."

The agents returned to Angel and heaved him up onto the bare prison mattress.

"Will you question him, also?"

"I'm not sure. I want to but, then again, I don't want to go anywhere near him."

"I can help," said Klaus.

"First things first."

A team of scientists in the cell arranged a tray of syringes and medical instruments to begin their study of the glove.

*

Melissa sat on her bed facing the window of her room. Tyler watched her through the doorway, from the sterile corridor.

"She spoke for the first time yesterday," said a

willowy nurse named Nema. "She's expecting you."
Nema left, her heels echoing a clipped beat.

Tyler entered. The bedroom was spacious but
uninviting despite excellent views of the clinic's exquisite
gardens.

"We have to get you out of here. I'll help you pack."

Melissa turned to peer vacantly at Tyler.

"Get me out?" she murmured slowly. "Where are we
going?"

"Home." Tyler found a bag and began packing
Melissa's few possessions. "This place isn't going to help
you get better. How do you feel?"

"Cold. Numb inside."

Tyler poked at an abandoned plate of salad with a
fork. "Not hungry, eh? I don't blame you."

"They have me on this hideous diet. It's supposed to
make be better."

"Do you remember anything?"

"What?" Melissa appeared to not understand.

"Do you remember anything from the cemetery?"

Melissa stared.

"We followed Angel into the cemetery and you went
to get closer. Do you even know what's happened to
you?"

Melissa shook her head and frowned, on the verge of
tears. Tyler dropped the bag and hugged her.

"Come on. I'm going to make you a bacon
sandwich."

*

The Roost: 1400 hours

Chapman met Tyler and Lucy at the door.

"I'm afraid I have to ask you to relinquish the

contrap before entering."

"Yes, Sir." Tyler reluctantly handed it over. "I get it back when I leave, right?"

"On my word."

Tyler and Lucy went in, heading straight to the interview suite where a bullet proof, two-way mirror wall separated them from Angel.

Thanks for nothing, Weaver.

On the other side of the mirror Angel, now free of the Mordecai chain, but straight-jacketed, wearing a biter mask and leg shackles, sat opposite Klaus at a table in the interview room. Klaus calmly observed Angel, awaiting Tyler's questions to be fed through his ear piece. Angel's face was bruising up with deep purple welts, a consequence of Chapman's earlier *interview*, and there remained only the faintest smudges of skin-toned makeup so that, even in the stark strip-lighting of the room, his skin shimmered an unnatural pale blue. A trickle of blue blood leaked from his left nostril.

"Ask him how Heydrich is controlling the reveries," began Tyler.

"How is Heydrich controlling the reveries?"

Angel laughed, smiling through the grill of his mask.

"You think I'm going to tell you anything? You are wrong."

"Ask him if he knows what a ring of gallows iron is."

Klaus asked. Angel chuckled again and Tyler registered the hesitation that pre-empted his reaction. *That meant something to you.*

"What is this *gallows iron*?" asked Angel.

"Why was Heydrich carrying a photograph of the Spear of Destiny?" asked Tyler. Klaus posed the question to Angel.

Angel stopped laughing and peered intently at Klaus. "What is the Spear of Destiny?"

"He knows very well what it is," Tyler told Klaus. "The spear was one of Hilter's many obsessions when he was alive."

"Maybe it's Mengele talking and not Hitler," said Lucy. "Mengele wouldn't necessarily know about the spear."

"True. Okay. This is pointless," said Tyler, heading for the door. "I'm done."

Angel looked knowingly at the mirror.

"You know, I have a question for you, about the last symbol."

Tyler paused and turned towards the glass.

"I'm listening." Klaus relayed her reply.

"I was just wondering: Have you learned its meaning?"

"Which is the last symbol?" relayed Klaus, but Angel only dissolved into hysterical laughter. As Tyler and Lucy left, he ranted at the glass in his thick, German accent.

"War is coming and you can't stop it! You and your kind will be liquidated and there is nothing you can do!"

*

A list of emails filled Tyler's laptop screen. She sought one in particular, a message from Chapman with an attached statement she'd made for the police about the Christmas Eve Incident. She found it, clicked it open, and read through the report she had written over four years ago, scanning for the name Streicher. She found it part way down the second page.

I witnessed scientists discussing some kind of weird experiments outside the NVF laboratory building in

Ducks Hill Road, Watford. One of them looked like he was a soldier, or perhaps a retired soldier, another had tattoos down his arms and a third, who was short and overweight, was named Streicher.

Tyler pictured the scene again, in lucid detail; a group of scientists taking a cigarette break out the back of their laboratory, talking carelessly, oblivious to her presence as she watched and listened with the *Past Eye*. She recalled their discussion about the gloved ghosts, something she only pieced together later with Melissa's help, and she saw again Streicher's rounded, boyish face.

Streicher was one of the scientists responsible for creating the GAUNT machine and bringing back Hitler and his associates from the dead.

Why, oh why, didn't I take German at school? I should have taken Melissa back to the corridor where Angel had been talking on the phone. I should have had her use the Past Eye *to find out exactly what Angel said. But then, with the contrap it's never too late.*

She turned her attention to the documents she had photographed in Angel's office in Buenos Aires, clicking on a folder to view images. Among a variety of invoices for seemingly innocent services, business proposals and purchases, she found a letter that also mentioned Streicher. Thankfully, it was in English. It showed no sender's name, but only a solitary initial where the name should be, and was addressed to Mr. A. Crane of Hobson and Crane Industries, at the Buenos Aires office address.

Dear Mr Crane,

I must report that the whereabouts of the man you

seek is still unknown. I have confirmation of his prior residence in Watford and a following address in London, the same as listed in the dossier disclosed to us by your source here.

Lucas Streicher has not lived at this later address for more than three years now and continues to elude our sources. I will, of course, inform you immediately should I learn more.

Regards,

D

Tyler copied the images to Chapman in an email, for analysis, and closed the laptop.

*

The mobile phone on Tyler's bedside table buzzed, shocking her awake. She peered into the shadows of her bedroom trying to work out what was happening. It was not only her phone she could hear. From the other girls' rooms other phones vibrated. She grabbed her mobile and answered the call, peering blearily at the dazzlingly bright caller ID.

"Ghost, get here now. The Angel has flown. Five minutes ago Crows Nest was blown clean off the face of the planet."

"What?" She managed to focus enough to read the red LED alarm clock on her bedside table: 1.06 a.m.

"The explosion was a diversion. The vast amount of our available agents went immediately to help. While we were distracted, Angel's people fell on The Roost, but there's no time. Get here, now, with Lucy and her bike."

"Angel's escaped?"

"Affirmative."

Lucy burst through Tyler's door.

"You heard?"

Tyler nodded.

"We're on our way, Sir." She threw on clothes and met Lucy in the hall where she collected her black ops mission bag.

They left Melissa standing in her nightdress, looking confused by the disturbance, to shoot through London's streets on Lucy's black Aprilia, speeding the whole way. At The Roost, Chapman waited to take them to a side door of the facility that was peppered with gunshot damage. They rushed past ambulances and paramedics aiding injured agents. A pair of paramedics carried out a gurney with a loaded body bag.

"He fled through this exit twenty minutes ago while his men held the place down with gunfire. He was bundled into a van right there and driven away." Chapman pointed to a spot across the road, opposite the facility's gates. "Use the contrap. Trace him. I want him back here within the hour. Lucy can carry you pillion."

"Yes, Sir." Tyler took out the contrap and, setting it to the *Past Eye*, searched back through the last twenty minutes, peering into the lens with one eye. Lucy brought the bike around and stowed the helmets on the back.

"We'll be better off if we ride without them," she said. "You need to see into the contrap and I need to hear your directions. Get on the back."

Tyler climbed on behind Lucy and pointed down the street to their right.

"That way!"

Lucy revved the Aprilia and took off.

"Wow! Slow down. They're in a van not a Ferrari!"

Lucy braked.

"Next left."

Lucy guided the Aprilia through London under Tyler's directions, crossing the Thames on Tower Bridge.

"I have a bad feeling about this," said Tyler, as they headed into Whitechapel.

"And what part of the last four years have you ever had a *good* feeling about?" They passed the Tower of London.

"I see your point. Bear left." In the contrap's lens, Angel's van sped through a break in the traffic, heading towards a rail bridge.

"Tyler, we're on a one way system. He can only have gone right."

Tyler tracked the van's progress as it threaded between cars.

"Uh-huh. He just went right."

"I think I know where he's going," Lucy called back to her. "South Sea House."

"Yes. He's turning into Whitechapel." Further down the street, Tyler watched Angel's van pull over and he bolted from the side door, fleeing into South Sea House, the pale, stone-built NVF HQ Chapman had previously investigated. It seemed the occupants were expecting him because, as he ascended the stone steps, the white front door flew open and he slipped quickly inside as the van drove away.

"He went in. Pull over. I'll call it in."

Lucy parked at the curb and Tyler hopped off the motorbike to phone Chapman.

"We tracked him to South Sea House, Sir. I'm pretty

sure he's still inside." Tyler peered through the contrap, training its lens upon the door to the stately house awkwardly with one hand, while holding her phone to her ear with the other. "Should we go in?"

"No. Wait. I'm sending a team. We don't know what you might face in there. If you go in alone they might overpower you. Conceal yourselves and watch the front. I'll have agents cover the back. Wait a minute. Are Albert and Zebedee with you?"

"Albert is. Zebedee's at home keeping an eye on Cog."

"Have Albert recon. Report back. It seems they used ghosts to get through our security and then initiate the escape from within. They really caught us off-guard this time. I'm afraid I've grossly underestimated the power of their ghosts."

"So it seems." Tyler tucked her phone away as she turned to Lucy.

"He wants Albert to check it out. We're to watch the door."

Albert remained invisible.

"On my way, Missy. I'll be back soon."

"Be careful, Albert!"

Alfric Crane

Lucy parked and chained her Aprilia safely out of sight and re-joined Tyler at the bus stop across the road from South Sea House.

"Déjà vu.   Do you think they know we're here?" asked Lucy.

"I'm not sure. I've been watching through the *Past Eye* so we don't miss anything, but that means I can't look through the walls.   Do you think I should swap to the *Present Eye*? I could take a look at what's going on in there right now, with that."

"But if you take the *Past Eye* off the door you might miss seeing Angel leaving and we'd lose him."

"Good point. I stick with this. Let Albert do his thing. How long's he been gone now?"

"About five minutes. He should be back soon."

Albert waived his usual etiquette, forming in the

street before them, looking frantic. Several pedestrians gave the bus stop a wide birth.

"'E ain't in there. I looked everywhere. Angel's gone!"

"What?"

"He must've used a back way before Chapman's men arrived."

"Right. Is *anyone* in there?"

Albert shook his head. "The 'ole place is empty. There's not even a ghost."

"Then I'm going in. We have to know where he is."

"You want company?" asked Lucy.

"No. Stay here and call it in."

Albert vanished as he accompanied Tyler across the road. She picked the lock of the grand, white door, and backed down the steps to use the *Past Eye* again, backtracking to the moment Angel had entered some twenty minutes earlier. She located the past moment and followed him into the dark building as two shadowy men guided him through the lobby and deeper into the building. They led him down a dark flight of stairs and through corridors, pausing only to turn on a lamp and give him a handful of passports. Angel took a moment to flick through the one on top of the pile and nodded approvingly. Tyler tweaked the contrap's lever to replay while she stepped closer for a better view. The top passport was British and she glimpsed the name.

Alfric Crane.

From a storeroom, Angel's helpers produced a black trench coat, a trilby and a scarf, all of which he donned, and they handed him a russet suitcase. Tyler whispered to Albert, now visible at her side.

"There're two men with him. They're giving him

everything he needs to escape the country." She called Chapman to update him.

"He's travelling under the name of Alfric Crane. I'm in pursuit."

"Be careful, Ghost. We've found more agents deeper in The Roost. They were stabbed to death by a narrow-bladed weapon. I'm having trouble making sense of what happened. There's no way anyone could have penetrated that far without being seen."

"Right." She pocketed her phone and watched Angel slip the passports into the inside pocket of his coat. He carried the case as his two accomplices led him down into a lower level of the house, this one undecorated and dusty. In the musty air of the cellar they paused, dragging away a rug to reveal a trapdoor that they hauled open. Angel peered into the gloom of the opening and dropped his bag through. His helpers lowered him down before closing the trapdoor and replacing the rug. They left, heading back the way they had come. Tyler lowered the contrap and examined the room. It was just as they had left it with the rug covering the door, disturbed dust on the floor around the edge revealing where they had been.

"Albert, there's a trapdoor." She pulled the rug aside. "I need to know what's down there."

Albert knelt to pass his head through the door and look around before resurfacing.

"It's very dark down there, but there ain't no ghosts. Not now. No sign of Angel."

"Thanks." Tyler lifted the door, took her Maglite from her bag and shone it into the hole. A dank floor, strewn with rubble and dirt in its further reaches. The light struck an ancient-looking, stone wall to one side, glistening with moisture and, as she searched, the other walls of a small chamber came to light. She gripped the edges of the trapdoor and lowered herself down.

"What *is* this place?" She fixed the beam on a low archway in the wall before them.

"I dunno," said Albert, gawping around. "I fink it's Roman."

"How do you know that?"

"I used to play in some Roman lead mines when I was a kid. That were before me and my Da moved to London. The walls kind o' looked like this. Smelt the same too."

"It *could* be Roman. The first London town *was* built by them." She ducked under the arch and followed a second chamber to an outlet of three tunnels where she stopped to consult the *Past Eye*. She levered back through time again and watched Angel take the tunnel on her right. She followed, knowing her use of the contrap might endanger her and yet not knowing what else to do. Angel was on the run and probably miles away by now. All the same, the dark, dripping tunnels she now tracked him through were eerie and she could not curb a shiver. She regretted leaving Lucy on Whitechapel and took out her mobile to call. *Dammit, no signal.*

"Albert, don't leave me."

"Never, Missy."

She plodded on, checking Angel's movements whenever she reached a junction. Further on in the underground passage she watched him place his bag down to search in the dark at the foot of a wall that closed off end of a side tunnel. Above him, around a metre from the ground, a small hole in the brickwork allowed a dull speck of light through. Angel found a crowbar, the thing he'd been seeking and, wedging it into the hole, began levering bricks free. He worked away at the wall until he had made a gap big enough for him to enter before discarding the crowbar. He shoved his case through to the other side and scrambled after it.

She crawled through to land, knee deep in water, but was relieved to smell the same stale, humid air as before, with no trace of a sewer's stench. Around her, tunnel walls glistened with dark, Tudor brick. Above her, way up at the top of a shaft, a drain grate allowed streetlight to filter in stripes from the road above. Angel had turned left, here, retrieving his floating case and wading on. She gripped the contrap and ran, splashing her way down the culvert, getting soaked from head to foot, but making good progress. Half a mile or so further on, she watched Angel ascend an access ladder up to a higher level. Climbing this, she came to another wall of modern concrete, offering a single exit by way of an iron door. She heaved on this stubborn hatch with all her strength until it reluctantly opened to reveal a dull yellow glow beyond. She tentatively looked out into a modern tunnel of sectioned concrete and recognised it as the Underground. Block lights punctuating the rounded walls to illuminate rail tracks and grime-blackened pipework. She willed her phone to work and, finding two bars of signal, waited for Chapman to finish barking commands to others at his end of the line.

"Lock this place down and find out where that tunnel leads. Yes, Ghost?"

"The passage beneath South Sea House leads out to an underground river. I followed it to a tube tunnel. But I don't know where I am. There's no satellite signal down here. Not much of any signal. I'll have to track Angel again just to find out how to get out of here."

"I'm checking a map. The closest subterranean river to Whitechapel Road is the Walbrook. You must be near Liverpool Street or Bank Station. If you're half an hour or so behind Angel, he could be at Heathrow by now. Ghost, hold the line. I have another call."

Tyler peered in either direction down the tunnel, and discerned the distant rattle and hum of a train. *Which way?*

Chapman came back online.

"That was Heathrow security. They clocked one Alfric Crane boarding a plane for Buenos Aires, but my call reached them too late. There were attempts to prevent the plane from taking off which, unfortunately, failed. Angel's airborne. We've instructed security at Jorge Newbery to pick him up when his flight lands. Good work, Ghost. Time to come home. Get some sleep and be in the office at ten hundred hours for debrief. We have some serious matters to discuss."

*

Melissa, in a dressing gown and sporting pink, fluffy slippers, stared at the computer's widescreen while scrolling through image after image, dazed. Tyler exited the shower and padded to her in the lounge, hair wrapped high in a white towel, another towel covering everything from her armpits to her knees.

"What you doing?" she asked before glimpsing the screen and instantly becoming more interested.

"I don't really know," said Melissa. "I keep getting this image in my head. It's like my subconscious mind is trying to work out something." On the screen more photographic and illustrative images of the Spear of Destiny scrolled. Tyler took a seat beside her.

"You remember!"

"I remember what? Why am I obsessing about the Spear of Destiny? I think I'm losing my mind!"

"No, Mel. You're finding it!" Tyler fetched her bag, took out her notebook, and retrieved the photo from its pages. She handed it over as Lucy, hair like a scarecrow, shuffled in from her bedroom to the breakfast bar in the open plan kitchen where she clicked the kettle on.

"What's this?" asked Melissa.

"Lucy, look at this!" Tyler beckoned her over and Lucy peered blearily at the screen.

"Yeah, I know. That's the Spear of Destiny. So what?"

"Let me get this straight," said Tyler to Melissa. "Nobody told you about this photo? About how we found it on you when we rescued you from the reveries?"

"No. Is that what happened?"

Tyler nodded.

"We were spying on Angel and Reinhard Heydrich. Heydrich carried you away on his shoulder when Lucy and I were trapped in a tomb. We tracked Heydrich and found you later in an underground tomb chamber, surrounded by reveries. We carried you back to the car and that's when we found *this* stuffed in your pocket. Mel, it could be important. How did you get this photo?"

Melissa gazed at the photograph and shook her head.

"I'm not sure. It's all pretty hazy. But I woke up this morning with this same image in my mind and I've been studying the Spear of Destiny ever since. From what I can tell, it's made up of at least ten separate components, of which only three pieces are from the original spear. Not that *original* is an appropriate term when talking about the spear that supposedly pierced Christ's side. For one thing, I've been researching Roman, military spears and there aren't many that look much like the Spear of Destiny, even if you take off all these extra bits and pieces that other people have added down the ages. It's also known as the Holy Lance of St. Maurice because of a legend about it belonging to a martyred Roman soldier, but it looks more like a seventh century spear to me. Look. See these branches sticking out on either side at the bottom? Designed to stop your quarry from getting any closer to you once you've jabbed him. The Franks and the Vikings used these spears. Sometimes they're referred to as hunting spears because of the barbs. These other bits of blade above the wings have been added later on. They're supposedly the knife blades that cut the robe of Christ when the Roman soldiers divided his belongings at the foot of the cross, throwing the dice to see who got what.

"Whatever the spear's origins, it's certainly been owned by some big names down the line; Emperor Constantine, Charlemagne, Napoleon and Hitler to name but a few. Hitler had the original spear locked away, but one account suggests he had a copy made."

Lucy glanced at Tyler.

"Well, I think we can safely say that Melissa's feeling better."

"Yeah. Back to her old, irregular self."

Melissa grinned.

"And another thing, it's also called the spear of *Longinus*, supposedly the name of the centurion who used the spear to pierce the side of Christ, but it's all myth that's been added to the story centuries after the historical accounts of the event."

"Right. So what are all these other bits of metal that were added later?" Tyler studied the various images on the screen which all showed a long, leaf-shaped, iron spearhead with a central section encased in gold.

"Well, it's been owned by many rulers throughout history, interestingly, in ten eighty-four, King Henry the fourth, a founder of the First Reich, had a silver band added to it. He had it inscribed with the words 'Nail of Our Lord'." Melissa clicked on a close-up image of the golden sheath and it filled the screen, the gothic, Latin words clearly visible. "You see, earlier on, someone else cut a section from the blade and fixed a nail in place; a nail said to be from the true cross of Christ. The spear is now on display in the Imperial Treasury in Vienna."

"Wait. Wait a minute." Tyler's head was buzzing. "A nail drawn from the cross that killed Christ? But wouldn't that make it..." Tyler met Lucy's eyes.

"Gallows iron!"

Gallows Iron

Melissa gave Tyler a blank look.

"What's *Gallow's iron*? Who is Gallow?"

Tyler turned a few pages of her notebook and picked out the parchment she had taken from Angel's office.

"Gallows iron. Not Gallow's iron," said Lucy.

"Well, thanks for clearing that up."

"*Gallows* as in the thing they hang people on. Gallows iron is iron taken from a gallows or a coffin, or some other iron associated with death." Tyler told Melissa about the parchment and read her Klaus' translation.

"Then yes, the nail set in the spear is gallows iron. And so is the entire spear, probably."

"We think this might be the way Heydrich controlling the reveries," explained Lucy.

"Yes. I see. Because of what the parchment says."

"So it follows that Mengele might have a vested

interest in the spear. Perhaps he's after it."

"Of course. Wait. I read something earlier about Hitler being obsessed with the spear, too."

"And Mengele is now also Hitler. It's too much of a coincidence."

"I remember!" said Melissa.

"What?"

"I remember how I got the photograph! I took it from Heydrich while he was carrying me! I was woozy and I couldn't see straight. I think I passed out more than once but, for a moment or two, I could see okay and I saw this thing sticking out of his pocket. I grabbed it without him noticing and looked at it. I didn't know what it was so I shoved it in my pocket before passing out again."

"We better tell Chapman. Get yourself ready. We're meeting him in an hour, and you're coming with us."

*

Chapman finished a call and nodded.

"Come in. Take a seat. It's good to see you back with the team, Agent Cog. I trust you're feeling better."

"Much, Sir."

"Tyler, good work getting his passport name. It's going to make all the difference as we try to mop up this mess. To put your minds at ease, I'll begin by telling you we have an air marshal watching Angel, and a team preparing to take him into custody when his plane lands in Buenos Aires." Chapman swiped fingers together on the briefing room's touch screen to zoom in on a map of the Atlantic and the Americas where Angel's flight path displayed as an extending red, dotted line. "Although this is already in place, I'd like you three to go out there. Chain him. Have your ghost friends check for any interference from other ghosts. Escort Angel home and make sure nothing else goes awry. Stealth is no longer an issue. As far as the rest of the world's concerned, he's an internationally wanted criminal and we have some damning evidence to back that up. Get him home, whatever it takes."

"Yes, Sir," replied the girls.

"Now, about these ghosts... I've met Albert Goodwin and Zebedee Lieberman, and I'm aware they are an established and trusted part of your team, but our opposition has ghosts, too. The fact they have a multitude of ghosts at their beck and call concerns me. Tyler reported as much after witnessing an entire army in preparation. My question to you is this: How do we recruit our own team of ghost spies? Surely if the enemy can use them, so can we. We'd be stupid not to. And you are my only experts in this field."

"There are the others who helped me in the chasm, Sir," said Tyler. "I can ask them to join us permanently."

"Are they all trusted? I mean truly reliable *and* trustworthy?"

"Yes, Sir. I'd trust them with my life. In fact, I already have."

"Do it. Ask them. Have them swear the oath. Enrol them. I'm making this your sub team. Agent Ghost will be the major. Cog and Pointer, you are her lieutenants. All ghost recruits will fall in rank beneath you. Recruit and organise. If this thing doesn't go away soon, we'll need the Ghost Squad, and you, ready for duty. Okay?"

"Yes, Sir."

"We'll help," said Albert, appearing with Zebedee.

"Of course!" said Zebedee. "We'll swear the oath."

"Good. I hoped you would."

"Sir, we have some intel of our own to report," said

Lucy, as Albert and Zebedee vanished.

"I'm listening."

"It's about the Spear of Destiny. Remember the photograph we found on Melissa?"

"Yes."

"Well, Melissa remembers taking it from Heydrich." Lucy explained what they had learned about gallows iron and from Klaus' translation, as Tyler produced the photograph and the Eucrates parchment.

"So you think Angel is after the Spear of Destiny? That Heydrich was bringing him the photograph to confirm the spear's whereabouts?"

"Something like that. Angel may have given the photograph to Heydrich, demanding he find it for him. We can only guess. We don't know because we were discovered and they called out the reveries. We interrupted their meeting."

"Do you remember anything else, Melissa? Anything from the meeting you spied on that might help us?" asked Chapman.

"Yes! Yes I do!" Melissa surprised herself by saying. "He gave the photograph to Heydrich. I saw it, just before the first reveries turned up. That's why I looked for it in his pocket!"

"And did you hear anything that was said when the two gloves met?"

Melissa tried to recall.

"They were talking about a *grand scheme*. Heydrich mentioned someone he called *the architect*, and Angel said something like 'We shall be able to bring back the others soon.' But that's all I heard."

"Never mind. Even that may be of value," said Chapman, jotting notes.

"So Angel might have also been consulting Heydrich about his ring of gallows iron," said Lucy.

"But that's just a myth, surely," said Chapman. "A ring of gallows iron cannot really control ghosts. And even if it were true, the Spear of Destiny, as you have so aptly pointed out, is almost certainly not the real spear that pierced the side of Christ. I can almost guarantee that the nail it carries is also a fake. It's well known the medieval church was always coming up with fake relics, hoping to raise revenue by attracting more pilgrims to their shrines. It's all nonsense. In reality, the spear and the nail might well have nothing to do with anyone's death, so they might not even be gallows iron."

"But there's something else," said Melissa. "When Hitler was alive he was obsessed with the spear. He had it locked away, deep underground so that not even the allies' bombs could reach it. That's how important it was to him. *He* believes it is powerful, whatever we think. On the twelfth of October, nineteen thirty-eight, Hitler ordered the spear to be seized and taken into his keeping. Less than a year after he took possession, he had grown so powerful that he was able to begin World War II by invading Poland. In the last few days of the war, Americans took Nuremburg and found the spear along with countless other treasures. One version of event says that ninety minutes later, and at the other end of the country, Hitler killed himself. It's like he knew it was all over once he'd lost the spear."

"You're saying it doesn't matter what power the spear actually has. It's the effect it will have on Angel if it falls into his hands," said Chapman. He polished the narrow lenses of his glasses on his tie before replacing them on his nose. "He'll gain a new confidence.

Possession of the spear would only encourage him, and that's the last thing we need."

"My point exactly."

"Yes, I see. I'll call the Austrian embassy immediately. Have them increase security at the Imperial Treasury in Vienna. By the way, I spoke to the PM earlier. We're closing South Sea House down for good this time."

Lucy muttered beyond earshot.

"Better late than never."

*

Tyler packed her bags for the Buenos Aires operation as Albert watched her.

"Will Klaus be there?" he asked.

"I don't know. Chapman didn't say. I suppose he might be part of the team already out there."

"Right."

"Why?"

"Oh, no reason."

"I just hope we can get Angel locked up soon. If he escapes us we'll be back to square one."

"For sure, Missy. We'll get 'im. Don't you worry."

She was finishing off and planning to make a start on recruiting for the Ghost Squad with the contrap when her phone rang again: Chapman.

"Change of plan, Agent Ghost. You and the girls better come back in. I'll be waiting."

*

"Bad news. Angel never made it to Jorge Newbery. There was an issue with the plane." Chapman swiped a map into position on the huge touchscreen and manipulated it as he explained. "We still don't know how it happened, but they lost fuel somewhere over the Atlantic and had to make an emergency landing before reaching Buenos

Aires. Ghosts in the machine, perhaps. They touched down at Fortaleza at fifteen forty-two hours, our time. The air marshal's body was found in one of the aircraft's washrooms after Angel had cleared the airport. He's escaped."

"We know he's travelling as Alfric Crane, though," said Lucy. "We can track him. Can't we?"

Chapman showed them an on-screen display of red, dotted lines linking London, Buenos Aires and Morocco.

"We *are* tracking his movements as far as possible, but he has other passports with other names, and that's why I've brought you in. We've tracked images of him at various airports and it seems he's been island hopping, trying to lose himself. I was going to send you to look for him in Morocco where he last touched down, but we just found a new image of him. One Reginald Meyer left Morocco on another flight twenty minutes ago. You'll never guess where he's heading."

The three girls exchanged glances and spoke in unison.

"Vienna."

"You're on the next flight out. Get to the Imperial Treasury, asap. Apprehend Angel before he takes the spear."

*

Tyler waited at Heathrow's terminal three with Melissa and Lucy, in the boarding lounge. *Forty-five minutes to waste here because Crows Nest has been blown to smithereens. That's forty-five minutes that Angel won't be wasting, I think it's safe to say.* She wished they had been able to hop on an MI6 plane and jet to Vienna sooner. With this in mind she worked on the Ghost Squad while hiding behind an opened copy of Hello. Across the lounge, others would see nothing but a girl reading gossip and images of celebrities. She set the contrap's switch to the spiral symbol and turned it to whisper into the lens.

"Kylie? Kylie Marsh, are you there?" She waited, glanced at Melissa, who was tapping away on her iPhone, scrolling websites and Google search results. On Tyler's other side Lucy texted endlessly. Tyler tried again.

"Kylie Marsh, I need to speak to you!"

"TAAN just tipped four thousand members and it's gone international!" said Lucy, leaning in towards the other girls. "Four thousand! That's an army! I'm considering training them up somehow. We have a new logo, too. It's the wings symbol from the contrap." She showed Tyler an image of the wings on her phone with TAAN written across the top in a bold, blocky font.

"That's great," said Tyler. Her Ghost Squad consisted of two people: a spidery, old man and a teenage chimney sweep. She looked back into the crystal but found only the usual, grey, swirling mist. She checked her watch again. *Forty-four minutes and counting.*

"Izabella? Danuta? Kinga?" She whispered each name hoping to call someone to the portal who might help. When no one showed she spoke to Albert, who she sensed standing invisibly in front of her, like a guardian angel.

"I can sense other ghosts in here. Are they dangerous?"

Albert drew close to whisper in her ear.

"No, nuffin' to worry about. There's an old girl over there by the door and a bent man haulin' a case up an' down the room, but they ain't showing us no mind. They ain't spies or nuffin'. Least, I don't fink."

"Good. Keep a look out for me."

"Will do, Missy."

Tyler called the names again, glad that Travis the Norman knight had ceased to pester her every time she used the portal. Albert had warned him off. She continued trying to find a ghost friend in the portal until she became so frustrated that she plugged in earphones and played music on her mobile. She listened to *Ghost* by Ella Henderson, which seemed to sum up her entire life. A while later, Melissa interrupted her thoughts, leaning in.

"Ever wondered how Mengele managed to avoid the Nazi hunters after the war?"

"Not really, no."

"I've been researching his history. The more I learn, the more astonishing it seems. You know, they captured a lot of these war criminals who fled including Adolf Eichmann, but a few have never been caught. There are even some still alive and running free today, according to this website. There's a list. They're still being hunted."

"Really? They must be pretty old, by now."

"They are, but my point is Mengele was one of those who was never captured. And he knows all about the contrap. The more I think about it, the more I'm convinced he knew about the contrap while he lived."

Tyler met her gaze.

"You're thinking Mengele once owned the contrap?"

"Well, think about it. He was the *Angel of Death*, an SS officer working as a physician at Auschwitz. He was the guy who separated the prisoners as they were offloaded from the incoming trains. He allowed some to live and selected others to be killed, all this while conducting horrifically *cruel and unusual* experiments on prisoners, supposedly in the name of Nazi science."

"I'm not sure I follow."

"I'm getting to my point. Who were the people who oversaw the collection and sorting of all of the valuables taken from the condemned prisoners? You know, they even collected their gold teeth! Anything gold or silver, anything valuable at all, was collected and stockpiled by the Nazis."

"I guess it would've been the SS officers who oversaw the whole process," said Lucy.

"Bingo," said Melissa.

"And among a whole heap of other bits of silver jewellery, there's a chance the contrap was collected," said Lucy. "There's a chance it lay in a heap with earrings, watches, bracelets and necklaces, just waiting for an officer to come by. Yes, they were supposed to pass on all these treasures for the war effort, no doubt, or otherwise add them to Hitler's growing stockpile of wealth, but..."

"The SS officers would have had first pickings. They were in charge, with no one to stop them doing exactly as they pleased," concluded Tyler.

"Precisely. It just seems to fit. What if Mengele took the contrap for himself or perhaps planning to gift it to a girlfriend, but he saw there was something different about it? What if he kept it for himself and began to learn how to use it?"

"A couple of years later he was running for his life and using it to keep himself safe."

"Well, that would account for his uncanny escape and survival while he was being hunted."

"And now he wants it back," said Lucy.

Tyler's attention was stolen by movement in the contrap's lens.

Finally, someone is coming!

The Spear

Izabella wobbled into view and glared at Tyler with her cataract-glazed eyes. She planted her hands on the flowery, billowing dress at her broad hips.

"Were you calling for me?" she asked, her Russian accent formidable.

"Yes," said Tyler.

"Well, I'm here. What do you want, child?"

"I'm forming a Ghost Squad and I want you in it. Will you join?"

"To what end?"

"To fight the Nazis, of course."

Izabella surprised Tyler by agreeing after only a moment's consideration.

"I suppose so. What do I have to do?"

"Nothing much more than you do already. You'll be a spy. I'll call on you from time to time when I need you.

It will mean me releasing you from the contrap, at least, periodically, so you can spy for me."

"All right. If it helps get rid of these stupid Nazis. I'm not sure what kind of spy I'll make. I'm not too quick on my feet these days."

"That doesn't matter. You'll make a great spy. No one will suspect you. Oh, you'll need to swear an oath."

"Very well."

"Can you do me one more favour?"

"What?"

"Find Kylie Marsh and tell her I'm waiting here for her."

"All right." Izabella turned and plodded away into the thickening fog of the lens. Ten minutes later, the ghost of a bookish schoolgirl with straight, dark hair, a narrow face and round-lensed glasses, and wearing a purple anorak, approached to stand looking up at Tyler with large eyes through the portal.

"Hi, Kylie. Thanks for coming."

"You're building a Ghost Squad. I want to be in it."

"Great. I was just going to ask you to join."

"What do you want me to do?"

Tyler had Kylie swear the oath then and there. She had an idea.

"Find Danuta and Kinga. Bring them here so they can be sworn in and then get Izabelle too. Apart from Zebedee and Albert, you four are the only ghosts I trust with this, but you won't be enough. The oppressor has a whole army of ghosts already and he's probably recruiting more as we speak. I need you four to work together and round up every ghost who's on our side. Make sure they understand what's going on. Swear them in. No reveries, obviously. Heydrich has a way of controlling reveries.

Can you do that?"

"Yes. I'll see you back here with the others." Kylie turned and jogged away, soon swallowed by the mist.

*

Tyler, Melissa and Lucy collected their bags. Chapman phoned before they had a chance to leave Vienna International Airport.

"News. The Imperial Treasury just reported the theft of the Spear of Destiny. Get over there, now."

Tyler swore.

*

Police cars and vans littered the vast entrance plaza of the Imperial Treasury Museum, flashing blue lights against whitewashed walls. Like worker bees, police cordoned off the area from the public with yellow crime scene tape and bollards. Tyler went in alone, showing officers her credentials before ducking beneath the tape to approach the open doors. Chapman had requested admittance for his team and, after much wrangling, officials had eventually agreed to allow one representative entry, purely as an observer. Tyler found an officer guarding the entrance.

"How many dead?"

"Two security guards. Knifed."

She nodded as an awful feeling rippled from her insides. The hairs on her neck stood like an army of pins. *Something horrible happened here less than two hours ago. If only we'd arrived sooner.* Knowing Albert was invisibly at her side, she took out her phone and put it to her ear, feigning.

"Albert, will you go in first. Take a look around and report back? I'll wait here."

"I will, Missy."

*

Albert slipped past the guard, noticing the shiver his proximity triggered. He paused and peered back through the doorway at Tyler, still faking a phone call. Had she noticed, as he did now, the charged air of this place? Something had happened here, and very recently. He could almost smell the fear, could almost taste the iron in the air, just like the time the trench-coated ghost locked Tyler and Lucy in the tomb.

He also sensed death close by, knowing it was the two security guards. He drifted further in, remaining invisible to humans, but visible to ghosts, as always. The iron smell led him to a hallway with large, glass cabinets displaying an array of ornate robes and exquisite vestments. He sensed their dusty age as he passed.

Strange, I'd 'ave expected to see some other ghosts by now. This place is right odd.

The iron charge in the air grew stronger as he neared the first of the fallen guards. He floated by, not wanting to see the grisly details. The guard's congealing blood pooled on the polished floor and crimson smudges adorned the glass and the frame of the closest cabinet. The glass of the cabinet opposite lay smashed and scattered, glistening like a thousand ice crystals.

Beyond the passage, the museum opened up into a capacious hall with enormous, regal paintings and more cabinets. Albert traversed this and a second similar chamber, stopping to gaze in wonder at a painting so vast that it covered most of an entire wall. It depicted the grand and colourful coronation of a king, set in a cavernous cathedral. He had only ever heard of such occasions when he had lived. He moved on, following the enduring scent and passing through many more rooms, all displaying majestic artefacts: gold crowns, jewel-encrusted sceptres and orbs, priceless reliquaries and historic dress, keys, goblets and sculpted busts. From each case glowed the lustre of gold and jewels, leaving him giddy. He'd never seen so many opulent riches all in one place.

My, my, some folks 'ave an easy time of it. He looked down at his ghostly, grubby shorts, bare shins and feet.

The second dead guard was slumped at the foot of a central display case in a large exhibition room. Again, fragmented glass told of a struggle that had taken place there; a struggle to death. He caught sight of the guard's many stab wounds and turned away, but not before noticing they were strangely small. An unusually slim blade had punched narrow slits in the guard's once white shirt, each no more than a centimetre across.

Albert turned his attention to the smashed display case where a gold altar cross, elaborately adorned with polished gemstones, remained in full glory alongside a smaller cross, inlaid with ancient wood. On the other side of the large cross, a red, velvet plinth was missing the Spear of Destiny, the spear's imprint still apparent in the flattened velvet.

He checked for other ghosts, still finding it strange that such a house of ancient objects could ever be so devoid, and a small movement caught his eye. He followed as a shadow recoiled through the far corner. In a chamber on the other side he found the ghost, a royal figure in black, complete with a ridiculous white ruff and a hat that Albert thought looked like an upturned, black pot. Seeing Albert following, the royal ghost backed away with widening eyes.

"Who are you? What do you want?"

"My name's Albert, Sir. Who are you? If ya' don't mind me asking."

"Huh! You mean to say you actually do not know who I am?"

Albert nodded candidly.

"Well, I've never been quite so insulted in all my... Well!"

"I beg your pardon, Sir. I didn't mean no offence, like."

The royal craned his neck closer and began waving his hands about wildly.

"Why, I'm Rudolph II, of course, Emperor of the Holy Roman Empire!"

"Right," said Albert, unimpressed. He'd never been one for kowtowing to royalty and, since he'd died, he'd learned that rank and social position and status were even less important than he had thought they were during his lifetime. "So, if you're such a bigwig, why's you cowering in the corner like a dog. And where's all the other ghosts?"

Rudolph nervously glanced around.

"They're hiding. Like me."

"Oh?"

"You don't know. You weren't here! You didn't see them."

"See who?"

"Such evil! They came with knives. Geists with blades! And such blades. They were not normal weapons of men. These were different. They sent terror through us all and we hid! Poor, old Josiah didn't hide quickly enough and they stabbed him. It was ghastly! He dissolved into thin air and hasn't been seen since! I only came out to see if they had gone."

"What, the ghosts? Yeah, they's gone ages ago, never you fear. So it were ghosts what murdered them guards?"

"Oh yes. It was dreadful. I've never seen anything like it! Such wickedness amongst geists. An abhorrence!"

*

Albert returned to Tyler and reported everything he had learned.

"Are there any living people inside?" she whispered, unnerved.

"No."

She entered and, once beyond view of the officer on the door, drew the contrap from its box. She used the *Past Eye*, clicking the lever carefully round the contrap's edge until she found the moment when the break-in began. Inside the lens, the room was dark. The first sign of anything amiss came with a rattling and shaking of the closed outer doors. The doors blasted open, the lights came on and the security alarm sounded, loud and piercing. She watched. Waited. The entrance became quiet, remaining empty. *Who opened the doors?* A moment later a shimmering in the air between her and the entrance caused her to question her eyesight. She backtracked with the lever and watched again to examine this patch of flitting light several times, realising, at length, that it was a fast moving line of narrow, glittering blades. Unseen ghosts were rushing in, each with a fine, but lethal, dagger. With difficulty she tracked the blades and a security guard dashed into view at the end of the tunnel. The blades flew at him and he staggered into a display case, smashing its glass before recoiling and grabbing at a growing number of bleeding wounds. He fell against the case opposite, groping for a hold to keep upright, but shock and internal damage were wrecking him. He slumped and slid to the ground, bleeding out over the floor.

Tyler closed her eyes, not wanting to see any more, yet she needed to learn all she could of what had taken place. She looked back into the lens and turned around seeking movement, having lost sight of the blades. Swinging back towards the doors, she watched Angel enter. He walked briskly in after the ghosts and their blades without pause and motioned for them to go separate ways, further into the museum.

"Seek them out. Kill the living."

Tyler caught the tell-tale glimmer of metal as the ghosts split up, taking different routes, rushing further into the museum. She tracked Angel as he chose his own path, making straight for the case displaying the spear. Drawing a hand gun, he put a bullet through the hardened, protective glass, which fractured but remained in one piece. He reached into his pocket as a security guard appeared in the entrance across the room, drawing a gun and running in. Blades zipped towards him and ghosts stabbed the guard repeatedly as he fell at the bottom of the case. Angel stepped away from the dying man and took a half brick from his own pocket. This he hurled at the case, exploding glass into hundreds of minuscule shards leaving the artefacts exposed. Fragments passed through Tyler as she watched. Angel grabbed the spear and left, ghost blades bobbing ahead.

So, that's how you roll.

Tyler boxed the contrap and glanced again at the fallen guard. She grimaced, dropping to one knee and, taking care to avoid the blood on the floor, examined the multiple narrow wounds. On closer inspection a particular wound different from the others drew her attention. She checked around to be sure she was alone before taking tweezers from her pocket and delicately drawing out a short length of broken blade from the wound. She examined it briefly before depositing it in a plastic evidence bag. She sealed the bag and tucked it and the tweezers into her jacket, glad to be leaving the site.

Outside she distanced herself from the other investigators to call Chapman.

"It was Angel, all right, and he's making the most of his ghosts. He has the spear." She told him all about the blades and the piece she had collected beyond her jurisdiction.

"Well done. Use your field analysis kit. Cog knows what to do. It'll be far quicker for you to do your own forensics."

"Right. He was here a matter of hours ago. I'm going to track him. See if I can't follow him back to a den."

"Good luck with that, Ghost. He's probably already left Vienna. Sorry we were too late."

"You and me both, Sir."

The Source

Fog. Nothing but fog. *Come on, Kylie. Where are you? I'm up against an enemy with an entire army of killer ghost spies at his service, not to mention a legion of reveries, and all I have are a few random ghosts. None of them soldiers or spies. None of them trained or highly skilled. What chance do I have?*

"Ky-lie?" she called for the tenth time. Again, she waited with the girls in a departure lounge. Having tracked Angel through the *Past Eye* for hours, she eventually witnessed him book in for a flight to Brazil. Chapman was right. Angel had headed straight for the airport, but by the time she'd painstakingly tracked him there, his plane had not only left Vienna but had also landed in São Paulo. She did not look forward to repeating the long process of tailing with the *Past Eye* when she landed in Angel's wake. *Still, at least we can rest while we fly.*

Four figures approached from obscurity until Tyler could name each; Kylie, Danuta, Kinga and Izabella. A pang of guilt hit her from out of nowhere. Claudia should be among her recruits but was lost to the evil waters of the chasm.

"You took your time!"

"Sorry," said Kylie. "Couldn't find Izabella."

"Now you're all here we can get on with it."

Tyler explained again about the Ghost Squad and what she needed from them before swearing-in Izabella, Kinga and Danuta.

"Kylie, I'm making you captain. You other three will be Kylie's sergeants. Recruit all the ghosts you can find who might be useful and bring them to the portal. Don't take anyone you think may betray us. And hurry!"

Chapman called.

"Yes, Sir. Waiting for our flight."

"Have you seen the news lately?"

"No, Sir. We've all been busy." Tyler glanced across at Lucy, who was texting again, building TAAN supporters, while Melissa researched feverishly on her iPhone.

"Iraq has just invaded Syria. We have reasons to believe they're being secretly funded by the NVF. Not that their cause has anything to do with the NVF, but their war clearly suits the Nazis. The Iraqis have also crossed the border into Jordan, breaking more international sanctions. The Turks are siding with Iraq. America, Iran and the UN are backing Syria. It goes without saying, we are, too. The ripple effect is feeding a monster. Enough countries are siding with Iraq to make this a serious threat to our national safety. Every nation is being forced to take one side or another. Libya is pushing into Egypt and no one even knows where their arms have come from. China and Russia have turned on our allied forces, making a bid for Arabian oilfields, but they're also at each other's throats. At least Germany is our ally this time. For the moment, there's a nuclear stand-off. No one wants Armageddon, but the balance is precarious. All hell's breaking loose.

"The PM will make an unscheduled announcement on the BBC in ten minutes to inform our nation that we are officially at war. Angel has had possession of the spear for less than a day and World War III has begun. I've consulted the department's criminal psychologists and they all agree, Angel will be a greater threat now he has the spear. He'll act more boldly and will take greater risks as he believes he cannot be stopped. Ghost, you and the team *must* get that spear back at all costs. I'm relying on you."

Tyler shared the news.

"Do you really think Angel's started the war?" asked Melissa, paling.

"If what Chapman just told me is true, he's been instrumental in setting it up. At the very least he pulled the trigger by funding insurgents."

"What should we do?" Melissa panicked. "Maybe we should go home."

"No way," said Lucy. "We take back the spear. Weren't you listening? It's even more important now than before."

"Sorry. Yes, of course. We'll go after the spear. Oh, I didn't even bring my gun!"

"There's no fighting going on in Brazil. We'll be all right."

"Yes. Yes, of course."

Lucy rolled her eyes at Tyler.

"How's the research coming?" asked Tyler, wishing to divert Melissa's mind from the war.

"It's very interesting. Ever heard of the Thule Society?"

Lucy and Tyler shook their heads.

"Its history can be traced back hundreds of years through associated groups, like the Order of the Teutons and the Skull and Bones Society, but it really began around nineteen eleven. A wounded World War I veteran from Berlin, Walter Nauhaus, started a study group. I'm not entirely sure what they were studying but it became an occult, secret society. I found some claims that the Thule Society was just another name for the German sect of the world-wide, secret society called the Brotherhood of Death."

"They sound like a nice bunch," said Lucy.

"Don't they? Anyway, when you get to the bottom of these societies you find they're all Satanic, wherever you look."

"I'm presuming you're going to tell us this is relevant in some way. I mean, you're not just rambling," said Tyler.

"Give me a chance. In nineteen nineteen Hitler, allegedly, joined the society. He was under the leadership of Dietrich Eckhart, who indoctrinated him into supposed occult powers. On his death-bed, Eckhart is said to have stated that *Hitler will dance to my tune*, and he said that he'd given Hitler *means to communicate with the powers*. Whatever that means. This is the stuff that came up when I did a search for *Hitler and the Spear of Destiny*. Weird, huh?"

"Yes, and it doesn't appear to have anything to do

with the spear."

"I guess Hitler is the occult association linking the spear and the Thule Society. To join, you had to swear an oath stating that you had no Jewish or black ancestry. They were white supremacists. Then the Nazi party began in nineteen twenty."

"What? That's just one year after Hitler joined the Thule Society," said Tyler.

"You're getting there. In actual fact it may've been less than a year. Apparently most of the founding members of the Nazi party were also members of the Thule Society: Rudolf Hess, Alfred Rosenberg, Hans Frank, Julius Lehmann... The list goes on. My guess is Hitler's doing all the same things again. He's seized the spear, and he's probably already created a new Thule Society."

"Or he's busy trying to reassemble the old one. Could that be what you overheard in the graveyard?" asked Lucy. *We shall be able to bring back the others soon.*"

Melissa nodded.

"That's what I'm thinking. What we don't know is *how* he intends to bring them back."

"I think I do. He's after Streicher. He wants to build a second GAUNT machine."

A distant, small voice from the contrap distracted Tyler. Kylie had returned and was observing her from the other side of the portal lens.

"We've brought a few ghosts along to get things rolling. There're not many but we can collect more."

Behind Kylie, Izabella and the twins, stood a ramshackle gathering of some twenty ghosts from various historical periods, each drawn from the distant city. To one side, a flaxen-haired Saxon warrior with long moustaches scowled from behind his shield. Among the others stood a barefooted, young girl in drab clothes who, Tyler guessed, was a Dickensian pauper, and with her stood a tall African with an iron slave ring around his neck. On the girl's other side stood Marcus, the silent fiddler. Tyler spotted several Jews and a handsome English infantry man in a smart uniform. She took in the gathering, wondering if it was possible to turn them into a crack team of spies.

"Well done, Kylie. Are all of you willing to swear an oath of allegiance? You are all aware of what this is about and the risks you may face in service?" Those gathered nodded. "Then we'd better get you sworn-in."

*

Tyler left São Paulo's bustling airport and set to work scanning through the *Past Eye* at each of the exits until she picked up Angel's trail. She followed him through busy evening streets as lights flickered on and the sun dropped beyond view over the city. An hour later she tailed him out of São Paulo as Lucy drove their hired car, and was relieved when he pulled up at the helipad of a private airfield. A stocky Brazilian man in ethnic clothes and sporting a thick nose ring that entered each nostril, waited, leaning against an old aircraft hangar. He left the hangar when he saw Angel approach and walked out to meet him on the open asphalt. Tyler ran from the car to get close enough to hear their conversation and watch through the lens. They shook hands. They spoke Portuguese, but Tyler got the gist. Angel opened his case and took out a brown parcel which the Brazilian accepted gratefully. He left as Angel boarded a small, white helicopter. The craft throttled into life and took Angel into the darkening sky. Tyler set the contrap to the flight symbol, but pulling the lever, she remained on the ground.

Dead. The ghosts must be worn out from all the tracking.

She boxed it, watching the chopper shrink into the distance.

Melissa took a bearing of the helicopter's trajectory with a compass app on her phone and then examined a GPS map.

"South South West. I think he's heading for the Urubici castle."

Tyler's gut turned at the thought. They would have to return to the castle; the dreaded Nazi fortress where she had almost died; the seat of Angel's underground empire. She didn't want to go back there.

Ever.

"Well, that's that. Let's find a hotel," she said, turning to Lucy and Melissa. "I'm exhausted. I'll get Zebedee to stakeout the castle tonight. We'll get over there in the morning."

As they pulled out of the airfield Tyler spotted Nose Ring again, this time talking with two others near the entrance. She signalled for Lucy to keep driving.

"Kylie? You here?"

"Yes! I'm here." Kylie appeared in the car next to Tyler.

"Are you ready for your first mission?"

*

Kylie, enjoying the lightness that accompanied her newfound freedom from the contrap, watched Nose Ring. He looked like a tribesman, better suited to the ancient rainforest than the barren asphalt of an old, out of town airfield. She followed him anyway. He walked with his two companions to a battered, blue pickup and climbed into the open back with one of his fellows as a dog had claimed the front passenger seat. The other man drove them away, bumping down a rutted road. Kylie flew after them, effortlessly turning when the pickup hit corners and navigated bends.

*

The three girls ate street food burritos ravenously in the car before booking into a hotel three-bed room where Tyler collapsed on her mattress and allowed her smarting eyes to close. She needed to rest the contrap, too, or risk finding it had shut down again at a time when she needed it most. Melissa donned surgical gloves to clean and examine the fragment of blade Tyler had recovered from the dead guard, manipulating it with tweezers. Taking a razor from the forensics case, she collected scrapings from the piece of mottled iron blade, mounting them carefully on a slide. She set this to one side and began unpacking and setting up a portable spectrum microscope and its many linking components with Lucy's assistance.

*

Windblown trees bowed their lament in the deepening night. A dilapidated farm fence creaked complaints of abandonment as wild grasses on the verge rustled.

Nose Ring hopped lithely from the pickup as it rolled to a stop at the cemetery gates. Kylie watched with shrewd interest, unable to pinpoint the source of an unfamiliar fear as more vehicles gathered; a van, an old minibus with a cracked window and a large, rusting saloon. Men clambered out at Nose Ring's command, an oddball wrecking crew of cheap labour, armed with heavy-duty tools, among them, a potbellied worker who hoisted a pickaxe over his shoulder and a slender man cradling a sledgehammer. The two from the pickup each carried spades and long crowbars. Ghosts gathered, too, ghosts yet to notice her. Kylie easily concealed her petite form behind a tree at the roadside opposite the gates. The other ghosts were evil. She sensed it with certainty, even before recognising their Nazi uniforms. She squinted into the night, trying to discern details.

Are they carrying knives? Solid knives that flash in the moonlight? Not ghost blades. Tyler had warned her of them.

The ghosts spread out around the cemetery, one forgetting about his earthly weapon and passing through the enclosure wall, at which point his blade plinked against the hard stone and, torn from him, fell to the ground so that he had to backtrack, retrieve it, and choose a different route in.

On his third swing, Sledgehammer broke down the cemetery gates with a thundering crash and marched in behind Nose Ring, who issued orders in a language unfamiliar to Kylie. Two ghosts remained at the roadside to guard the gate.

Once inside the cemetery walls the crew separated to seek out burials. They smashed tombs open, hauled off great, stone slabs uncovering the dead, and prised doors away from their hinges to drag out coffins. They grasped claw hammers and nail pullers from their pockets and belts, and set about splintering wood, drawing rusty nails from every casket. Kylie watched them desecrate graves through the open gates as they ripped away all the metal fittings they found: plaques, crosses and coffin handles, all of them dumped in Nose Ring's sack. *Surely someone from one of the houses nearby must notice the lights and the noise.*

A while later, the first police car arrived, speeding up with coloured lights blazing. It pulled in behind the ramshackle vehicles and a single policeman ran from the car to block the crew's escape. He was not standing long, as the two ghost guards, wielding their slim blades, flew at him in a stabbing frenzy. He screamed, attempting to ward off his invisible assailants, and fell to the ground as the wrecking crew bolted for their vehicles and more police sirens sounded further down the road. The crew loaded up swiftly, rammed the police car aside and drove away. The Nazi ghosts shot into the darkness of the surrounding countryside.

Appalled and alone, Kylie turned and headed back towards the city to seek out Tyler, wanting to get far away from the unnerving, metallic taint of blood and iron in the air.

*

Melissa shook Tyler awake.

"We've tested the blade. Interesting results..."

Tyler propped herself up on the bed, trying to shake a muggy haze from her head.

"Yeah?"

"It's mostly a rough kind of wrought iron with fibrous inclusions, about zero point ten percent carbon with some serious contaminants: flakes of iron oxide, that's rust in layman's terms, silicon, manganese and an unusual amount of phosphorus. Basically it contains more than the usual two percent slag, which means it should, technically, be called coldshort iron. It's the contaminants that made the blade fragile enough to break. A better quality iron would be stronger and more flexible. Coldshort iron isn't used much these days but a while ago it was considered good enough quality to make things like nails."

"And you just know all this stuff?"

"Research," explained Lucy.

"With these contaminants, it's still strong enough to slip between a man's ribs?"

"Oh, yes," said Melissa.

"It's gallows iron," said Lucy. "That's what Albert could sense in the Imperial Treasury. That's why the other ghosts were terrified. Gallows iron, hammered from coffin nails and the like. And if we're going to form any kind of effective ghost army, we're going to need to get some, too."

Tyler planted her feet on the floor, perching on the edge of the bed.

"Yes. I hadn't thought of that. Albert, what do you think about this blade? Can you carry it, or are you afraid of it?"

"I don't know, Missy." Albert appeared at his usual place, gazing from the window. "I ain't never tried."

Tyler carried the broken piece of blade to him and he gingerly took it.

"Yeah, no problem. I guess it gives the power to whoever wields it. Like a ring of gallows iron empowers the wearer. Like the contrap works for whoever holds it." He held the blade shard up to study it. "It's very thin. Don't weigh much at all. Easier for ghosts to carry, I suppose."

"So if we supplied you and the others with these knives you could use them against the Nazis and against the Nazi ghosts?"

"Don't see why not."

Tyler froze, sensing the approach of a ghost from the other side of the wall. "Wait, someone's coming!"

Knife's Edge

The girls tensed until they recognised Kylie. She noticed the partial blade in Albert's hand and shuddered.

"I followed the man with the nose ring." She explained what she had witnessed in the cemetery outside the city.

"That confirms it. They're collecting gallows iron. The more the merrier," said Lucy.

"Wait a minute." Melissa put a hand to her temple. She sat at the desk in front of her laptop and started searching the internet for images of gallows. A moment later her face relaxed. "Yes! Look at this. If you were seriously after a quantity of gallows iron, you'd be better off finding one of these." She pointed to the grisly image of a suspended gibbet caging a ragged corpse. "Bands of iron, riveted together to form a body cage. You'd get a lot more iron out of that than you would digging up a hundred wooden coffins." She hurriedly dialled

Chapman's number.

"Sir, we need you to place guards on every museum, exhibition and private collection in Britain that has a gibbet. Once we know they're safe we need them collected and taken to a secure location. It's all gallows iron and we need to get it before the Nazis do."

"Good thinking," said Lucy, as Chapman fired questions on the other end of the line. Melissa explained, adding "Tell the CIA, also. There're gibbets in museums across the States. They're sitting targets and will be snapped up as soon as these stupid Nazis realise."

Lucy could not resist high-fiving Melissa.

"I'm pretty sure we'll soon have some gallows knives of our own," Lucy said to Tyler. "That should even up the odds for our ghosts."

"Sir, would you repeat what you just said? Listen." Melissa put Chapman on speakerphone.

"I said there've been multiple reports of graveyard vandalism over here, up and down the country. I didn't know what it was about. Never made the connection. But I'm now sure they've been exhuming graves for gallows iron."

"They're doing the same here," said Tyler. "The captain of the Ghost Squad just told us."

"Right. I'm glad to hear you have things in order all ready. I'll have police guard the bigger graveyards, but there won't be enough to guard them all. This has to stop."

Lucy started texting frantically.

"The blade fragment Tyler collected is also gallows iron. We think they're using it to ward off other ghosts, but they work well enough to kill the living. It appears to have some kind of power. Albert said the ghost in the museum reported at least one ghost dissolving into nothing when struck with one of the blades."

"I see."

"We need to arm our ghosts with gallows blades or we don't stand a chance."

"I'll collect what I can. By the way, Klaus should be with you in the morning."

Albert vanished as Chapman ended the call and Tyler and Melissa turned to Lucy, whose mobile was chirping incessantly.

"I sent a text out to every member of TAAN," said Lucy. "I'm getting hundreds of replies. Tonight, TAAN will be guarding cemeteries wherever they can. I told them to leave the ones with police guards well alone. TAAN and the police are *not* good bedfellows."

"Better warn them to go armed, too," said Tyler. "They could come up against anything."

"Roger that."

*

The approach to the Urubici castle was devoid of snow, unlike the last time they were there and, in daylight, looked very different. A carpet of dense trees gave the foothills a vibrant, green glow and even the higher slopes were emerald with vegetation. Klaus parked the camouflage-green Land Rover on a rocky plateau, sheltered by trees, switched off the engine and opened his door.

"We're on foot from here on. The four by four won't cope with that." He pointed to a mountain that continued to rise before them, spiked with jagged outcrops. "The castle is a little way beyond this peak."

Tyler studied a map. They were far from the sloping valley that ended with the castle's cliffs, where they had parachuted before, and the castle was in between them and that vale. She used the *Present Eye* to zoom through the mountain and on to the arête where the hidden castle nestled. She recalled bolting, half-drugged, down unfamiliar corridors and rooms, fleeing for her life alongside Melissa as Nazi soldiers pursued. *Are they in there right now?* Later investigations of the castle had failed to prove any Nazi associations, but she had no doubts. The place was full of evil. She shivered and chewed her lip, subduing the onset of a panic attack.

Why am I doing this again?

Klaus scanned the summit and green slopes through field glasses before consulting a handheld GPS. He opened the rear door and handed out climbing ropes, harnesses and bunches of cams as Zebedee appeared.

"Good morning, all."

"Zebedee, is he still there?" asked Tyler, boxing the contrap.

"Oh yes, he's there all right. He's preparing for something, though I'm not sure what. I learned something of interest last night."

"What?" Tyler and the others gathered closer.

"They're making the knives here. The gallows blades. Boxes of the things, stockpiled in a storeroom beneath the ground. There's a consignment leaving tonight, scheduled to be flown out at midnight and dispersed to Sturmabteilung. Whatever they are."

"Storm troopers," said Melissa. "Ghost storm troopers, I'm guessing."

"Are there soldiers in the castle? Are the knives heavily guarded?"

"There are soldiers stationed throughout and ghosts too, but not many of either. Nothing we couldn't cope with, I'm sure. Most of the living are factory workers and clerks. The ghosts are all soldiers. If you want me or Albert to venture back in there it might be sensible for us to go disguised or we'll be noticed by Nazi ghosts. I had quite a time trying to stay hidden all night. Might I suggest a short jaunt into the *Ghost Portal* to seek out a couple of Nazi uniforms?"

Tyler nodded and turned expectantly to the others.

"Tyler, I know that look, but we can't," said Melissa. "It's not our primary objective. Chapman would freak if he found out."

"We can't let our ghosts go to war unarmed against an enemy armed with gallows iron. Don't you see? This is perfect!"

Lucy eyed Melissa and Tyler, deciding whose argument to adopt.

"I'm with Tyler," she said, after a moment. "It's too good an opportunity to pass by. Chapman might even agree if we consulted him."

"Which we're not going to do. Klaus?"

Klaus smiled and threw up his arms defensively.

"Hey, I'm just here to help. But as far as I'm aware, Tyler's the boss of this team, so I say we do it."

Zebedee grinned and puffed merrily on his pipe.

"Jolly good show!"

"Albert? What do you think?" asked Tyler. Several moments later, Albert appeared a short distance from the others, looking out over the valley with his back towards them.

"Albert?"

He turned, grim-faced.

"Who cares what *I* fink?" He turned back to the view.

"Wow. What's wrong with *him*?" Tyler asked the others. They shrugged. "Right. Well, get your stuff together. We'll take a break once the castle is in sight and send in ghosts to check it out. If it all looks good, we'll go for the gallows blades. If it's too well defended we'll recon Angel for a possible extraction. Maybe he'll hang around here long enough for us to take him out."

Albert disappeared but materialised next to Tyler a moment later.

"I'll go with Zebedee into the portal."

"Okay. Are you both ready?"

Zebedee and Albert nodded and Tyler opened the portal.

"Good luck. Phasmatis licentia." The two ghosts became ethereal, blue light and spun into the contrap's lens. "Compenso pondera."

Tyler felt a pang of regret as she began a long and exhausting hike up the mountainous slope with the others. Albert was no longer at her side and she was almost at the threshold of the castle. She felt vulnerable without him, but she sensed no ghosts around the mountain side, only barrenness. An hour later, the incline became a rock face too steep to walk.

"Can we take a break? I'm shattered." Melissa found a boulder and sat down, dumping her rucksack on the ground and rolling her shoulders.

"Five minutes," said Tyler. "Then we climb." She checked the portal for any sign of the boys but, finding only mist, boxed the contrap and puffed with reticence at the climb ahead, steeling herself for untold danger ahead.

*

Klaus lead the way, setting cams and ropes for the girls to use and Tyler marvelled at his efficiency. He was fast and sure, testing each cam once before confidently entrusting it with his weight. She climbed behind him and Melissa followed with Lucy at the rear. Tyler helped haul Melissa over the crest at the top and once Lucy joined them, pulling herself up easily from the cliff, they rested and ate while keeping a watch on the grey, rock-toned fortress. Smoke rose from its centre to dispel on the breeze.

"How are we going to get in? Are we going to wait until nightfall?" asked Melissa, catching her breath.

Klaus passed his field glasses and pointed along a curving ridge that ended part way up the camouflaged walls below a turret.

"See there? The rock ends only thirty feet below that window in the tower. We can edge our way along it keeping always on the south side of the arête. No one will see us there. When we reach the end we can put a grapple through the window and climb up."

"Perfect," said Tyler. "The ghosts can go ahead and tell us when it's safe to make the assault, make sure no one's around to hear the glass break. Albert's probably strong enough to close the door to that room and limit the sound traveling." Klaus grinned. *Klaus, I'm becoming obsessed with your beautiful teeth!*

Tyler used the *Present Eye* to search the castle, recognising halls and doorways and the large, circular, pillared chamber where she and Melissa had once been trapped. Finding it unchanged she boxed the contrap to save its power. *Any closer and the gloves in the castle might sense it.*

Melissa nudged her and whispered as Klaus regained his binoculars to study the battlements and towers.

"Hey, I think I might know what's up with Albert."

"Yeah?"

"Yes. It's obvious really."

"To *you* maybe."

"Oh, come on, Tyler! It's this *thing* you have for Klaus. Albert's jealous. He's in love with you."

Tyler began to protest. "I don't have a thing for..." *No, wait. I do!* "Oh!" *So ghosts get jealous, too? Interesting...* She took out the contrap again to check the *Ghost Portal* and saw Albert and Zebedee waiting, dressed in Gestapo uniforms.

"Good work, boys."

"We would've brought more but they're quite hard to come by," said Zebedee.

"You two will be enough for now." Tyler climbed further beneath the peak where she could release them without the dazzling light alerting the castle's occupants.

"Phasmatis licentia." She waited while they coalesced, and muttered the balancing spell before replacing the contrap in its lead box and tucking it away in her coat pocket. Zebedee brushed his uniform down, gave Albert an appraising look and nodded approvingly.

"Quite smart, really."

"We'll do, right enough," said Albert, glaring into the distance.

"The blades go out tonight so we don't have much time. I need you to check out the castle again and give me a full report. Find the quickest route to the storeroom and find out who we're likely to encounter along the way. Be quick, watch each other's backs and don't get caught."

"We will do our utmost, Miss May."

"Meet me at the end of the ridge when you're done." Zebedee and Albert nodded. "And Albert, come back to me quickly. I don't like it when you're not here."

Albert turned and looked into her eyes with

determination.

"I will, Missy. Never you fear."

*

Klaus lead them precariously along the treacherous arête as they hugged the mountainside. In places the terrain demanded more cams and ropes and in others the girls were able to clamber more freely and even walk along narrow ledges, clinging to the rock face. Several times, their passing sent fragments of stone skittering down into the steep ravine below. As they approached the craggy knife edge, Albert returned to them, whispering and remaining invisible.

"Look out! There's a patrol headin' this way and they got dogs!"

The climbers ducked lower behind the arête and froze, hoping the patrol would pass them by as Melissa shook, causing little rivulets of stones and gravel to tumble away.

"Get a grip!" hissed Lucy, next to her.

"I can't help it! Dogs freak me out, ever since Ingarata." Melissa looked up at the mountain edge above her and saw a man's face and a peaked cap protruding. Lucy clamped a hand across Melissa's mouth to stifle a shriek. The guard surveyed the mountainous view for a while, unaware of the climbers below, before whistling for his hounds and walking away.

Lucy released Melissa, who clung, pale-faced and panting.

"That was close."

"Yeah," said Lucy. "Too close."

They climbed on to the castle wall where Albert and Zebedee were waiting for them, invisible to mankind.

"No guards on the store room," explained Zebedee.

"But there's officers everywhere. You'll 'ave to let us go ahead of ya. We'll warn you if anyone's around."

"All right, Albert. You two go ahead. Look out for traps, too. When we were here last there were loads of traps."

"What about the turret room up there?" asked Lucy, pointing at the overhang above their heads. "Is it all clear?"

"I'll go an' see," said Albert. He returned quickly. "Two men, talking an a'drinkin'. We'll 'ave ta wait 'til they've gone away."

Tyler resisted the urge to take out and use the contrap as they waited, huddled against the wall. The late afternoon sun glowered over the mountains, turning clouds to shades of rose and threatening to drop below the frowning horizon. The climbers perched uncomfortably until Albert checked a second time and brought better news.

"Empty, and the hallway and all the rooms nearby. All empty!"

"Do you think we should wait 'til later?" asked Melissa. "I mean until they've all gone to bed."

Tyler checked her watch. *Gone seventeen thirty hours.*

"No. It's a big place. If we take too long getting to the storeroom we could be too late. The consignment's being picked up at midnight, so there's a good chance it will be carted up and taken out to the helipads before then. We could miss our chance. We'll go in now and hope they're busy eating and drinking." An image flashed in her mind; a band of armoured contrapassi feasting wolf-like around a long table heavily laden with all manner of food and drink.

Klaus fished out a grappling hook from his pack and used a karabiner to clip it to a climbing rope slung over his shoulder. He freed enough length to swing the rope and let the grapple dangle ready to swing.

"This is going to make some noise as it goes through the window. You two go up and check the way is clear. Do what you can to delay anyone who takes an interest."

"Right you are," said Albert.

Klaus gave the ghosts several seconds to take their positions and Albert peered down at them from the turret window to give a nod.

"All clear," whispered Tyler.

Klaus scanned the rugged landscape on the plateau side of the arête. A long, broad road and a helipad amongst barren rock stretched ahead, but little else. No sign of the patrol or their dogs. He swung the hook on its rope and brought it sweeping overhead in a great arc four times before releasing it. The grapple shot up towards the castle, smashing through the glass of the window loudly. Shards of glass rained. He tugged, checking the hook was secure, and climbed.

Melissa shuddered while pulling on gloves.

"We're all gonna die."

Blades of the Sturmabteilung

A cruel wind licked up the mountainside as Tyler heaved herself over the windowsill. Remarkably, the smashing pane and rattle of steel against stone brought no one to investigate from within. Klaus knocked out the few shards remaining around the frame to make it safer to negotiate. Tyler made a silent prayer of thanks while treading broken glass, and pulled up the rope to coil it and slip it over her shoulder with the grapple tucked into her pack. She followed the others out of the small lookout room and, with her tools, locked the door behind her to lessen the chance of somebody happening upon the broken window and raising the alarm.

"What if we meet Angel?" asked Melissa. "Are we going to tackle him?" She checked her Taser was loaded and held it at the ready.

"Have tranquilisers, will travel," said Lucy, tapping

her pack.

"We'll deal with that if it happens," said Tyler. "But it wouldn't be easy to get him out of here. Not like we have a van on standby. Better to wait until we can get him alone like before."

"This way, Missy." Albert appeared and beckoned them on, drifting along a corridor past several doors and pausing at the top of a broad stairway. "Keep left just 'ere." He pointed. "There's a floor panel that triggers a trapdoor. We 'ave to go down. The knives are right underground, but there's somethin' you needs to see first." He became invisible as the team descended. At the bottom of the stairs an atrium offered a choice of hallways. "Psssst." He showed himself briefly to wave them on. They followed and wondered at a distant clamour, a clanking, hammering din of echoes.

"What's that?" asked Tyler.

"Sounds like someone's building a railroad."

The noise grew louder as they neared the bottom of a second flight of stairs leading out into a long passage that Tyler recognised. She'd been there before when Albert led her to an arched window halfway down the passage, overlooking a vast courtyard filled with a ghost army in training. He pointed through the opening at the ground below. The yard was full of the noise and glow of industry. Ironsmiths hammered and forged, the smoke of their fires and a grimy, metallic taint, filling the air.

"They're making gallows blades."

Melissa and the others joined her at the window.

"So that was the smoke we saw from outside. Hobson and Crane Industries is a cover for the production of the knives. While they pretend to ship out handcrafted ironmongery, this is really what they are producing en masse."

"We have to stop them," said Tyler. The girls and Klaus ducked lower as a supervisor walked into view at one end of the courtyard to strut from smith to smith, examining their work.

"Remember, you must not overwork the iron or it will lose its desired qualities." He paused at one furnace and upturned a box of newly forged knives, letting them clatter onto the flagstones. Knowing better than to stop production and gawp, the other workers quickened, hammering iron on anvils and bellowing furnace flames with increased vigour. The supervisor berated the hapless smith.

"You have been working this shift for five hours! Why is your pile of knives so small?"

The smith mumbled an answer that did not reach the window, but was received badly by the supervisor. He backhanded the smith across the face. When no further excuse or explanation was forthcoming, the supervisor took a baton from his belt and pummelled the smith to the ground, where he lay unconscious. The supervisor strolled on casually, searching for other slackers.

"Did you notice anything about the workers?" asked Melissa as her team left the window.

"Yeah," said Tyler, brooding on her answer. "Blacks and Jews. All prisoners. The Nazis are back and they're hard at work."

"We have to help these people. We *must* free them!"

"And we will, if we can. First let's get the knives. We can arm our own ghosts and then at least they'll stand a fighting chance." With renewed incentive the team tailed Albert and Zebedee through a door at the end of the corridor and down more stairs where Zebedee held up a hand to slow them.

"Don't tread on the fourth step down. It triggers a mechanism that flattens the stairs into a slide. It will also open a pit at the bottom, into which you will fall."

They went on, careful to avoid the fourth step.

The girls recognised the large, circular, pillared hall when they passed an open door and, glimpsing a meeting in full flow, they quickened their pace. Zebedee appeared looking startled and drawing a finger to his lips. They halted and flattened against the curving wall edging the chamber as voices echoed to them from further on down the passageway. Tyler searched for somewhere to hide. *A doorway, a stairwell, anything!* They were stuck half way down a long, featureless corridor. A shout shook them and footfalls told them that Albert was drawing the threat away. As the sounds quietened, Zebedee led the way again, passing doors and navigating passages and, reaching the next level down, they headed towards an intersection where their path joined another. Zebedee rushed to the team, slipping through the wall.

"Hide! Five officers heading this way!"

They searched about for a hiding place, finding only one recessed doorway with a locked door into which Klaus shoved Tyler before beckoning for the others to follow as he tucked himself in after. Melissa and Lucy frantically tried to cram themselves into the doorway but there remained only enough room for one of them. They turned, desperately seeking other options, glancing down the barren passage. Tyler watched in horror. *Too long. No hope there.* Footsteps marched ever closer as the officers neared the junction. Frantically, Melissa and Lucy struggled again to fit into the cove, pushing each other, and Lucy took the place, shoving Melissa out into the path of the oncoming men.

Tyler watched helplessly, pinned in the doorway by Klaus, and dreading the appearance of the gloves. Melissa watched the officers, stunned, and checked their faces: no gloves, but all unfamiliar faces. They stopped and gazed soberly at her for a hideous moment as she stepped further from the cove to draw their eyes away from the others hiding there.

"Er, hello. I was looking for the bathroom but I seem to be lost. Can you help me?"

The foremost of the officers smiled, as the others chuckled. He spoke with perfect English while eyeing her curves.

"Of course. This place is a bit of a maze, isn't it? You will find the bathrooms down there." He pointed back the way he and his companions had just come. "Take the first right. The room you require will then be on your left."

Melissa nodded, gratefully.

"Thank you! You're very kind." She passed them, as though following his directions.

Tyler breathed a sigh of relief as the officers moved on. She left the doorway and waited as their footsteps distanced and finally disappeared. A moment later, Melissa returned and stood eying Lucy with wrath, hands on hips.

"Thanks for that!"

"My pleasure," said Lucy.

"What I mean to say is *what did you do that for?* You could've got me killed!"

"I thought it was the best idea. We didn't all fit so someone had to make a play."

"Yeah?"

"Yeah. And if one of us is going to get caught, it's better if it's you. Klaus would have raised suspicions. He looks too much like a soldier. I couldn't very well shove Tyler out to get caught. They'd have taken her because she's clearly not Arian and they'd have found the contrap. You're blonde and might pass for an officer's daughter."

"You could have gone yourself!"

"Yeah? And you're going to rescue me are you? Better that I'm the one doing the rescuing, I think. You're all, like, *I wouldn't hurt a fly* an' everything. Anyway, you have bigger..." Lucy cupped hands towards her own bosom. "...you know. Much more likely to distract..."

"Again, thank you!"

"It worked, didn't it? They couldn't take their eyes off you!"

"Shush! It doesn't matter now," said Tyler. "You did well. No one's dead."

"Yet," said Melissa, tilting her head at Lucy.

Tyler peered around the corner into the next passage as Albert arrived.

"More coming from back there. Move! Follow me!" He dashed ahead in the direction the officers had taken, and turned left to descend stairs which led out onto a landing where more stairwells rose and fell, and a lift waited.

"Don't take the lift," said Albert. "Too risky. You don't want ta' get trapped in there." He led them down more stairs zigzagging back on themselves as they descended further levels. Tyler figured they were now well beneath the courtyard they had seen from the window. Albert ran ahead to check for dangers, returning to take them to a bolted and locked door where he stopped. Zebedee appeared behind them.

"I'll keep watch this way."

"The daggers are in 'ere," said Albert, tilting his head towards the door. Tyler picked the padlock, drew the bolt and opened the door to look inside. The storeroom was divided by row after row of metal racking, some bays empty and some with boxes.

"Over 'ere," said Albert, pointing to a bay with two large boxes. She heaved one down to the ground with Klaus's help as Lucy and Melissa did the same with the other. Inside, the knives were packaged into smaller boxes, knife length. Tyler tore open a box. The knives were so narrow and thin that she estimated each of the smaller boxes contained around a hundred blades. They loaded the smaller boxes into their packs until they ran out of room.

"We can't take them all," said Klaus.

"They weigh a tonne," said Lucy, heaving her pack onto her back. "What do we do with the others?"

"We could break them," said Melissa. "If they're the same as the fragment I studied they will fracture easily."

"No time," said Tyler. "We need to get out." She noticed Klaus was removing grenades from his pack to make more room for the knives.

"I like to come prepared," he said with a smile. When he had filled his pack he set timers and placed two grenades in each of the large boxes, hiding them with some of the smaller packages.

"That should do it."

"Nice," said Tyler. "How long do we have?"

"Fifteen minutes." He set the bezel of his watch to count down the minutes. "If they blow as we're leaving the castle, so much the better."

She looked around for Albert. "Albert?" He

materialised close by.

"This way, Missy."

"Wait! Albert, take a blade. You might need it." She offered him an opened box and he took a knife, marvelling when he lifted it with ease.

"It's real light. Don't weigh much at all."

"Yes. They've made them really thin so that even their weakest ghosts can use them. You don't fear it?"

"No. Not when I'm holding it."

"Good. Our own ghosts can use them too."

Blade in hand, he led them on as Zebedee flitted back and forth checking the way ahead. They dodged more figures, making a slow ascent back towards the turret with the broken window. As they climbed stairs near the lift a ghost patrol of two soldiers drifted into view, spotting Tyler and her team as they withdrew. Gallows blades at the ready, the two ghost soldiers launched at them. Melissa screamed as Albert confronted the attackers. Tyler dug in her pack frantically to arm herself with one of the blades.

"It's gallows iron," she told the oncoming ghosts who, recognising the blades, lost confidence. They wavered in their approach as she joined Albert in front. The others were arming themselves now, slipping packs from their backs and tearing open boxes. Outnumbered, the ghost soldiers backed away. Tyler and Albert gave chase as they fled.

"Lucy!" called Tyler.

Two gallows blades purred through the air finding their marks in the backs of the bolting ghosts. The ghosts dissolved like mist leaving the blades to clatter to the floor. Lucy reclaimed her weapons and slipped them into her back pocket as Zebedee appeared in the doorway ahead.

"Well, what do you know? Gallows iron does kill ghosts!" she said.

"Where were you?" asked Tyler running to Zebedee. "We just got attacked!"

"Ah. Sorry about that. I thought I saw Angel and followed to be sure."

"You know where he is now?"

"I do. But he's preparing to leave, packing bags in his room."

"Go. Stay with him. Find us later when he's sleeping."

Zebedee vanished with a nod.

They came to the level below the arched window where Tyler stopped.

"The ironsmiths must be on this level. Can we take them with us, Klaus?"

"We can try, but if we make it to the mountainside they'll have to climb without harnesses. We don't have spares. Once we're far enough away from the castle we can organise an airlift or some other way out of the mountains."

"Albert, take us to the blacksmiths."

"Tyler, ten minutes and counting."

They followed Albert through another tunnel that brought them to a doorway of the noisy, smoke-filled courtyard and paused while he checked for problems.

"There's a ghost guarding each door," he warned them. "There's a door on each side of the yard, so four guards in all. Didn't see no livin', but they got gallows blades."

Tyler thought for a moment before beckoning the others closer.

"Okay, this is what we'll do. I'll use the contrap. Release the Ghost Squad."

"But the gloves are bound to sense it," said Melissa.

"Yes but only for a second or two. I'll box it as soon as I'm done."

"Okay."

"The Ghost Squad can each take a dagger. Take the guards out. Then we'll be free to extract the workers."

"It's dangerous," said Lucy. "We'll be trailing a whole line of clumsy blacksmiths through the castle. Doubt we'll go unnoticed for long."

"The Nazis still don't know we're here. The Ghost Squad can escort us. Any trouble, they'll be around to help."

"What if you can't find the Ghost Squad? The ghosts in the contrap aren't always hanging around the portal. You could be calling for them for hours."

"They're waiting for me by the portal. They'll be there. Trust me."

Ghost Squad

Tyler took out the contrap and swiftly set about releasing Kylie and her sergeants. They formed from dazzling, blue light until the entire squad stood crowded in the corridor and seeping into the walls. Tyler quickly closed the portal and tucked the contrap away in its lead box.

"Everyone take a gallows blade. There are four ghosts guarding the doors in the courtyard. I need you to take them out while we free the prisoners they have working in there." The ghosts nodded.

"We'll do what we can," said a Jewish woman with a resolute expression.

"Don't let any of them escape. No one knows we're here. Let's keep it that way. Any questions?"

They shook heads.

"If we get separated find me later on the slopes of the mountain. Kylie, lead the way."

The ghosts collected blades from the boxes offered and Tyler inched the door open to allow the knives to slip through as the squad filed in; a strange, silent, deadly gang of armed spectres with grim determination in their eyes.

Tyler spied through the gap in the door as they spread out, skulking around behind furnaces and the flotsam of industry. Steam hissed from quenching troughs. Bellows blasted to engorge smouldering fires. Smiths pounded rods of gallows iron.

A shriek rose above the clamour as a small group of Jews reached the first of the ghost guards, stabbing. His transparent form dissolved like memory mist on the wind. The workers stopped, aware of the commotion. A second ghost guard found himself suddenly cornered at knife point. He dropped his weapon and tried to run until the huge Saxon caught him and thrust a gallows blade between his ribs. Across from Tyler's door, the supervisor entered to see the courtyard in uproar, and bellowed orders to the workers as the remaining ghost guards were hemmed in.

Tyler rushed through the door and sprinted across the yard, barking commands as the last guards dispelled, peppered with gallows blade wounds. She pointed to the supervisor, levelling her own gallows blade.

"Surround him! He mustn't escape." She reached the centre of the yard and turned about, addressing the smiths as the Ghost Squad hedged the supervisor with blades.

"Follow me! We're taking you out. *Quickly!*" The scattered smiths turned to her with uncertainty.

"You're taking us out?" asked one, close by.

"If you want to leave. Yes. But it has to be quickly

and it has to be *now!*"

They edged towards her, dropping their tools, and she lead the way back through the door to join the others, tailing Albert down the corridor and banking left. They climbed stairs and passed the arched window. Tyler glimpsed the Ghost Squad still surrounding the supervisor in the courtyard below. Albert beckoned her on and she ran with Lucy, Melissa and Klaus as the great trail of freed workers followed. Albert warned them each time they approached hidden traps and several minutes later they were threading through the door of the little turret. Tyler anchored the grappling hook and, glancing out to see the mountain top devoid of people, readied to launch the rope out of the vacant window.

"Wait!" Klaus grabbed her arm before she could swing, and peered at his watch. From far below an explosion rumbled, shaking the air. "Okay. Now."

She threw the rope and watched it fall, straightening below.

"You first," she told Klaus. "If anyone gives chase from the castle the workers will need you with them."

"Okay." Klaus climbed through the window and descended, hand over hand. Tyler sent the workers next in a long, laboriously slow line, all the time fretting that they would be discovered and those remaining in the turret apprehended, but smoke riding the air reached the little room and she knew Klaus's grenades had started a fire on the storeroom level. *They must be busy firefighting! Perhaps it will buy us enough time.*

While the smiths climbed, Tyler eased tools into the keyhole to lock the door. Melissa climbed down after the last of the smiths with Lucy close behind. Tyler shoved a heavy bench across the closed door before easing herself out of the window onto the rope. Below, a line of jittery smiths negotiated the arête. She suffered a moment of panic. *This is ridiculous! We're going to get caught!*

Half climbing, half slipping down the rope, she descended, burning her palms with the friction. It didn't matter. *If I make it out alive I shan't care!* Soon she was leaving the rope and clambering over to the hidden side of the arête to join the others, amazed they had made it this far. They would be seen if anyone higher up in the castle happened to look over the mountainside but, peering back, she saw no one, only...

The rope!

A *very* obvious climbing rope dangled some ten metres from the turret window to the mountain. *Nothing I can do about that now and, anyway, there's nobody around to notice yet. Just get out of here!*

She joined the line of terrified smiths and wished they would speed up. The fear of imminent discovery and capture, or worse, death, never far from her mind.

The temperature had dropped with the rising wind as they'd entered the castle. Now it was plummeting as twilight took hold and the wind offered no respite. *What to do with twenty escaped prisoners on a mountainside? We need to get away fast, but how can we when our escape route is a mountainous climb?* Klaus had left the cams and ropes in place for their return journey, but that was before he knew he would be leading all the extra climbers. They gathered at the rise where they had breached the ridge on their ascent, and clustered, clinging to the rock like island birds.

Tyler risked a peek over the top, wondering if they were being hunted.

Muted cries in the distance removed all doubt.

Men and dogs issued from the castle doorways to search about on the plateau and down the opposite side where the land dropped into a valley, sweeping round to the base of the castle's cliff. She knew that valley. It was the way she, Melissa and Lucy had entered when they had put Himmler into the contrap. It would have been a much easier passage for the escapees but it was no longer an option.

Probably a bad idea anyway. Nowhere to hide.

She squinted into the wind. The low sun dipped below the horizon, casting a deep shadow over the side of the castle with the turret and the dangling rope. *Thank goodness for that! The rope has yet to be noticed.* The hunting parties were still a good distance from the ridge where she spied. Hardly believing her luck, she turned to Klaus, Melissa and Lucy across several huddling men who whispered words of fear and worry. The wind was loud enough to cover her words from those on the castle side of the arête.

"We can't take them all down the mountain, surely!"

"We must. We have no choice," Klaus called back to her. She nodded. He was right. *What else can we do?*

Klaus and the girls began their descent, spreading out among the smiths and coaxing them down, guiding and showing them remembered foot and handholds as they free-climbed. An unspoken urgency surpassed thoughts of the four harnesses. With much relief they gathered, at length and after a long and precarious climb, at the foot of the rock face where they congratulated one another uneasily on their survival.

"You'll be glad to hear it's easier from here on out," announced Klaus. "But keep your eyes on the trail. You could still take a bad fall." They tramped after him, sinking lower into the rolling landscape, finding rutted ridgeways and rugged slopes. The trees engulfed them like a welcome blanket, bringing a tentative sense of safety. Tyler walked with a blade at the ready, unable to trust the feeling. *At least we're hidden from the heights above and the trees give some shelter from the worst of the cold wind.* Klaus stopped amid a particularly dense spread of low trees, noticing that some of the older men were exhausted from the climb and the hike.

"We can rest here a while. Five minutes."

They sat among ferns and the scrub of the forest floor, but quickly began to feel the cold. Tyler's team had Gore Tex climbing jackets but the smiths were wearing little, having fled straight from the heat of their furnaces. Melissa noticed an older man shivering and suggested they move on. She added another thought.

"They're bound to send ghosts after us. We should arm the smiths with the blades. At least then they'll stand a chance of defending themselves."

Tyler nodded and they opened a box of knives and passed them around until everyone was armed with at least one blade. Lucy filled the side pockets of her combats until they would take no more, and the small army marched on. At the head, Klaus spotted the Land Rover first and signalled for everyone to drop low to the ground. The vehicle had been discovered. Figures loitered nearby, their automatics clearly visible even from the distance between.

"We can't go that way," he whispered, as Tyler, Melissa and Lucy drew level, ahead of the others. "You see them?"

"It doesn't matter. We would only fit a handful of them in anyway. Looks like we're marching out of here on foot."

"You do know how far these mountains stretch?"

"I know, but what else can we do. Any hope of an air rescue?"

"I tried to radio a while back. No signal. I'm not getting any phone signal either. In any case, we'd need a Chinook to get this lot out. That would take time to organise and then there's the flight time. It's best if we presume that won't happen."

"There are caves in these mountains," said Melissa. "I don't know where, but they exist."

"Okay. We'll look out for a cave. In the meantime let's get as far away from the castle as we can. The further away we are, the harder we'll be to find."

"Agreed."

A movement off to the side in the underbrush drew their attention.

"Someone's there!" hissed Lucy. Brandishing a blade, she stalked out towards the movement, relaxing when Izabella and Kylie came into view. The rest of the Ghost Squad came in close behind to join the others. The smiths, being used to the ghosts of the castle, did not blanch.

"Were you followed?" asked Tyler.

"No. At least, I don't think so," said Kylie. "We dispatched the guards and waited, holding the boss man at knifepoint. When we were sure you'd had enough time to escape we fled. We were quick and we didn't meet any one on the way. We heard an explosion down in a lower level and saw smoke. I think everyone was busy down there."

"Good. I have another job for you all. Spread out and find us a cave. It's getting dark and we need to shelter and rest up. Keep a look out for enemy ghosts."

Izabella pushed to the front.

"Is all this rushing about truly necessary?"

"It is," said Tyler.

Kylie and the other ghosts of the squad nodded and dissipated into the surrounding forest as Izabella lagged at the rear.

Klaus tried to radio for help again, failing to secure a signal. He and the girls checked the phones but those, too, were out of range.

"A cave is sounding like a good option right now," he muttered.

"Yeah."

They heard the whir of a helicopter passing overhead.

"They're looking for us."

"Better hope they don't have thermal imaging," said Tyler.

They waited, vigilantly as a tense, slow hour passed and the ghosts finally returned. Kylie reported.

"We found a cave. It's a few miles downhill from here at the bottom of a gorge but it's big enough to hide you all and it will keep you out of the wind."

"Sounds perfect," said Tyler. "Lead the way." She turned to the others. "We're moving out." She peered out from the sprawling tree canopy to search the sky for helicopters. *All quiet.* Kylie drifted out into the open passing through vegetation and the occasional boulder. She led them down a steep slope that eased to a gentler gradient and for a few moments they walked a gravelly trail.

"Wait a minute," said Tyler, as Klaus, Lucy and Melissa walked alongside. "This is a path. They'll be watching paths and roads. We need to stay off-road."

"Good point," said Lucy.

"Get off the path. Kylie, I need the squad to scout around again." Tyler glanced up at the darkening sky. "I've a bad feeling."

Kylie sent out ghosts to flit away into the wilderness, scouting, while Tyler took the small army off-track to be lost among trees and shrubs. The vegetation changed as they dropped lower into foothills. The trees grew taller and a multitude of ferns and tree ferns covered the inclines where a deeper soil lodged, and still they passed rocks and skittered their way down scree slopes. Kylie's scouts returned one after the other, firstly, the Dickensian pauper girl, with her nervous habits of wringing her hands together and fiddling with the braids of her long, raven hair.

"Yes, Bronwyn?"

"There's dogs, Miss. Men with dogs." Bronwyn stopped twiddling her hair to point up a valley that led back towards the castle's peak. "They're coming down the mountain over that way."

A tall, Jewish ghost with a moustache and wearing a blazer came in behind Bronwyn to report in a strong Polish accent.

"I saw ghosts tracking around from the higher ground to the west." He pointed in the opposite direction. "If we move fast we can make the cave before they cross us."

"Thanks, Leon."

Tyler turned to her companions and risked calling out.

"We have to pick up the pace. Hurry!"

Albert's Death

The unrelenting wind pummelled the army of smiths as they sank into the gorge. It moaned against the stones, chilling everything within its greedy reach. Ahead, a scree slope two hundred metres long, descended, the wrong side of steep. Tyler watched as Lucy launched herself down with glee. Klaus followed, lodging himself half way to reach out and help prevent others from veering out of control. Melissa stayed with Tyler at the top, steadying the line as the smiths ventured over the ridge onto the slippery shale.

As the last few smiths readied themselves for the plunge Wulfric the Saxon appeared by her, the frosted air whipping through his softly shimmering essence and billowing, long hair.

"They come, man and beast. Be swift!"

Tyler turned to those waiting on the ridge.

"Go now!" She waited until she alone remained before leaping over the edge to hurtle down the scree. At the base Kylie, Lucy and Klaus led the others deeper into the gorge. The gale was softer here and soon they saw the dark shape of a cave's mouth ahead, and hastened to scramble in to shelter. The Ghost Squad assembled, watching protectively from the entrance.

"Do you think we were spotted?" Tyler asked Kylie and Izabella.

"Who knows, child? These mountains could hide a thousand souls but, if we were, we'll soon know about it."

"I suppose we should be grateful for that." Tyler tensed, fearing a distant, new sound. It drifted to her again, the baying of dogs carried on the wind. The hounds were close, perhaps at the crest of the scree slope. "We need to hide deeper. They're coming. Go as deep as you can."

"Okay, I'm SCO," said Melissa.

Klaus frowned. "Huh?"

"Seriously creeped out," said Tyler. She hoped the driving wind would obliterate their sent trail in the gorge as she took a torch from her pack. Further back in the darkness of the tapering cavern she huddled with Klaus.

"What now?" she asked.

"We wait. Try to keep warm. No fire. Not yet at least."

"Agreed. We don't need to send them an invitation."

"If we're lucky they'll get bored and cold, and go home. The longer we remain hidden, the safer we'll be."

Tyler looked up at the nearby sound of skittering stones.

"They're coming down the scree. We need to do something!"

Klaus peered with concern at the entrance where moonlight illuminated the cave floor.

"Kylie, can dogs sense you?"

"I don't know."

"They can sense us ghosts," said Albert. "Makes 'em bark an' folks finks they gone mad."

"Take some ghosts and draw them off. If it's just men and dogs they'll be no match for you but you'll drive the dogs crazy. The men won't know what's going on. Stay invisible. You'll have to leave your blades behind. Lead them away from the cave. When they're gone come straight back and arm yourselves."

Kylie gathered the squad and they passed into the walls of the cave.

Those remaining, huddled in the furthest reaches, also hoping to become invisible in the pitch. The scattering, gravelly sounds from the slope ceased, replaced by the closer patter of men and hounds running. The dogs sensed the ghosts, growling and baying intensely as they crossed the cave's mouth to sprint through the gorge.

Close, but it worked. The Ghost Squad were drawing the hunting party away.

Klaus slipped an arm around Tyler and hugged her for their mutual warmth. Others were doing the same, gathering in groups. Albert turned away and vanished. The fridge-like cave was only marginally warmer than the night beyond where the wind groaned to mingle with the howling of the dogs as their din grew evermore distant.

Tyler believed they might actually survive the night, and allowed herself to relax to a degree. Hunger gnawed at her stomach but she said nothing of it. Talking about it would only make it worse and remind others of their pangs. The smiths seemed to be doing okay. They muttered together in small, close groups; hard men glad to be free of their captors even if they were chilled and empty. She broke away from Klaus to visit several of the groups, whispering words of encouragement. She needed them to stay positive and helpful, knew that if they turned against her they could ruin everything very quickly.

A while later she noticed Albert venturing to the mouth of the cave where he stood, peering into the night, unaffected by the relentless wind. She walked to him, leaving the others in the deeper shadows.

"They've been gone too long," he said without turning. "Somefin's wrong."

Tyler said nothing but watched the night wind tug at grass on the gorge wall opposite. He finally looked at her.

"I'm going after 'em."

"No! I need you here!" she said, but Albert walked out into the gale and soon vanished in darkness. She ran after him, immediately feeling the wind's bite. "Come back!" she called, against every sensible notion in her head. "*Please.*"

But Albert was gone.

*

Seconds ticked by to the rhythm of water dripping from the limey cave roof. Minutes, then hours passed with no sign of Albert or the squad. Tyler had no more words for the smiths or her friends. Her hope was slowly eroding like the wind-pummelled faces of the ancient gorge and she sat alone hugging her knees to her chest, feeling incomplete.

When the squad finally returned, Albert was not among them and, knowing she should be cheered by their safe return, she fretted, thinking of all the things she should have said to stop him.

Why did you go? Why now? Why wouldn't you listen to me?

Pacing to the mouth of the cave, she peered out with dwindling hope, only to withdraw to her spot on the unwelcoming floor where she resumed her foetal position. A voice, deep with a heavy, Nigerian accent stirred her.

"Miss Tyler, are you all right?"

She looked up at the large African from the squad.

"I'm fine."

He sat at her side with his back against the cave wall.

"In times of great sadness my people used to sing."

"We can't sing here. They might hear us."

"Indeed."

"So what's your story?" She studied his face with its broad cheek bones, prominent brow ridges, full nose and mouth. The whites of his eyes shimmered softly as he watched her.

"They call me Yakubu. I was one of three hundred and thirty-two slaves on board the Phoenix, bound for the sugar plantations of Virginia, when the ship began to take on water. We'd had no food or water for two days, but were shackled and crammed in the hold."

"What happened? Is that where you died?"

"When water began flooding the ship the white crewmen were forced to release the slaves to help bail out. My people were desperate. We would not take orders. The crew put half of us in irons, but some broke loose and tried to break the gratings. The seamen were too afraid to come down into the hold and so they murdered fifty of the strongest of us. Over the next five days the ship limped on with no sign of land. Four of my people died, and a woman..." Yakubu paused, not wanting to continue.

"What about the woman?"

"She could take no more of the misery. She drowned herself in the hold. No one had any drinking water, not even the white men sailors. For ten days we drifted, thinking each hour that we would sink to the bottom of the ocean. Then another ship was sighted. The King George came alongside us and rescued the thirty-six crewmen."

"And the slaves? How many of the slaves did they rescue?" She turned to him and he smiled as though she had missed something.

"Miss Tyler, the water in the hold had been steadily rising for ten whole days."

She dipped her head and he put a ghostly arm around her shoulder.

"Do not be sad for my people, Miss Tyler. It will not help us, and look around you. We are not in a sinking ship."

"Are you sure about that?"

"Quite sure, Miss Tyler."

Melissa and Lucy found her fighting back tears.

"What did Albert say before he left?" asked Melissa while Lucy scratched a skull smiley on the cave wall with the tip of a gallows blade.

"Just that he was going after the squad. He was worried about them. Thought something bad had happened to them. Now I'm wondering the same about him."

"I was thinking," said Melissa. "We should send a ghost to Chapman, like when you sent Zebedee last time we were out here. Get some kind of rescue organised."

"Sounds like a plan. Who do we send? Zebedee and Albert have gone."

"What about Izabella?" said Lucy. "She could do it."

"She might need some persuading," said Tyler. "But it's worth a go."

"It has to be. Anything's better than sitting in this freakin' fridge, doing nothing."

"Fine. Go do it. Good luck." Tyler could not think about escape. Not when Albert was still out there, lost to a mountainside peppered with malicious, armed ghosts and dog patrols. She had seen the remarkable effect the gallows blades had on ghosts. The iron left none wounded, took no prisoners. Busy worrying, she did not at first notice the figure drifting in like flotsam on the wind from further up the gorge.

Albert?

She ran out into the squall. Snow had begun to fall since she'd last ventured out and it pelted her face and eyes as she strove to see who the ghostly figure was. She caught a flake and examined it.

No, not snow. Ash.

She peered at the figure again. A blade caught her attention and she stopped and called out to the others behind her.

Not snow! Not Albert! Nothing is as it seems here.

"Klaus! Lucy! Mel! We have company!" She turned and bolted back in as the ghost Nazi officer pursued, grinning with narrow jaws and waving on more ghosts that massed from the gloom. Lucy was first to join Tyler as she came to her senses, whipping a gallows blade from her belt. Lucy's knives purred through the air to pierce ghosts, taking two, then three of the enemy spectres into oblivion. More replaced them to form an advancing wall. Tyler and Lucy backed into the cave, joining a defensive line.

"Kill them all," commanded Tyler. "If a single one escapes it will bring the others down on us!"

In response, the gaunt ghost officer sent two envoys back into the night with a flick of his bony hand. Lucy continued to hurl knives with great effect as, to her side, ghosts clashed hand to hand and several of the squad dispelled as iron pierced their transparent forms.

"After them!" shouted Tyler, and the twins erupted from the flanks to give chase. Other ghosts appeared from the walls further in and, hearing the bellowed warnings from the terrified smiths, several of the squad turned to tackle the new threat. The smiths joined battle, tentatively closing on the enemy ghosts. Wulfric sliced and stabbed alongside the British infantryman, dispatching enemy ghosts trapped between ranks as the smiths pressed in, spearing more ghosts. Tyler briefly considered using the contrap but knew it would be next to useless. The portal would swallow ghosts indiscriminately and she would lose as many of her squad as she would the enemy, and she feared it would reveal their location.

Kylie saw Wulfric shatter his blade on the cave wall and tossed him another.

"Wulfric, here!"

He snatched it from the air and in one fluid motion, thrust it into the heart of an oncoming officer. Bronwyn was small enough to be missed by those among the enemy who had eyes on larger, more intimidating figures. She darted back and forth between the melee, jabbing at the unsuspecting. Still more Nazi ghosts appeared from the rear walls of the cave, taking smiths by surprise and wounding several in their backs. An old man fell, dead, and the battle raged on around his body.

Danuta and Kinga returned to join the fight and the enemy ranks thinned as more ghosts received gallows iron, dissolving into mist. The squad surrounded the last few and sent them the same way. Tyler found herself in the middle of the cavern turning, blade ready, but without foe. She walked slowly to the dead man and stood with others around his body.

"I'm sorry," she said.

"At least he died a free man," said one of the smiths.

"He was very grateful to be rescued," said another.

She dragged her aching body back to the rear of the cave where sleep overwhelmed her.

*

She woke to a hot, wet stickiness. Her left forearm was throbbing, heated, sore and covered with blood. She looked around the cave. The others were still sleeping. The wind had died and the deep night beyond the entrance had softened to pre-dawn greys. Her eyes settled on the smith's body, arranged respectfully on the floor at the end of the cave, and she shuddered, guilt stricken.

Perhaps he would still be alive now if I'd left well alone and just staked out Angel as planned.

She staggered to her feet, cold in every part of her body except her burning arm. Peeling back her sleeves she found a knife wound, mid-forearm, that she did not remember receiving. Her clothes were pierced and clogged with cooling blood, but the wound had stopped bleeding already. She bound it with a field dressing from her kit and dragged her sleeves back over it. A voice startled her.

"What you done, Missy?"

She looked up, wondering if her mind was playing tricks. *Albert!* He walked into the mouth of the cave, surveying her and the sleepers beyond.

"Where have you been?" she asked, still doubting her senses and unsure if she was angry with him or overwhelmingly relieved to see him.

"Your arm. What 'appened?"

"It's nothing. Ghosts found us and attacked. What happened to you? You've been gone ages."

"Yeah. I searched for the others. Couldn't find 'em anywhere. Then I 'appened upon a group of Nazi ghosts out searching for us, and 'id. There was too many for me to take on, so I spied on 'em for a while. Didn't learn much, but I know we need to move on. There's a troop of 'em never reported in after last night."

"That'll be the troop we killed."

"The men at the castle are broadening the search now it's daylight."

"We'll move out soon. Albert, I thought you were dead. Thought you'd been caught and stabbed. You've no right to just go off like that!"

"Didn't know you cared, Missy."

"Of course I... That's not the point." She fumed during an awkward silence. Albert removed his cap and beat it against his thigh to free ghost soot before replacing it.

"How are the others?"

"A few are wounded and one of the smiths is dead. Killed by the ghosts when they came, and we lost three ghosts of the squad."

He nodded grimly.

166

"Albert, I *do* care about you. I care about you very much."

"But..."

"You know what the *but* is. Do I have to spell it out?"

"No."

"So?"

"So what?"

"So what's the problem? Why are you acting like you've been acting?"

"I don't know. It's 'ard, watching you with 'im." He jutted his chin towards Klaus, asleep on the floor across the cave.

"Listen. No one will ever replace you. I want you to understand that. I mean, whatever happens. No one will ever be able to replace what you mean to me."

The beginnings of an honest smile blossomed at the corner of Albert's mouth.

"You really mean that, Missy?"

"Yes, and one day, if I'm still around when this is all over, I'm going to track down the chimney where you got stuck and died, and I'm going to buy the house. I'm going to find your body and give you a proper burial. I'm going to live in that house."

"You'd do *that* for me?"

"I plan to stay as close to you as I can. Is that creepy?" Albert's tragic death triggered a thought. "It was the manner of your death that prevented you from going to rest, wasn't it? You know, where all the other ghosts go?"

He nodded. "No grave, no resting place, no rest."

She thought about Albert's chimney and the gallows iron, iron from coffin nails and other grave associated artefacts, as others in the cave stirred from their sleep.

"What do you suppose is the reason for the power of the gallows iron? Why does it work like it does?"

"I don't know, but I guess no one likes being trapped in a closed box underground. Not even ghosts. Perhaps it's a bit like giving them a grave."

"Do you think that's where it sends them, back into their graves?"

"Naw. I fink it sends 'em on. You know. Somewhere else. Some other place. Heaven or Hell, or whatever, but I ain't allowed to talk about that."

Estancia la Candelaria

Tyler rewrote her list and stared at it feeling the need to tick something off. She figured the fourth item was pretty much covered. She added two new items.

Extract Angel from Buenos Aires √
Locate and recover the Vice President of Brazil
Find out how the NVF are recruiting their ghosts
Find out what the ghost spies are doing √
Put Reinhard Heydrich and Adolf Eichmann into the chasm
Acquire the Spear of Destiny
Extract Angel (again)

She burned the list and stamped out the last of the flames to minimise the smoke.

Zebedee fell through the cave ceiling and landed in a heap at her feet.

"Oh. There you are!" He peered up, dazed. Albert helped him up and passed him his cane. He brushed his tailed suit down and checked his broken pocket watch. "Thought I'd better find you. Angel's on the move. I can't tarry long or I'll lose him again."

"Okay. Stay on him." Tyler boxed the contrap. "Find me when he's stopped travelling so you can show me where he is."

"Right you are, Miss May." Zebedee looked up at the ceiling before launching into it.

Klaus visited her.

"I'm going out. Need to find a signal so I can get us some help. Stay here."

"Be quick. Albert says we don't have long."

"Don't worry. I will." Klaus trudged past to peer up and down the gorge from the entrance before heading off. He returned triumphantly twenty minutes later.

"Bingo. We're moving out."

*

The extraction point was six miles south of the cave. They found it, a long plateau devoid of trees, amazed to have not encountered any further ghost patrols or tracking dogs. Tyler watched the smiths and her team scramble aboard the Chinook and followed as the surrounding vegetation jostled violently in the downdraught. She collapsed onto a bench inside and, feeling safer than she had for the last day, fell asleep before lift-off.

*

She woke with a headache and a dry mouth, sensing the Chinook set down.

"You need to hydrate," said Klaus, passing a bottle of water. She gulped it and checked her watch.

"How long have I been out?"

"Half an hour."

"Right." Tyler took out the contrap and stared at it. *What do you signify?*

The enigmatic heart symbol incised in the silver casing taunted her.

She recalled Zebedee's visit and wondered where he was. Another thought struck her. *How did he find me in the cave?* The contrap was in its lead box at the time, so that couldn't have led him to her.

The others were disembarking. Medics helped the injured smiths into ambulances. Lucy looked back from the steps.

"You coming?"

Tyler boxed the contrap and followed.

Klaus, Melissa and Lucy waited in a white car, arranged by Chapman, and no one spoke during their ride to the hotel. At reception the man behind the desk stared at their bedraggled appearance. Tyler looked down at herself before glaring at him.

"We've been hiking."

She took a long shower, put a clean dressing on her wounded arm, and slept in her hotel room's silky, spotless, white bed. She stirred a while later with a feeling that she was not alone and looked up to see Zebedee perched on the end of the bed, puffing on his pipe, blowing smoke rings and watching her.

"Good morning, Miss May."

"Hello, Zebedee." She dragged sheets closer around her neck and shuffled up against the headboard. "What're you doing here? Can't a girl get some privacy?"

"Ah, sorry. You did ask me to find you when he reached his destination."

"Angel."

Zebedee nodded. "He's staying in a hotel named Estancia la Candelaria. It's in Lobos, outside Buenos Aries. From what I gather, he's there for a conference organised by a charity calling themselves Ethnic Equality International. It's being sponsored by Hobson and Crane Industries."

"Honestly? That's priceless. He's attending as a delegate?"

"No. As a representative of Hobson and Crane. He's there to make a presentation."

"Okay. Good job, Zebedee. I'm gonna get dressed now. Could you..."

"Oh, yes. Pardon me. I'll see you later."

"Wait. How did you find me? I mean, the contrap's in its lead box. How do you and Albert keep finding me all the time? You found me in the cave..."

"Ah. I wondered when you'd ask. Think back to when you were a ghost in the machine. Do you remember what it was like?" Tyler nodded. "You had a way of sensing things that was not of this world, yes?"

"Yes."

"It's like this. Out here we can sense those we hold dear. I found you because I care about you very much. Albert... Well, suffice to say, he does not need to be able to sense the contrap. You see, love is a very powerful thing."

*

Lucy huffed.

"Great. Another castle. I thought you said it was a hotel."

"It *is* a hotel." Tyler drew the lever around the contrap's edge to focus in, using the *Present Eye*. "Mel tried to book rooms for us but they're full because of the conference." She telescoped through the hotel's creamy stone walls and watched guests as they moved around, shifting her view from room to room.

"Anything?" asked Klaus from the driver's seat of their hired car.

"Not yet." She lowered the contrap to squint between the huge trees surrounding the road. Estancia la Candelaria did look like a castle. At each corner stood a rounded tower with a pointed, grey roof and towards one side of the front loomed a high, squared tower, topped with battlements. Gigantic palms spotted its immediate grassy grounds, and denser woodlands and treed avenues encompassed all to give a vast, emerald backdrop.

Albert appeared in the car next to Melissa, making her lurch.

"Great. Thanks for the heart attack." She clamped a hand to her chest.

"Sorry, Mel. 'E's in there, all right."

Zebedee appeared on her other side. Melissa leapt again.

"My apologies." Zebedee tipped his hat. "Room nine. The register was open on the reception desk. I flipped a few pages but I don't think anyone noticed. He's booked in as Mr A. Crane."

"Do you think we can get on with it now? I've had enough of castles to last me a lifetime." Melissa grimaced.

"It's *not* a castle," said Tyler. "It's a *hotel*."

"Yada yada yada," said Lucy, checking the magazine of her P99. "What's the plan, exactly?" She slipped the gun into her shoulder holster.

"Got him. I want to know what he's up to." Tyler followed Angel with the *Present Eye* as he crossed his hotel room to stand before a mirror, putting on a tie. "I don't think we should attempt a capture and extraction. We don't know his movements. We're in unfamiliar territory and there are just too many people about." She lowered the contrap to watch more delegates arriving and filing into the hotel.

"It's not a very big hotel for a conference," said Lucy. "I expected something larger."

"I'm sure it's for a very select crowd," said Melissa. "You realise this charity, Ethnic Equality International, is just a cover for something else dodgy."

"Yes." Tyler put the contrap away and sat back. "So no C and E, and we're on unfamiliar ground. That just leaves a recon. I'm not sure of the best way yet. Kylie, are you here?"

"Affirmative." Kylie remained invisible.

"Great. Have some of the squad set a perimeter around the place to guard it. Take knives but be discreet."

"Will do."

"If we all go in we'll be recognised for sure," said Lucy, passing out gallows blades to thin air beyond her window. The blades flitted away into the grounds as the ghost squad dispersed.

"If we just sit and watch everything with the *Present Eye* we might miss something important. I can't look everywhere at once."

"Send the rest of the Ghost Squad," said Melissa.

"I can go in, too," said Klaus. "They don't know me. That will be a substantial presence in the building and you can still watch from out here."

"Sounds good. I know it's a long shot, but grab the spear if the chance offers."

"I'll go and change."

"You mean you brought a suit?"

"Of course." Klaus flashed a grin as he left the car. "Didn't you?"

Tyler watched him walk the length of the drive to the hotel doors where he entered beneath five arches and, from there, she followed him using the *Present Eye* until she realised he was going into the gents to change. She felt heat rise to her face and placed the contrap quickly back into its box.

"Guess we'd best get in there too," said Albert, vanishing. "We'll fetch the squad." Zebedee followed. Lucy's phone buzzed and she checked the incoming text message.

"Oh no. It's all going terribly wrong."

"What is?" Melissa peered over Lucy's shoulder.

"It's TAAN. Remember I sent a request for members to guard the graveyards?"

"Yeah."

"Well, three TAAN activists were killed last night doing exactly that. A ghost wrecking crew came for gallows iron in a graveyard in Chelmsford and they brought ghosts. This morning police found the graveyard plundered and the three TAAN guys dead."

"I'm sorry," said Melissa.

Lucy's phone buzzed again.

"Wait." She read another text and swore. "Five more were murdered guarding a cemetery in Reading." She pocketed her phone and stared at the back of the seat before her. A moment later she exited the car, looking pale. "I'm going for a walk. I feel... I'm not sure what I feel." She slammed the door and stomped away into the woods.

"Wait," said Melissa, winding down the window. "You shouldn't go off alone. We should stick together." Lucy ignored her.

"Give her some space. She's upset."

Klaus' voice came through their in-ear receivers. "You hear me okay?"

"Roger that."

"Great. I'm going in."

Tyler scanned through the building again with the *Present Eye* until her view settled upon Klaus. She watched him exit the bathroom and join a congregating crowd, slipping in at the back of the room as a presentation began. PowerPoint slides of maps and ethnic minorities illuminated a big screen behind the presenter and a smartly dressed, grey haired man waffled on about Ethnic Equality International and its fight against racism, and the world trading rights of third world countries. A voice in her ear interrupted her wandering thoughts.

"Tyler! Mel!"

"Lucy, you okay?"

She and Melissa exchanged a concerned look as hiss and crackle drowned Lucy's voice and the line died.

"Lucy?" No reply. "Mel, are you getting anything?"

"No. She's in trouble."

"Right. You stay with the car." Tyler boxed the contrap, checked her handgun and opened her door. "I'll go after her. Albert, if you can hear me I need you." She left the car, running after Lucy but was soon wandering in the woods with no idea of Lucy's location. She tried the comms again.

"Lucy. Come on, Lucy. Answer me!"

"I'll let you know if she returns to the car," said

Melissa.

"Okay. I'm in the woods, north west of the hotel. I could use some help." She searched on, turning among the trees, and getting nowhere.

What am I doing? Use the Past Eye! She took out the contrap and flicked the switch while jogging back towards the car. She spotted the car through a gap in the woods and drew the contrap's lever ten degrees clockwise, peering at the car through the crystal as time visually reversed. She saw herself running backwards to the car and a few moments later Lucy was there, doing the same. With a minor adjustment she watched Lucy leave the car at normal speed to stalk away into the woods, and followed her progress, falling in behind her and walking for what seemed an age. Lucy had cried and Tyler was glad she could not see her friend's face from where she was. She felt bad enough as it was, spying on her in a private moment, even if it was necessary. She went deeper into the woods and Tyler glanced back towards the hotel and the car but saw only trees. Returning to the *Past Eye*, a darting shadow caught her attention. A ghost Nazi officer swept in from the edge of the crystal's view and Tyler called out.

"Lucy!" She stopped. The Lucy she was watching could not hear her, nor did she see the ghost's approach. In an instant a gallows blade pressed at Lucy's throat as a second ghost arrived. Lucy tensed and reached for a blade of her own, but the ghost applied more pressure with the blade, shaking his head to say 'don't try it'.

"Tyler! Mel!"

The second ghost snatched the comms from Lucy's ear and pinned the device to a tree with his blade.

"Your friends can't help you now. You're coming

177

with us."

Melissa screamed in Tyler's ear.

"Tyler! Get back here! They're coming! They're coming for me! They're..."

"I'm on my way." Tyler abandoned her pursuit of Lucy and fled back through the trees listening to Melissa's struggle. The comms fell silent long before Tyler reached the road.

Too late!

The car was empty, Melissa's door hanging open. Tyler's stomach knotted.

This can't be happening!

"Mel. Come in, Mel." She stooped to pluck a smashed comms unit from the gravel.

"Klaus, they have Lucy and Mel. Abort. Get out now!"

The Haunted Forest

Tyler climbed in and started the car, ready to bolt at the first sign of trouble as she taxied round to the entrance beneath the arched, stone pillars.

Come on, Klaus.

The hotel doors opened and Klaus slipped through and into the passenger seat. Tyler floored the accelerator and, wheels spitting gravel, sped them away. Neither spoke until, several miles down the road, she pulled in, trying to calm. They gazed at endless, sprawling fields on all sides: the middle of nowhere.

It's going to be all right. It'll be all right. Think it through. Make a plan.

"Here, let me drive." They swapped places, circling the bonnet.

"You okay?" asked Klaus.

Tyler nodded and then shook her head.

"Not really. They have Mel. They have Lucy. I don't

know what to do anymore. This is all getting way out of hand."

"Don't worry. We'll get them back. Zebedee will stay with Angel, and Angel will take the girls with him. They're perfectly safe as long as Angel doesn't get the contrap. That's what he wants, isn't it: the contrap and you?"

"Yes, of course. You're right. We need to set up a meeting with Angel. I need to make a trade."

"That's not what I meant. You can't give them the contrap, Tyler. That would be the end of everything."

"They want the contrap and me. You said it yourself."

"Yes, but..."

"I can't let them do anything to the girls. It's Lucy and Mel."

"But trading yourself would be quitting. Chapman would forbid it."

She stared at him. "Chapman's not here." She tried calling the girls but their lines went straight to an out of service tone. When Albert materialised in the back seat he found Klaus waiting while Tyler fretted.

"The squad set the perimeter and spied on all them people, like ya' said, Missy. Zebedee's sticking with Angel. Where's Lucy and Mel?"

"Angel has them, Albert."

"Blimey."

"Our perimeter didn't work. We were too late, too unprepared. I let my guard down. Their ghosts must've already been planted around the hotel and now Angel has Lucy and Mel."

Tyler's phone buzzed. She checked the caller ID.

"Oh, great. It's Chapman." *Just what I need.* She

fought an oncoming panic attack and steeled herself with a deep breath to answer the call.

"Ghost, what's going on? I see you girls have separated. Is everything all right?"

Tyler shrugged and glanced at Klaus, who overheard every word from the phone's miniscule speakers.

"No. Everything is not all right. Cog and Pointer have been taken. Angel must have known we were on to him. We should never have tried to book rooms. It's my fault. I..."

"We'll deal with the blame game later. We need to focus on getting them back safely. Any ideas?"

"Yes, but nothing you're going to like. For now we're working on the principle that Angel will keep the girls close. Zebedee's tailing Angel, so we should be able to find them easily enough. It's the extraction that's the problem."

"Wait until they've stopped moving and we'll reassess. They're heading north west in separate vehicles, approaching Chivilcoy. It'll be interesting to see if you're right about Angel. I'm sending their coordinates through to your phone now. Go after them."

Klaus started the engine.

"Yes, Sir."

"And, Ghost, pull yourself together. My agents are depending on you." Chapman ended the call.

No pressure then.

Klaus turned the car and drove as Tyler navigated with coordinates from Chapman.

"What went on in there?" she asked, wanting to escape from her welling guilt.

"It was very odd. I think they were using a code. For a few moments I thought it might actually be genuine, but then I noticed some things the presenter said didn't add up. It was made to look like a talk about ethnic minorities and equality but there was something else going on, too. When the speaker finished he invited Angel up to the podium and Angel presented a cheque for twenty-three million dollars towards the cause."

"Yeah, right. 'Cause he's big on equality for none-Arians."

"For sure. It's obviously a front for one of his Nazi schemes."

"More funding for the rebels, maybe. Anything else?"

"Not really. That was when you told me to get out."

"What about the Ghost Squad, Albert? Everyone okay?" She felt another pang of guilt for having waited until now to ask.

Wake up, Tyler. Wake up! Think!

"I don't know. I sensed you'd left an' followed. Suppose the others are still back there."

"Go back and call them off. Be careful. The place is teeming with Nazi ghosts."

"I'll be back soon." Albert vanished.

"Stop the car," said Tyler. "They may have bugged it. They could've placed a tracker, too." Klaus pulled over and they swept for transmitters.

"It's clean. Maybe they didn't have time. They just grabbed Mel."

"Yeah, I was only gone a minute or two. All the same, I'll feel better when we've ditched the vehicle."

At the next town they parked up and hired a new car. They drove for the rest of the day and took small, uninviting rooms in a shabby motel as it grew dark. Tyler dumped her bag on the worn carpet and collapsed on the creaking bed to stare at peeling paint on the ceiling. For a long time she lay there trying to figure out what to do. Chapman had said follow, recon, but she had already formed the basis of a plan and it certainly did not involve risking the lives of anyone else.

Trade the contrap and me for the girls. Once they are free it's up to me to escape and I'll have the contrap, at least until the handover is complete and the girls are safe. Maybe at the last minute I can use the portal. No. There'll be too many of them. It would only take one of them to shoot me, and Angel would have the contrap. Unless I get him first. I guess Chapman's right. We don't know what we're dealing with yet. Wait and see where they take the girls. Stake it out. Make some informed decisions then. But the waiting is killing me!

She wrote out her list and reread it before adding another item.

Extract Angel from Buenos Aires √
Locate and recover the Vice President of Brazil
Find out how the NVF are recruiting their ghosts
Find out what the ghost spies are doing √
Put Reinhard Heydrich and Adolf Eichmann into the chasm
Acquire the Spear of Destiny
Extract Angel (again)
Free the girls!

Feeling useless, she burned her ever-growing list in the room's metal bin, predicting the smoke would not set off the yellowed, antiquated detector in the centre of the ceiling that probably hadn't seen a battery change for ten years. She showered in tepid water and realised she was famished as someone knocked. She wrapped herself in a towel and, hiding her PP9 behind her back, answered the door.

"Hungry?" asked Klaus, looking fresh in a clean set of clothes. She noticed his aftershave, an enticing, invigorating scent, and pictured warm spices. "I spotted a diner across the street."

"Ravenous. Give me two minutes."

*

They found a table in the far end of the diner, well away from the other two customers eating next to the bar. A TV, mounted in the corner nearby showed a news program, relaying footage of war-torn districts of the Middle East.

"Steak and chips twice, please."

"How d'ya want the steaks?"

"Rare."

"Medium."

"You want drinks?"

"Coke for me."

"Same here."

"Alrighty."

Tyler gazed out of the grimy window at the faded motel sign as the stilettoed waitress with the blue headscarf wobbled away. She drew a finger across the greasy, red, vinyl table cloth.

"You really know how to treat a lady."

"Yeah. This place is the best."

Tyler's laugh dwindled as she sensed a ghost approaching.

"We lost another one of the Jews," said Kylie, remaining invisible. "Judith."

Tyler swore under her breath. "I'm sorry. You know

about Mel and Lucy?" asked Tyler, pretending to be speaking with Klaus so that the diner staff would not notice anything unusual.

"Yeah. We didn't know they had Lucy but a couple of us saw what happened to Mel. We tried to stop them but there were too many Nazis. It was all we could do to escape. Like I said, Judith didn't make it. She took a gallows blade in the back. It was a mess. I tried to gather the squad but they were stationed all over the hotel. We did what we could."

"Don't worry. The *whole thing* was a mess. It wasn't your fault. It was mine. I'm sorry about Judith."

"You said that."

"Where're the rest of the squad now?"

"In your room, resting. Everyone's pretty tired. Albert's there, too."

Their meals arrived and the news article switched from the presenter to scenes of British soldiers clambering aboard helicopters. Vast trains of tanks zoomed by the camera, and fighter planes landed on aircraft carriers in the Pacific. American soldiers fought on the streets of Palestine and Iran. Protestors rioted in Paris, blockading roads, and hurling petrol bombs at police. Russia fought to occupy Kazakhstan. Syria bombed Egypt and was, in turn, attacked. *The world in uproar. Whatever we're doing, it isn't enough!*

The news reporter began a new story on recent graveyard atrocities. Images flashed across the screen in time with a barrage of place names: Caen, Paris, Birmingham, London, Madrid, Pietermaritzburg, Santiago, Venice, Rome, New York, Washington DC. The seemingly-endless list continued and, at each place, graveyards lay plundered and destroyed at the hands of wrecking crews. *Nowhere is immune to the new scourge.*

Tyler pushed her plate away as her phone rang. *Think I've lost my appetite anyway.*

"Yes?"

"They've sped up and entered a forest zone with no roads. Must be in a plane or a helicopter, but their signals now show as one so at least we know they're together."

"That's good isn't it?"

"If they know they are not alone, it is. It would be preferable for their psyches. Of course, for us it also makes them easier to track. Any news from Zebedee?"

"Nothing yet."

"Okay. I see you've stopped for a break. That's good. Forget any thoughts of pursuit tonight. You fly out of there early in the morning. I'm sending through details now. Get some sleep. I need you thinking straight tomorrow. There's work to be done."

"Yes, Sir."

"Goodnight, Ghost."

"'Night, Sir."

*

The Mi-17 helicopter set down in a field behind the motel, billowing dust and dry grass into the air. Smaller than the Chinook, but an obvious military craft decked in striped camouflage, it bobbed briefly before resting. Weaver opened the door and jumped down from the cockpit with Freddy close behind.

"Chapman didn't tell me," shouted Tyler, hauling her gear in the downdraft.

"He wasn't going to send me. Knows about me and Lucy. But I kind of freaked out and gave him a few ultimatums."

She handed him her bags and Klaus shook hands

with Freddy before throwing his bags in the back.

"Headsets on. We can talk on the way."

They climbed in and buckled up, and Weaver throttled them away from the ground.

"Chapman's relaying the girls' tracking signal," he said when they reached two hundred feet. "But it's not moved since zero three hundred hours. You're not going to believe where they are."

*

A rich, green, living carpet rolled out beneath the Mi-17 as far as could be seen. Weaver pointed downwards with a gloved hand, holding the Mi-17 joystick steady with the other and speaking into his headset.

"That's the Javari River, a tributary of the Amazon. The girls stopped moving five miles downstream from here. This is where you get out. Any closer and they'll know we're coming. They may have already clocked us, but we really don't know their capabilities out here. The nearest set-down is fifteen miles to the west on a patch of high ground. You go ahead. Freddy and I will catch up later. You had any jungle survival training?"

Tyler shook her head.

"No, but Klaus is pretty handy."

"In normal circumstances we would prepare for a trip like this," said Klaus.

"Yeah, well these aren't normal circumstances. The kit you have will serve you well. You have some drinking water and some rations. We threw together some basics when we saw they were heading out this way."

"We don't have time to prepare properly. We have to go now. Who knows what they're doing to the girls?"

Freddy handed Tyler her bag, heavier now with the added kit and bulky with a sleeping bag rolled and strapped across the top.

"Stay out of the river," he said. "Everything in there wants to eat you. Be careful beneath the canopy. Pretty much everything there wants to eat you, too."

She peered down at the tiny trace of the Javari that the jungle canopy allowed to see daylight. *There's nothing but river or canopy.*

Freddy nodded. "Yeah. That's my point."

"Good luck," said Weaver. "You're gonna need it."

"Great. Thanks."

"We'll be fine." Klaus kicked the rope out of the open door and, pulling on gloves, turned to Tyler. "I'll see you on the ground." He headed out, climbing from the helicopter onto the wind-torn drop line. Tyler pulled on her rucksack and switched the contrap to the flight symbol.

"Thanks, Weaver, Freddy. See you later." She drew the contrap's lever clockwise and took off from the edge of the stage to descend towards the trees. She passed Klaus and negotiated a mass of branches and leaves to alight on the forest floor long before he reached it. He joined her, shedding his backpack onto the ground and peering around as the rope rose with the Mi-17.

"Well, it's not Kansas."

"You got that right."

Mulungu

Tyler checked her phone for the girls' GPS location as the helicopter's drone distanced. "No signal. Weaver said downstream, right?"

"Yes. At least we seem to be alone, for now."

Albert and the Ghost Squad appeared, mingling with the abundant tree trunks, hanging vines and sprawling undergrowth.

"Maybe not alone, exactly."

"It's odd Zebedee hasn't returned. Do you think Angel's moving again?"

"I suppose he could be."

"I hope Zebedee's all right."

"Yeah."

"I'll scout ahead," said Albert, slipping through trunks and vegetation to lead the way.

"Thanks, Albert."

Tyler turned to Klaus. "What do you think they're doing out here? I mean, it's pretty remote."

"Just like the Urubici castle. They seem to prefer these unreachable places."

"But there's nowhere to land. How are they getting in and out?"

"I don't know. Perhaps we'll find out."

With the din of the helicopter gone the forest became alive with new sounds. Frogs chirped and croaked, and birds and other creatures, nameless among the huge leaves and fronds of tropical plants, called with unfamiliar, exotic voices.

They trailed after Albert along the river's edge giving the water a wide berth and fighting a prickly path through unrelenting scrub.

"Look out for snakes and spiders in the foliage and on the ground." Klaus paused to lash a large combat knife to a branch to wield as a machete. "Hey, Albert, wait up. We can't move through this stuff like you ghosts."

Albert did not respond, and Tyler and Klaus glanced at each other with concern. Klaus hacked at undergrowth, trying to beat a path to Albert.

"Albert?" Tyler tried to peer ahead through the enormous leaves and drooping creepers. "Albert, are you all right?" They waited, listening to the jungle's living hum. Klaus broke a path through to a clearing where they found Albert standing and staring. Before him, the ghosts of six Amazonian tribesmen gazed back inquisitively, painted and naked except for belts that extended downwards between their legs. For a moment nobody moved.

"Are they friendly?" asked Tyler.

"Who knows?" said Klaus.

"Blimey! Ain't never seen no ghosts like them before."

"Me neither." Tyler stepped forward. "Stay back, Klaus. They could view you as a threat." She turned to the tribesmen.

"Hello. Do you understand me?"

The men muttered among themselves in their own dialect. Several of them ventured closer to examine Tyler, deeply curious. One of them poked around her bag.

"Hey, stop that!"

They circled her before returning to their companions.

"We understand you," said the tallest and boldest of the men. Feathers adorned his hair and wrists, and red paint striped his face crossing his broad nose. "This is our land; the territory of our sons and our daughters, our fathers and our forefathers. We are the Korubu. Why have you come?"

"We have friends who were brought here, to a place close by. We've come to rescue them. We'll return to our own lands when we have them safe. Have you seen others like us? We must find them. Will you help us? We mean you and your people no harm."

"Men have come before you. Bring bad smell, bad magic, building on our land further down the river. They are evil men. If they are your friends, you are our enemies."

"Those evil men have captured our friends," said Tyler. "The bad men are our enemies."

"You are strange but, if you speak truth, we will help. We want the bad men to leave."

"So do we. Can you lead us to them? Is it far?"

"Not far. Follow us." The tribesmen turned and sped nimbly away into the jungle. Klaus and Tyler battled on through branches and clinging plants until, exhausted, Tyler called out.

"Wait! We can't travel as fast as you. You will have to slow down."

They slowed and Tyler, Klaus and the Ghost Squad followed. A few minutes later the leader of the Korubu turned back to Tyler.

"You are very slow. Move like wounded pig."

"Thanks. We're doing the best we can."

"We must move faster if you want to get there before nightfall."

"All right. We'll try, but we'll need to rest soon. This is hard work."

"Woman can rest when we get there."

"My name is Tyler."

"Tyler, I am Pioka. We go now." Pioka headed off again and Tyler followed behind as Klaus hacked a path. Large droplets of rain drummed on leaves and Tyler checked for clouds but saw only the endless canopy of treetops towering above. The rain fell in a deluge, soaking everything in seconds. Pioka returned to warn them of a poisonous tree snake ahead and they cautiously bypassed the area. He pointed out more dangers along the way, and plants that his people found useful.

"Do not eat these leaves. They are poisonous."

Tyler paused to marvel at a vivid red and black frog that gripped a huge rubbery leaf. Pioka materialised in her face.

"Do not touch the brightly coloured frogs, unless you wish to join us on the other side. My people catch them to poison their darts with their skin. The fruit of this tree looks good to eat but do not even go near it. Ah, acai! The purple berries are very good. Eat some. Rest here for a time. My men will scout ahead."

Tyler and Klaus stopped to pick and eat berries from the plumes at the sides of the acai palm, trying to shelter beneath its leaves. Pioka pointed out the hanging fruit of another tree.

"Take one of these and cut it open. Grind the seeds into a paste and paint it on your faces. It will protect you from evil spirits."

Klaus lopped one of the spiky, pear-shaped fruits down and carefully opened it with his machete. He mashed the fleshy red seeds inside into a pulp and they daubed each other's faces in stripes.

Catching Pioka's knowing smile, Tyler asked. "Does this really work?"

He laughed, and the other tribesmen joined him until they were all in hysterics.

"No. It does nothing. My living ancestors still do this, but they don't know any better, and we let them carry on because it amuses us."

"Okay. Very funny." Klaus rubbed paint from his face. He squatted to rest his back against the tree and tighten the binding on his makeshift machete.

Pioka continued. "No, but seriously, if you take a thorn from the sago palm and pierce it through the base of your nose, no evil will ever befall you, as long as you wear the thorn."

"Really?"

Again he laughed. "No. Don't do it. It will achieve nothing and it is excruciatingly painful." His men fell about laughing.

"You know a lot about the forest, Pioka," said Tyler,

laughing with them dispassionately.

"The sacred knowledge of the forest has been passed down through generations for thousands of years. Without this knowledge it is impossible to live here, but with the knowledge, the forest is great provider. She gives us everything we need. She is our mother." Pioka spotted another plant. "This is Mulungu. Its bark and roots can be ground to make a sleeping potion to ease those with a troubled spirit."

"Well, there're enough of those around here." Tyler glanced at Klaus, busily working on his machete. She stripped some of the Mulungu bark from the tree and quickly stuffed it into her pocket while he was not looking.

"You've been very helpful, Pioka."

*

The rain ceased, leaving them cold, wet and weary as the daylight waned. Ahead, the Korubu tribesmen scouted for danger. To Tyler's left, Albert, Izabella and half of the Ghost Squad drifted. The rest of the squad covered her on other sides so that she and Klaus were surrounded by ghostly companions of one sort or another wherever she looked. She marvelled at the strange sight as they shifted through the trees.

"It won't be long before dark," said Klaus. We'd better think about making camp. We should get a fire going to warm up and to keep animals and mosquitoes away during the night."

The thought concerned Tyler and she realised she had been avoiding the inevitable. She called back Pioka.

"How long before we reach the bad men?"

"At the speed you move, half a day."

"Then we'll make camp here."

"It would be wise to go a little further from the river."

"Lead on." Tyler checked her water bottle, finding it half full, and Pioka took them deeper into the jungle to a small clearing. Klaus hacked down a few bushes at the edges to give them enough room to make a camp fire and sleep close to it, clear of undergrowth. After struggling with damp twigs and branches, he coaxed a small fire into flame and piled more wood scavenged from the jungle floor to dry near the blaze. By the time it was dark and they had heated packets of army rations from their packs and boiled water for hot drinks, the fire was blazing away and they had collected and dried enough fuel to get them through the night. Klaus rigged a tarpaulin as a shelter. They strung hammocks to keep themselves off the bug-infested ground and slept close, in sleeping bags, as Albert and the other ghosts watched over them.

*

A noise disturbed Tyler. She blinked, blearily peering out into dark jungle.

"Psssssst! Missy!"

She turned and found Albert in the murk. Beyond him in the shadows movements fleeted. She squinted.

Enemy ghosts!

She reached across to Klaus and shook him awake, pressing a finger to his lips when he blinked at her, and she pointed.

"They found us!" she whispered, slipping from her sleeping bag and hammock to grab her pack. She took out a gallows blade but thinking again reached for the contrap instead, letting its empty lead box fall back into the bag. She set the switch to the *Ghost Portal*.

"Get behind me," she whispered to Albert, stepping

between him and the enemy ghosts stalking through undergrowth as Klaus armed himself with two gallows blades. Tyler glimpsed the ghostly buttons and stripes of their uniforms, and their haggard, ghoulish faces glaring back from the trees. "Tell all the squad to get behind me." She aimed the crystal ahead as the squad cleared the way. A cold glow lit the Nazi spectres before her as they closed with blades poised. They hesitated.

"Phasmatis licentia!" Ghost soldiers shrieked into the crystal, lighting up the jungle with quick blazes. Others fled as she circled the camp, seeking out more enemies. Abandoning all stealth, a moustached Captain shouted commands to attack, but Tyler swept the contrap at anything that moved. Ghosts charged into the campfire's glow at the edges of the camp. The portal locked onto another entity, and he screamed as his essence spiralled into blue light to be consumed. Two other soldiers retreated, their domed helmets bobbing away and vanishing. Three others had the sense to become invisible as they closed in but, shutting her eyes to help focus, Tyler sensed them and, one by one, collected them before they reached her. When she was sure she had cleared the ground of enemies she uttered the balancing spell and returned the contrap's switch to the *Safeguarding Skull*.

The crystal's glow died and she followed the light of the fire back to camp.

"Some of them got away," said Klaus. "Should we send the squad after them?"

"No. I don't think they'll try that again."

"But they'll return to Angel and he'll know we're coming for the girls."

Tyler thought for a moment. "That's just as well.

When we get there tomorrow I need to talk to him."

Klaus eyed her with concern.

"Let's get back to sleep. Albert and the squad will warn us if anything else happens."

*

Morning light struck her, warming a patch on her cheek. She rose to find Klaus gone, and discovered numerous, itchy, insect bites on her ankles and arms. Albert came to her.

"'E's out collecting more wood. Said 'e wants an 'ot breakfast."

Tyler tossed the last of the firewood onto the fire and peered into the bush.

"Today's the day, Albert. I'll be joining you in your realm before nightfall."

He looked at her, stunned.

"What?"

She busied herself, packing away her string hammock and rolling up her sleeping bag, all the while feeling his eyes on her.

"So what you plannin'?" he asked at last, but Klaus returned laden with sticks and small logs and she said nothing more. An awkward air fell over the camp and, although they cooked and ate a reasonable breakfast of porridge from foiled army ration packs, and drank tea, they spoke little. They broke camp an hour later and set off again into the jungle. After several sweltering hours passed, Pioka emerged from a bush to warn them, pointing towards the river they had followed.

"We are very close to the place. The bad men are just over there."

Tyler squinted into the jungle but saw nothing.

"Where?"

"Across the river. You will not see them. They have built there and hidden their building. It is covered with trees that are not trees and ground that is not ground. Come. It is easier to show you." He led her and Klaus past another three trees and squatted behind a massive, fallen trunk near the river bank, gesturing for them to do the same. Before them, two precarious-looking bridges, each consisting of three strands of rope bound from vines, crossed the flowing water side by side. Downstream, the Javari meandered in a broad arc to be swallowed by jungle. Pioka pointed across the river where the land rose in a vast dome. "See, where the land climbs? This is the giant hut of the bad men. Beneath the hill, they are many. We see them come and go."

"How do they do that? There're no roads. No airstrip."

"They fly in metal birds. They have built a hut thatch that moves and a metal bird comes from the ground and flies them in and out."

"A helipad with a false roof," said Klaus.

Tyler nodded and checked her phone again. "No signal, but the girls must be in there."

"Yes," said Klaus, pointing to a spot beyond the water where the ground vanished into a dark hole. In the shadow, Tyler made out the tell-tale lenses of field glasses. "We're being watched. What do you want to do?"

"I don't know. Let's go back to the others. I need to think."

They returned to Albert and the squad to inform them.

"If they already know we're here, there's no harm in lighting a fire. I need a hot chocolate. It always helps me think better."

"I'll get a fire going," said Klaus, leaving to collect wood.

But Tyler had lied. She did not need time to think. She knew exactly what she needed to do.

They nursed a fire into life and heated water in a small mess tin from Klaus' pack. While Klaus worked on a shelter, Tyler fed the fire and waited for the water to boil. She sprinkled in chocolate powder from sachets and set to work grinding the Mulungu bark into a fine dust using a couple of kit spoons. By the time Klaus returned to the fire for a rest she had stirred the bark dust well into the drink. She poured some of the concoction into a tin cup and passed it to Klaus before taking some for herself and pretending to sip. Behind Klaus, Albert narrowed his eyes at her. Izabella made her jump, appearing suddenly at her shoulder and whispering in her ear.

"Are you sure you know what you're doing, child?"

Klaus blew on the hot chocolate and swirled it in the cup. When it had cooled a little he drank thirstily before looking up.

"All right?"

"Fine." Tyler glared at Izabella. *Keep out of it!* "There's a drop left if you want it, Klaus."

"I have enough, thanks." He swigged some more. "Have you thought about the situation? I suppose we'd better make a proper reconnaissance of the place. You can use the contrap. Might as well, now they know we're here and because of last night they know *it's* here, too."

"Yes, we'll do that. Find the girls' exact location and check they're okay. Maybe we'll learn something that'll help."

Klaus drained his cup dry.

"Maybe." He reclined and Tyler looked over the shelter he had so easily thrown together; a lean-to of angled branches thatched over with the tarpaulin, camouflaged with palm leaves and floored with layers of moss and grasses.

"Hey, this looks okay. You done this before?"

"In basic training. They teach you to use whatever materials are to hand, but here we're spoilt for choice." He let his head rest on his pack, knotted his hands over his chest, and closed his eyes. When Tyler asked, "Do you think it's waterproof?" he did not respond. She asked him again, stepping closer to examine his face. Satisfied that he was sleeping, she left him by the fire and gathered the squad.

"I want you all to stay here and watch over Klaus. Make sure nothing happens to him. Look after Lucy and Mel. Carry your blades at all times and keep a lookout for enemy ghosts. There's something I have to do."

"Look after Lucy and Mel?" questioned Kylie.

"But *I'm* coming with ya', ain't I, Missy?" asked Albert.

"Not this time, Albert. I don't have time to explain but, for what I'm going to do, I must be alone."

He scowled at her before turning away and vanishing. Tyler grabbed her bag and walked, unaccompanied, out of the camp for the last time.

Crossing Over

Tyler quickly threaded her way back to the fallen trunk at the river's edge and ducked behind it to scan through vegetation into the covert neo-Nazi base through the *Present Eye*. For a moment she thought she was the one who was drugged as, beneath the fake rainforest facade, it all seemed uncannily familiar. She followed corridors and anti-chambers, staircases and secluded passageways. She traced her way deeper and found a vast, circular hall edged with twelve stone pillars. She focused in on the centre of the floor where a large, black swastika was inlaid and surrounded by a ten-pointed star. It looked, unquestionably, like the inside of the Urubici castle. She rested her back against the trunk and closed her eyes.

How many of these hidden locations do they have?

The knowledge that, below the surface, it was a copy of the first castle came with an equal measure of relief and fear. She found the place terrifying and she had nearly died there, trapped, yet if she could just get inside she knew she would be able to find her way around and perhaps locate the girls. Steeling herself, she turned to search again through the *Present Eye*, knowing that Angel was likely to be sensing the contrap's presence, or even watching her somehow.

She found the pillared hall again and spied on several officers in Nazi uniform meeting and passing documents, before dropping her view through the marble floor. Beneath lay a vaulted crypt with a central pit where a fire burned. She drew the focusing lever round the contrap's edge, bringing a tomb into view, one recessed into the crypt's wall with mouldering bones and a Nazi flag mounted on the rear wall. She shifted up again, looking through walls and passing chambers until a familiar arch caught her eye: the window from where she had watched the courtyard below. She thought of the smiths, their forges, and the hammering of gallows iron. Focusing through the contrap she recoiled, nearly dropping it. The crystal lens showed her a familiar, troubling scene, reminiscent of the Brimstone Chasm. Malnourished prisoners laboured, sorting piles of clothes and shoes, a sorry collection of humans; Jews, Puerto Ricans, Amazonians and others whose origins she could not name. The scene brought to mind harrowing black and white images of concentration camps she had seen, only here the prisoners were crammed into this one courtyard so that they appeared as one sprawling mass.

Tyler searched again for the girls, once more forced to question her plan. If she gave herself up in exchange, what was to become of these prisoners? *Is Angel doing this in other similar secluded places?* The thought was horrifying.

She found Lucy and Melissa, and relief flooded her being. They were alive and talking to each other, although shackled to the wall of a small prison chamber. Zebedee was there with them, also bound, but his manacles were transparent and ghostly. They had stripped him of his Nazi officer's disguise, leaving him with only his white vest, undershorts and gartered black socks.

So that's where you are. One more prisoner to bargain for in the exchange.

She had seen enough. She tucked the contrap into her shirt and rose, climbing onto the fallen trunk and waving her arms to attract attention. The neo-Nazis were watching and it was only a matter of time. A minute later a cluster of them gathered on the opposite bank, training automatics on her. Tyler shouted across to them.

"Where's your new Führer? I want to speak to him. I'll only speak with him."

"Do not move or we will shoot," called one of the officers across the water.

She smiled at his lack of understanding and knew she could drop behind the trunk in an instant with a fair chance of them missing because of the distance.

"Don't worry. I'm not going anywhere. Bring out your Führer!"

Two from the line ducked away, returning to an entrance she could barely see among creepers and foliage. They soon reappeared with Angel, who gripped the Spear of Destiny and smiled at her with obvious, new-found confidence. Tyler glimpsed the spear and again doubted her plan, remembering the mission to retrieve the spear that Chapman had ordered.

"Fräulein May. I wondered when you would come and, now, here you are. I trust you are..."

"I'm not here to chat, Mr Crane. I'm here to make a trade. The girls and Mr Zebedee Lieberman for me and the device. What do you say?"

The jungle was strangely quiet. Tyler waited.

"The terms seem fair. You have a deal, Fräulein. Will you cross and we can shake hands?"

Tyler laughed.

"Release Zebedee and send the girls out across a bridge. I'll cross to you at the same time on the other one."

Angel pursed his lips and nodded before sending men to fetch the girls. Zebedee appeared from the entrance on the other bank escorted by ghost German soldiers, his hands now bound with ghost rope.

"Let Zebedee go free now or the deal's off. You can call it a goodwill gesture."

"You drive a hard bargain, Fräulein May. Here is your spy." The Führer turned to his men and gave orders beyond earshot. Tyler watched as they released Zebedee.

"My effects, if you please," he said, waiting patiently until they presented his walking stick, his pocket watch and his pipe. He took them before crossing the river to join Tyler: a strange sight, walking several feet above the water, wearing only his underclothes, and tapping away with his cane.

"What do you think you're doing?" he asked, glaring tensely at Tyler when he reached her. "Have you taken leave of your senses?"

"I have to get the girls free somehow. I'm counting on you and the others to look after them once they're across the river. Wish me luck." She left him by the trunk and leapt down to follow the bank in full view of the soldiers on the far side. Climbing up to the closest rope bridge she stepped out and grabbed the side ropes while balancing on the lower, central line. She shouted.

"Right, then! Send the girls across, now, or the deal's off, Crane!"

On the far bank, soldiers escorted Lucy and Melissa to the other bridge and, at a word from Angel, cut them loose so they could cross. The girls hesitated, staring at Tyler.

"Don't worry," she called to them. "Just cross the bridge and you'll be free." Nervously, Melissa nodded and edged out onto the bridge causing it to wobble and bounce. Melissa glimpsed the coursing, brown river five meters below and froze.

"Keep going," urged Lucy from behind. They neared Tyler at the centre of the bridge, both looking drawn and exhausted.

"Klaus is sleeping a short way into the jungle from the bank. Find him. The Ghost Squad's waiting with him. He has food and a little water. Weaver and Freddy are somewhere close behind."

"But what about you?" asked Melissa, pausing on the bridge a few yards across from Tyler.

"Don't stop," said Tyler. "They'll suspect something."

"But what's the plan?" asked Lucy, as they passed. "You *do* have a plan, don't you?"

"Tyler, don't go. You don't understand what they're doing in there."

"I drugged Klaus. Find him. Find Weaver and Freddy. Get out of the jungle." Tyler continued along the ropes and checked behind to be sure the girls were doing the same. She slowed as she neared the end of her bridge where two enemy soldiers awaited, their automatics trained on her. She looked back again and watched Melissa climb down onto the bank. A shout sent birds fleeing into the air with an explosion of their calls.

"TYLER! WAIT!"

Turning to look beyond the fallen truck, she saw Klaus, Weaver and Freddy emerging from the jungle. Klaus shouted, his face ferocious.

"NO! COME BACK! YOU CAN'T MAKE THE TRADE!"

"TYLER, NO!" called Weaver.

Tyler glanced at her enemies to her side on the other bank. Even the two at the end of the bridge were distracted. She bolted the last few strides of the unsteady bridge to drive between them, shouldering them out of her way. Recovering quickly, they turned their guns on her and fired but she was already darting between trees and leaping into the entrance beneath the huge dome of the hidden lair. More gunfire sounded as the soldiers shot at her friends across the water. She heard a more distant tone of gunshot and knew Klaus, Weaver and Freddy were returning fire, probably backing away into the forest.

Inside the doorway Tyler paused, flattening against the wall to listen as out on the bank Angel laughed.

"Don't worry. Where can she go? She's trapped."

She ran deeper in, turning down a pristine corridor, white and featureless except for its endless row of glaring ceiling lamps. Footsteps sounded ahead and she waited against the wall until they had passed. She sprinted as soldiers reached the outer door and, finding a staircase, descended, skipping the fourth step where she remembered a tread triggered a trap in the Urubici castle. At the end she hurried through a doorway on her right, entering a length of passage without doors. She worked her way cautiously from there, listening for the beat of soldiers' boots overhead. The marching came and went, and she slipped along more clean, white passages, seeking a good place to hide and plan her next move.

The next turn took her directly into the path of two Nazi ghosts and she fumbled with the contrap to open the Ghost Portal and take aim.

"Phasmatis licentia."

The ghosts were sucked into the portal with a shrieking hiss that she was sure the entire world could hear. "Compenso pondera." She switched to the *Present Eye*.

Hardly daring to believe that she was still alive and in possession of the contrap, she peered through walls and the surrounding chambers to check for occupants. She noticed a strongroom and wondered what was held on the other side of the thick steel door where a large handwheel secured a locking mechanism. Focusing into the chamber she saw bundles of dollar bills and a pallet of gold bullion. Along the walls were aligned eighty or so deposit boxes and she quickly scanned through the contents of each box as best she could until she reached box number fifty-two. This box contained the Spear of Destiny. Its gold sleeve glimmered softly in the chink of light that penetrated from a gap in the lid.

Surely Angel has the spear, so how can it be here? Two spears, then. The true spear and a copy. But which is which?

Knowing she did not have long before they would find her, she traced a route to the strongroom with the contrap, and set off. She found the steel door and studied the internal workings of the complex lock through the

Present Eye, panic rising at the sounds of a small army's approach. She felt ghosts closing the net around her. Urgently, she turned a smaller dial on the door, watching a column of pins disengage inside, one after the other until, with a click, the column was free. She hauled on the handwheel, spinning it loose, and opened the door. She glanced behind. Soldiers were running towards her down the tunnel, shouting. She closed the safe door behind her and spun the inner wheel, sealing herself inside and realigning the pins to secure the door. Fists pounded on the other side of the door and angered voices reached her, even through the thick steel. It was still only a matter of time, she knew. They had her trapped and, inevitably, they would take the contrap. She watched through the crystal lens as a man on the other side turned the dial to release the pins; one, two, then three pins, disengaged. She chose her moment and forced the dial to engage them again. The game continued as she thought desperately. She could keep them out for a while by forcing the dial, but that was only delaying their access.

What else can I do? Again, she considered putting herself into the *Ghost Portal*, but the Nazis would enter and find her dead body and the contrap. *Game over.* They would have a powerful weapon that would only accelerate their plans for world domination and the mass execution of all races except theirs. She would be trapped in the contrap and no less at their mercy. She abandoned the notion, eyeing the wall of deposit boxes.

Albert materialised and glared at her.

"There's some very angry people out there."

"If I don't keep turning this dial, there's gonna be some very angry people in here. Albert, I need help. Do you have the strength to turn the dial?"

"I can try, Missy." Albert took her place and gave the dial a twist. "Yeah, I can do it."

"Great. Keep it moving if possible." Tyler crossed to the wall and pulled down box number fifty-two. She opened the lid and lifted the spear tip from its bed of red velvet.

"Is it the real one?"

"I don't know," she said, turning it in her hands. "But I think I might have a way of finding out. Are the others okay?"

"Yeah, they all got away. When they saw you'd gone into the lair they ran back into the forest. Freddy got shot in the ankle but he'll be all right."

Tyler set the contrap's switch to the *Ghost Portal* and clamped the spear to the contrap.

"What ya' doin'?"

"I'm going to summon ghosts using the spear as the artefact. It should tell me if this is the real spear."

"Ain't that..."

"Dangerous? Yes, very. It could be disastrous, but if I don't like the ghost that is drawn to the spear I should be able to trap it in the portal, if I'm quick."

A presence smoldered out of the air to coalesce before them. Tyler backed up, lowering the spear and aiming the crystal as details formed. The turbaned ghost of a Persian man gazed back at her with steady, brown eyes. She waited, wondering if he was going to be a problem, but calmed as he contemplated her before glancing at Albert.

"And you are?" Tyler continued to aim the contrap.

"My name is Tahir ibn Khalid." He looked serenely back at Tyler. She held out the spear head.

"Did this belong to you when you lived?"

He frowned and reached out to touch it, allowing his fingertips to pass through the point.

"Yes, I think I did, but it did not have all this gold wrapping when I owned it, or these other embellishments. It was a simple spear. I traded for it with a Dane who journeyed far across the sea."

"So this spearhead was made by Vikings?"

"It was."

"This is the real spear," said Tyler, recalling Melissa's observations. "It's not the spear that pierced Christ's side, but it is what they are calling the Spear of Destiny. Not a copy."

"But what good is it to us? You're trapped, Missy!" Albert fought with the dial but the men on the other side of the door were gradually freeing more and more of the bolts. Each one clicked as it snapped loose of the locking column.

"I don't know."

Tahir peered at the door as though looking through it.

"There is an evil on the other side of this door. A great evil comes."

"Yes, and they're coming for me and for this." She showed him the contrap, knowing she was about to be captured.

"The symbols are strange. Some I know and others are foreign to me."

She stared at him intently. Hoping for some morsel of knowledge that might help, she pointed to the heart symbol.

"You don't know what this is, do you?"

"It's a heart."

"Yes, but what does the setting do?"

Tahir shook his head pensively.

"Missy, they're coming! I can't stop them!"

"All I can tell you is that my people believed the heart was the house of the soul; where the spirit rested. It was not until many years after my death that people understood that the head was the centre of thought and all else."

"So the heart signified the soul, or spirit?"

"Indeed."

Tyler's mind raced as she recalled the words of Onuris IV, translated by Klaus.

Where the heart is concerned, one can only muse (deliberate). Perhaps this was selected as a substitute image because the more accurate (truthful) device was already engaged (in use).

So the heart was used because the spirit symbol had already been used.

"The heart symbol signifies spirit, but why? What does the setting do?" she asked again.

"Maybe it's another *Ghost Portal*," said Albert.

She turned the contrap and set the switch to the heart symbol.

"Whatever you're going to do, do it fast, Missy!"

She drew the contrap's lever full-circle around the edge of its silver casing and pushed it like she had never pushed it before, no longer fearing it breaking.

If I don't try something now, it's not going to matter anyway. In fact, better to break the contrap so they can't use it.

With a loud click, the lever snapped back to its original position. She stared, astonished. At the same moment, the door mechanism also clicked as the last of the locking bolts disengaged. Albert turned.

"They're comin'!"

The Heart

Albert gawped at the contrap. It faded, becoming transparent as Tyler tried to keep hold, but it was ghostly and her fingers clawed through it.

"Stone the crows! I ain't never seen that before!"

"It's turned ghost! Take it, Albert! Get it out of here!"

Albert snatched the contrap from where it hung in the air and vanished through the side wall of the vault as the door flew open. Soldiers spilled in, grabbing Tyler, slapping her up against the wall and cuffing her hands and ankles. She laughed as they searched her. The rough hands of men fumbled over her body, but she couldn't stop laughing. She was still laughing when they dragged her into the corridor before Angel. He grinned, pretentiously.

"The device, if you please, Fräulein."

Tyler met his gaze.

"I lost it. Sorry."

"Search her," he demanded, losing his smile. An officer nervously stepped forward and handed her mobile, her watch and a handful of gallows blades to Angel.

"This is all we found, mein Führer."

Angel waved the phone in her face.

"You won't need this where you're going." He slipped it into his jacket pocket and passed the rest of her things to his guard. "Search her again. Trace her path from the entrance and have the medical team strip her. I want her X-rayed."

Soldiers hauled her away by her arms and she no longer cared. They didn't have the contrap and that was all that mattered. She only feared Albert may have been apprehended by enemy ghosts as he tried to escape.

The soldiers took her to a medical unit where doctors in white lab coats strapped her to a steel gurney and injected her with a clear fluid. She did not fight but hoped it would knock her out, or better, kill her swiftly. If she became a ghost now, she would be able to follow after Albert. Maybe even help him get clear of the lair. The doctors left the room and she felt the world around her softening. As her vision blurred she saw a figure draw near to stoop over her.

"Tahir?"

Tahir ibn Khalid watched her with his steady gaze and, as Tyler passed out, she heard strange animal yelps and howls echoing from elsewhere in the building.

*

Albert fled the strongroom, dodging several Nazi ghosts by dipping into floors and walls on his way out of the lair. He ducked into passages to avoid other ghouls and was approaching the exit when a ghost officer stepped out from the wall to block his path. Albert froze before glancing down at the contrap in the palm of his hand. The officer called out to bring guards before closing in.

"The device! But..."

Albert switched the contrap to the *Ghost Portal* and took aim.

"Phasmatis Licentia!"

The officer morphed into a blue fog and spun into the contrap's lens.

"Gor blimey, it worked! Compenso pondera." Albert exited the lair to plunge through the river, passing piranha, a lurking caiman and a host of small, shimmering fish beneath its surface. He bolted into the jungle, only slowing at the sound of voices ahead, beyond a screen of undergrowth.

"Mel, Lucy, it's me, Albert." He passed through the foliage and joined the others as the Ghost Squad lowered their blades. Klaus, Weaver and Freddy lowered automatics.

"They 'ave Tyler." He told them about the spear, Tahir ibn Khalid and the heart symbol, and held up the ghost contrap for them to see.

"Then all is not lost," said Izabella. "Although they'll have killed Tyler by now, she will fight on as a ghost."

"What should we do?" asked Melissa. "What if she's still alive? We might be able to rescue her."

"We need to know before we try anything," said Lucy. "Or we're just endangering more lives, and that's exactly what Tyler was trying to avoid."

"*We* can go to her," said Zebedee, standing with Albert. "We can slip in and find out what's going on in there."

"Not dressed like that you ain't," said Albert, tossing Zebedee the ghost contrap. "Use the portal. The contrap still works even though it's ghost! Find another Gestapo uniform while I go back in." He turned and vanished into the jungle.

Zebedee set the contrap to the *Ghost Portal* and aimed the crystal at himself.

"Phasmatis licentia." He flashed into it. Izabella took the contrap from where it hung, turning gently in the air.

"I have something that might help," said Weaver, opening his pack. "A little something Chapman had constructed." The others looked through the gaping zipper to glimpse a chink of silver.

*

Tyler opened her eyes, feeling groggy and a strong sense of déjà vu. She also felt a slight pang of disappointment.

Oh. I'm still alive.

The room around her was clinical and stank of disinfectant. She tried to focus on the movement at the foot of her gurney. Two doctors whispered to each other while examining X-rays she presumed were of her body. She glanced around. Tahir had gone. She tried to rise but her head hurt whenever she moved and the tight straps across her chest and knees restricted her. She looked again at the doctors and smirked.

You won't find it there.

Wondering why they had kept her alive, she tried to empty her mind and shut it down. She didn't want to be there; didn't want to have to think about anything. She wished they *had* killed her. At least *then* she might be free to go and they could do nothing more to hurt her. Alive they could torture her and use her as a bargaining chip.

I can't let that happen. I'll kill myself at the first opportunity.

From her gurney, she studied bottles on a shelf, looking for poisons. The doctors noticed she was awake and made measurements of her body and collected blood samples. They took her temperature, tested her reflexes and peered into her eyes with bright lights. When they had weighed her and strapped her into a wheelchair, they wheeled her into another room where they attached wires to her head and taped heart monitor sensors to her chest. She tested the straps binding her arms to the armrests of the chair and found them unyielding.

"Why are you doing this?" she asked a bearded doctor who peered at her over his bifocal glasses.

"We have been ordered to give you a full medical examination and conduct certain tests. We are only acting on orders. Don't worry. The Führer has instructed us not to harm a hair on your head. Now, sit back and relax. You will be asked a series of questions."

"Some kind of lie-detector test?"

"Something like that."

They blindfolded her and a few moments later the doctor spoke again.

"What is your name?"

"Tyler May."

"Your age?"

"Eighteen."

"Where were you born?"

"Watford."

"How do you feel?"

"Tired. Very tired."

"Do you feel anything else? Do you sense anything

around you? Before you?"

"What do you mean?"

"Please just answer the question, Miss May."

"No, I don't sense anything in front of me."

"And now? Has anything changed?"

"No," she said, wondering what this was all about. She *was* starting to feel something; a creepy notion that these weirdoes were up to something odd. "Listen, what is all this about?"

"Just answer, please. How about now?"

A sudden chill hit her, sending the hairs on the back of her neck on end. She stopped herself from replying.

I'm not going to play your game, whatever it is.

The feeling was the one she had each time a ghost was close by and she sensed that the ghost closing in on her now was evil. Sweat beaded on her brow as she fought to hide all signs of her awareness. Angel spoke at her side.

"Very good, Fräulein May. I can see you tried hard to conceal your unusual ability but, I'm afraid you did not succeed. Tell me, how did you acquire this capacity to sense the presence of ghosts?"

Tyler waited. *So that's what all this is about.*

"Answer me, child, or I will cause you great suffering."

She could not suppress a smirk.

"You are a constant and never-ending cause of great suffering to many and you are already a cause of great suffering to me. What more do you think you can do to me?"

"Oh, don't worry about that. I have special plans for you. I have plans for all of your kind. Firstly we will annihilate the Jews. Then we will rid the world of every other abomination, each and every black-skinned nation." He lent in close to whisper and she felt his breath on her face, smelled its sickly, stale reek. "We must, inevitably, turn our gaze upon Africa and, when we are done, there won't be a single rat living on that perverted continent. Of course, it may be some years before the land will be habitable once more, but we are in no hurry. We will wait and, in time, your homeland will be re-populated with the master race."

"I'm not from Africa," said Tyler, sensing him only centimetres from her face. With a sudden lurch she stretched her restraints to butt him. "I'm from Watford." She listened to him recoil and spew a tirade of German expletives. A sharp blow across her cheek sent pain reverberating around her skull before she passed out.

*

She came round in chains, trapped in a darkened cell. One small, high window allowed a chink of light to show her surroundings. She recognised it as the same cell the girls had been held in and noticed, on the same wall, a second set of manacles hanging vacant. To one side a skull smiley was etched into the bleak wall plaster.

Lucy was 'ere.

She tested her chains and found enough slack to rub at the aching welt on her cheek.

Albert coalesced before her.

"Albert! Did you get the contrap out?"

"I did. Left it safe with Zebedee and the others. He's gettin' a new disguise."

"Good."

"They're waitin' in the forest. They don't know what to do. Thought you might be dead or somefin'."

"Okay. Get out of the jungle. All of you. Go back to

Chapman and tell him what's going on here. They're using this place like a concentration camp. It has to be stopped."

"But what about you, Missy? They... We all want to get you out."

"It's too dangerous. Get far away from here. Get the contrap far away from *them*."

"But they could hurt you. You don't know..."

"They can't hurt me if I know you and the girls are safe. Not really. Don't you see?"

Albert shook his head.

"It ain't like you t' give up, Missy. The others won't leave you 'ere anyway. And don't forget, I can bring you the contrap and take it away again without them Nazis knowing anythin' about it. Ain't there somethin' we can do to get you out?"

She stared at him briefly.

"Did you use the contrap?"

"Oh yeah. I used it all right. I slapped a ghost right in the portal."

"So it works even when it's a ghost contrap."

He nodded.

"But I don't need to use it to bring it back to you. I found a way in where no one else goes. There's a big tree with a big root that ends just below this floor. I can get in and out of this cell without even meeting a single ghost."

A spark of hope kindled in Tyler's mind.

"Okay, change of plan. Bring me the contrap, but be ready to take it away again should they come for me. Quick, go! Someone's coming!"

The Rite

The cell door clunked and clattered as men unlocked and opened it. Angel stepped inside, closely followed by four armed guards.

Not taking any chances, eh, Angel?

Tyler noticed the bluish bruise on his forehead and smirked. A guard rifled through a bunch of keys before unlocking Tyler's manacles.

"Come with me," said Angel. "I've something of interest to show you."

Rubbing her sore wrists, Tyler reluctantly followed him out of the cell and through tunnels. Animal noises echoed.

What is that?

The yelping and howling grew louder as they passed the end of another corridor and Tyler noticed another skull smiley scratched on the wall, its eyes leering permanently towards the sounds. The noise abated as they climbed stairs to a higher level and she recalled the time she had approached the Urubici castle two years previously. Back then she had parachuted from a stealth plane and heard similar sounds as she stomped through snow.

They passed an open doorway and Tyler glimpsed the room inside. At the center stood a hulking trilithon, a stone doorway with head-sized recesses carved into the stone of the two uprights. All three stones were age-worn, the lintel so decayed that it was partially missing. She noticed a long table covered in red velvet and adorned with a great assortment of old objects. Among them were many World War II German artifacts: soldiers' helmets, daggers, guns, medals, toothbrushes, combs, boots and coats, and other wartime memorabilia.

Angel led her along a final, curving walkway and into the pillared chamber with the swastika floor where armed soldiers lined the wall. She looked again at the huge symbol and wondered why it was emblazoned on a backdrop of a ten-pointed star.

Tyler had a bad feeling.

The doors opposite her opened and, led by a familiar woman in a sharp grey business suit, two men in white coats wheeled in a shrouded cage and shunted it across to Angel.

"Here he is, my dear," said the woman, heels tapping over marble. Tyler recalled her name.

Valda Braun, we meet again.

Angel removed the cloth covering the cage to reveal a trapped baboon. The powerful creature shrieked, eyeing them with suspicion from beneath its bulging brows. It bared its long, yellow teeth and shook the cage as its raucous howl rebounded from the arching walls and pillars. Tyler glared at Angel.

"You brought me all this way to show me your mother? Really, you shouldn't have."

"Let's see how long you bravado lasts. Come closer and see the markings. Perhaps they will explain best what we have in store for you." Angel swept a hand towards the vast marble floor and as Tyler stepped closer to the center she saw them: strange symbols chalked all around the edge of the swastika, one in each of the ten points of the outer star. They brought to mind images she had seen of witches' pentangles and she recalled Jonathan Hatherow's secret backroom.

"Welcome to our sanctuary. This is where you will eventually die," said Valda Braun. "We have everything prepared. We have performed the rite many times before, so you see, we are quite practiced. The art is all in the preparation and timing."

"We had some interesting results during our trial period," added Angel. "Though the din was attracting some unwanted attention and so we moved our experiments to this location where the sounds of the animals would not be out of place. Quite a fortuitous move, as it happens. It opened up a whole new realm of possibilities to us. For the rite, I mean. The jungle is an amazing resource."

"What rite?" asked Tyler, immediately wishing she had kept quiet.

"To extract your soul from your dying body before it escapes to other planes," said Braun. "That is where the beast comes into its own. You see, your soul will be transferred into its physical body and we have it trapped in a cage: A win-win situation, I think you'll agree. You will be dead but your ghost will remain trapped; our property. No silly-business after you've gone."

"Unless you give us the device," added Angel, stepping closer to poke a piece of apple through the bars of the baboon's cage." The baboon chomped it hungrily.

"I can't give you what I don't have. Let me get this straight," said Tyler. "You think you can turn me into a monkey?" *You really are nuts!*

"Not exactly, Miss May," said Braun. "But close enough and, when the transfer is complete, we'll liquidate what is physically left of you. Watch. You will learn how it will be."

Guards dragged in a bound and gagged, Brazilian prisoner. Tyler stared, knowing she had seen him before but unable to place him. As they strapped him to a chair and heaved it into the center of the swastika she saw beyond the grime, his rags, and unkempt beard and hair.

The Vice President of Brazil.

Angel wheeled the cage over to the edge of the outer star symbol and carefully positioned it at the tip of a point containing an inverted heart symbol. Unprompted, guards carried tall candle stands to each of the remaining nine points and lit the wicks as the Vice President, eyes wide with terror, wrestled with his bonds and moaned through his gag. Braun and Angel entered a side chamber and reappeared wearing black robes. They drew up large hoods.

"I always like to be properly dressed for the occasion." Angel turned to the men who had brought in his victim. "You may leave us." They exited as he and Braun took positions at the edge of the swastika and chanted in a language Tyler did not recognize. A guard remained posted either side of Tyler. Angel drew a dagger and jabbed it into the flesh of the baboon through the side of the cage. He dragged his finger along the blade to collect a smudge of animal blood and smeared this onto the bound man's forehead before returning to his place at the edge of the swastika. A blade in Braun's hand flashed in the candlelight. Tyler bolted towards the Vice President, but the guards around her slammed automatics into her gut and she doubled over in agony. A moment later the prisoner's pleas and moans ceased as his throat was cut and the baboon released a resounding howl.

A guard burst through the doors, disturbing the rite.

"My Führer, we have the device!"

Turning, Angel threw off his hood.

"You have it? Where? Where is it?"

"Our men are bringing it here as we speak. The spies across the river wanted to bargain for the girl. They came to the bank but our soldiers opened fire. The spies fled but one of our men saw them drop the device. It has been reclaimed."

Angel turned to Tyler.

"It seems we'll not need the animal after all. Before long, you will be enjoying all the delights of the chasm." He laughed, and Tyler swallowed a wave of nausea.

The guard stepped away from the entrance and a troop of soldiers marched in, at their head, a man carrying a silver amulet on the flattened palms of his hands. Angel took it and grinned. Tyler gazed, disbelieving. *Angel has the contrap! That's it, then. He's won and I'm doomed.* He looked at her and nodded.

"I will make it quick for you, Fräulein May." He stopped, sensing nothing from the device in his hand.

"This is a fake, you incompetents." He drew his

handgun and shot the man who had delivered the imitation, and tossed it to the next in line. "Take it away! GET IT OUT OF HERE!" As he spoke, the fake contrap sprang apart in the soldier's hands releasing a swarm of NanoSects that dispersed into the air. Tyler smirked as the silver pieces skittered to the marble floor.

"Nice one, Mr Crane. I had my doubts but, yeah, you guys clearly *are* the superior race."

"CATCH THEM!" screamed Angel, waving his gun at his men. NanoSects buzzed around his head and through the open doors into the corridor. "I WANT EVERY ONE OF THOSE BUGS ELIMINATED!" The bugs hid in corners and beneath furniture, and slipped away from the chaotic, pursuing guards and soldiers to secrete themselves throughout the lair.

*

Guards unlocked her cell door and forcefully shoved her back inside.

"The true device, Fräulein May." Angel was once more in his business suit; Alfric Crane, the generous and charitable benefactor and industrialist. "Or the next soul strapped to that chair will be you. Think on that."

The guards locked her into the manacles and left with Angel. Tyler slumped against the wall as they secured the door. There seemed only one thing left for her to do. When Albert returned with the contrap she planned to put herself into the Ghost Portal and have him take the contrap out of the lair. It would kill her, she knew, but she would be able to fight on as a ghost. She could head up the squad and nothing much would have changed.

Except I'll be dead, of course, and there is one unknown factor. Albert. Would he be strong enough in this realm to set the switch to the heart symbol and force the lever into position when the contrap was not in a ghostly state? If he failed, Angel would find the contrap in the hand of my dead body and I would be his prisoner still. Will Albert even agree to the plan in the first place?

She sensed a ghost approaching and knew it was him long before he peered cautiously out of the floor.

"It's okay, Albert. We're alone."

He rose to stand over her, reading her face.

"Albert..."

"No. Whatever it is, no." She did not know if he had seen it in her eyes or worked it out for himself, but Albert knew what she was thinking. "Don't get me wrong, Missy. I wants ya' to be with me, but not like this! Not 'cause o' them."

She watched him.

"All right. If not that, then what?"

"I don't know. 'Ere, take it." He drew the contrap's lever full circle, anticlockwise and it clicked back into place. The contrap became solid, falling from his grasp. Tyler snatched it as it dropped and hung the chain around her neck. "Try somefin'. Anyfin'!"

She told him about the Vice President and the rite.

"I won't let 'em put you in the chasm, Missy. Never!"

"You may not be able to stop them. I don't have long. He'll sense it's here." She switched to the *Present Eye* and traced her way through the lair to the corner where Lucy had left a skull smiley. She followed this corridor as it turned and passed several doors, backtracking when she glimpsed another mark carved into a door. She focused in to get a closer look. *Another smiley.* Lucy had marked this door. She drew on the lever to look into the room beyond the door where guns were arrayed around the walls, and shelves carried a vast collection of munitions.

"There's a munitions store with enough explosives to blow the entire place. It's somewhere between us and the sanctuary. If I could get there I could really go out in style."

Albert glared at her. "Missy, you gotta stop finkin' like that!"

She tracked back to the corner with the smiley and retraced her journey with Angel, looking for the room with the strange standing stones.

"There it is. Wait, someone's in there!" She told Albert about the room with the artefacts and the standing stone doorway she had glimpsed.

"What's it all for?" he asked.

"Who knows?" She watched a worker placing artefacts in the niches of the upright stones. Sensing the approach of another ghost, she stopped, fumbling with the contrap. Tahir slipped through her cell door.

"You are wondering what the stone arch is for."

Tyler nodded.

"They are trying to summon more ghosts. They are growing their ghost army any way they can."

"And does it work, this stone doorway?"

"I do not know, but it would be better to destroy it anyway."

"I like the way you think, Tahir."

"Oh, Missy, I forgot. Some of the others are waiting in the portal. They've come to 'elp get you out."

Tyler set the contrap to the *Ghost Portal* and released Zebedee, Izabella and Kylie.

"Phasmatis licentia."

They stood around Tyler, an odd assortment of

spectres in her cramped, dim cell.

"Everyone, this is Tahir ibn Khalid. He's one of us." The other ghosts nodded a greeting.

"At your service." Tahir bowed graciously.

Tyler switched the contrap to *Ghost*, set the lever and watched as the silver casing and chain became translucent.

"You take it, Albert. Put it in your pocket. Even if you get caught they won't search you for it. They don't know it can do that."

Albert pocketed the contrap.

"What now, Missy?"

"You're risking your lives, coming in here without blades." *What an odd thing to say to ghosts.* "You'd best all hide. They're coming for me."

The Cage

Tyler's ghost friends ebbed away into the walls as guards unlocked the door.

Angel entered, seething, and jabbed the spear against Tyler's cheek, pinning her to the wall. With interest he watched a drop of blood run to her chin from the wound where the spear dimpled her flesh.

"Oh, so you *do* bleed, then. You and your people think you're clever but you will see who is the brightest amongst us. My plans are coming to fruition despite you and your English friends. War is breaking out across the world. The spear is doing an excellent job." He released her and stepped back, calming with great effort.

"You think these facilities are our only respites, this and our mountain castle? You are wrong. We have hundreds, here and in many countries. Already, we are poised for the domination of all territories. Our enemies burn behind closed doors along with any who dare to stand in our way, and the world remains blind. There is nothing you can do to stop us and now you will burn, too." He turned to the open door.

"Bring it." A guard entered, cradling a bowl of grey liquid which he held to Tyler lips as other guards clamped hold of her, keeping her still. "Drink. The potion will prepare you for the ceremony."

Tyler tried with all her strength to pull away but they held her fast. She smelt the odd mixture. *What is that? Fermented bananas and ash?*

"NO!" she shouted through the fingers digging into the sides of her mouth.

"Drink!"

She struggled but they tipped the bowl. No, not a bowl; a slice of human skull! They poured the liquid down her throat and she was forced to swallow or drown. Gulping, she broke a hand free to dash the bone and its remaining contents against the wall. Her world spun and the cell broke into morphing shards of colour. Angel transmogrified into a fire-breathing dog, barking at her as she slumped in the guards' arms.

"Enough! Bring her." He escorted Tyler back to the pillared hall and watched as guards bound her hands and legs to the chair at the centre of the room. Tyler tried to focus. Angel was still a fiery dog. The pillars of the hall were fat, writhing snakes. The swastika on the floor flashed with neon colours. Striding to her, he waved a hand to delay the guard waiting to secure her gag. Angel lifted her head with the tip of his spear beneath her chin.

"Last chance, Fräulein. The true device, or your soul."

"I told you, Alfric. I can't give you what I don't have.

Geez, you'd think the Master Race would catch on a lil' quicker."

"So be it." Ignoring her quip, he motioned for the guard to gag her, and crossed the room to slip on his robes as Braun arrived. "Bring in the recipient." A moment later, a guard wheeled in the cage and tugged its cover off to reveal another baboon, this one bigger and more agitated than the Vice President's. He positioned it at the edge of the star, as before.

Guards relit the candles at each of the ten points. Flames glimmered, reflecting on the glossy floor. Angel turned to his men.

"I don't think our guest will be causing any more problems. You may leave us."

*

The Ghost Squad and Tahir searched for blades, darting through passages and rooms. Reconvening in Tyler's empty cell, Zebedee reported.

"One gallows blade, but it's in the hands of a Nazi ghost. Looks a nasty piece of work."

"If we work together, I'm sure we can overpower him," said Tahir.

"We'll need to be quick, or we'll be too late," Zebedee urged.

Kylie stared at the others. "What are we waiting for?"

*

Shadows played like demons as Angel and Braun took positions at the edge of the marble star. The baboon jabbered and rattled the bars of the cage, baring its huge canines. Tyler glimpsed it across the room, a vast beast with teeth like sabers, hungry for her soul.

"He's quite a specimen. Don't you think?" asked

233

Angel. "A real beauty. But enough timewasting. Let the rite commence!"

Braun began the chant and soon Tyler heard the baboon yelp as Angel jabbed in his knife. He crossed to her and daubed baboon blood on her forehead. He looked round and interrupted the chanting.

"Wait! It is near. I sense it!" He scanned the room.

Albert!

Angel searched but found nothing out of place. "No matter. We will find it sooner or later. Continue."

Braun resumed her incantation as Tyler searched for signs of Albert through the haze of hallucinations. She found one almost immediately when a small movement caught her attention. The bolt fastening the baboon's cage wiggled as though all by itself. A moment later it wiggled again.

The baboon shrieked at Albert, unnerved by his invisible presence. Angel and Braun glanced up but seeing nothing out of place, looked away again. Albert tugged at the bolt again but it was a tight fit and hard to draw. He managed to loosen it a little, seeing that with some work he might draw it free altogether. He paused when Zebedee stole into a shadowed edge behind the pillars on the other side the hall.

At a faint buzzing, Tyler looked up. A NanoSect hovered before her.

In the shadows, Zebedee stooped to retrieve the gallows blade he had slipped beneath the door. He straightened to see Albert raising his hand to gesture 'wait!' Zebedee glanced at the two robed figures occupied with the ceremony, and froze. From his position, Angel would be able to see Zebedee's blade gleaming in the candlelight if he moved it even an inch. Zebedee waited.

At length, Angel turned, the edge of his cowl now blocking the corner from his view. Albert waved Zebedee on and he flew to Tyler, and her eyes widened as she glimpsed the blade dancing towards her. Zebedee worked away at the ropes on her legs with the knife.

Biting on her gag, she shot a nervous glance at her two captors. They were busy with the rite, still at the edge of the swastika, eyes closed, enraptured with their chant. She felt the tug of the blade as Zebedee sawed away and, a moment later, the ropes slackened. The ropes on her arms were next. The floating blade sawed frantically, fraying fibres with each passing stroke. Across the chamber the cage bolt jostled and shifted. Sensing its imminent release, the baboon howled and thrashed. Tyler felt her arms free and threw off her ropes. Propelled by rage, she ran for Angel as the cage door burst open. The baboon leapt out as Angel turned, but Tyler was on him, charging like a ram. She drove head-first into his gut, knocking him from the ground.

Albert darted for the cloakroom.

"No!" screamed Braun, but a gallows blade danced before her, holding her at bay.

Angel hit the floor and slid to a halt, recovering.

Guards streamed into the darkening room as Kylie focused all her energy into the tips of her fingers to pinch out candles, flame after flame.

"Kill her!" screamed Angel, battling to rise.

Gunfire echoed as guards entered the chamber. Across the swastika floor, Tahir worked his way around the points of the star to kill the last flame as Albert emerged, heaving a cloak to Tyler. She took it and threw it on before fleeing as chaos reigned in darkness, lit only by the staccato blaze of automatics. The baboon attacked guards, biting and mauling, loosing blood from its victims. Angel clambered to his feet but slipped on the bloodied floor.

Albert and the others each took a robe from the cloakroom and followed Tyler into the passage. A blaring alarm startled them and a voice reverberated from secluded speakers throughout the lair.

"All armed personnel report to the sanctuary without delay. All armed personnel report to the sanctuary without delay."

"Split up," said Albert. "Use the cloaks. Protect Tyler."

"You'd better protect yourselves. This place will swarm with armed ghosts any moment now." Tyler fought to discern reality from hallucination. The ghosts pulsed with vivid hues. She tried to shake off the drug.

Albert and the other ghosts heaved on robes and, hampered by their earthly weight, chose different paths. Tyler made for the munitions room but reaching the first of Lucy's smileys, which winked at her, had another idea. The enraged baboon had brought chaos, and she knew where there were more. She sprinted past the store, following the sounds of the animals as they raged at the reverberating siren. The tunnel broadened into a long chamber with four doors on each side, the first of which she opened to face a renewed cacophony as baboons howled. She ran down aisles of cages slipping open every catch. She darted into the next room as the hairy troop streamed out into the corridor to head off at will. In each room she found a different species of ape, releasing them all into the mounting bedlam of the lair.

Returning to the munitions store, she shut herself in and searched for nitro and detonation timers. She took one timer and ripped out its detonation cables to use it as a basic countdown clock, a replacement for her watch, which Angel had taken. She threw an automatic over her shoulder and shunted a full magazine into its housing. She stuffed a second clip into her belt along with a loaded handgun but hesitated, hearing that buzzing again. A NanoSect hovered in the air, watching her. Feeling the drug's affects easing, she gave it a nod.

"Hi guys. Glad you could make it. No chance of a miraculous rescue, I suppose. No, thought not." She found the explosives and held some up for the insect to see before working on a bomb. "No doubt Albert's told you about the prisoners. The layout of this place is an exact copy of the castle, except it's all underground, of course, so you'll remember the courtyard. I don't have much of a plan and I have even less time, so I'm kind o' making this up as I go along, but I intend to blow the roof off this place. Get us an evac. crew. I'm guessing three hours should be enough to beg help from our friends at Langley. After that, don't bother. There won't be anyone left to rescue."

She completed the bomb and set the timer to count down from three hours. She programed her wireless timer to match and set it counting down. The NanoSect buzzed closer to examine the timer. Tyler offered the flat of her hand where the bug settled. "You'd better come with me." She placed it carefully on her shoulder. "Hold tight." She hid the bomb under a box at the back of a shelf and, taking a bag from another rack, collected more explosives before opening the door an inch to spy out. The din from the outside was a mix of shouting, howling and the stomp of soldiers' boots. A cloaked figure shot past the door and Tyler closed the gap to a hair's breadth.

The chasing soldiers caught the figure further down the passage and celebrated.

"We have the girl!"

The tugged off the cloak and it fell to the floor.

"Nice try," said Kylie, looking back at the soldiers. She smiled and pushed her glasses further up her nose before vanishing. The frustrated soldiers stormed away. Tyler waited until they had gone and stole out of the store.

Now to buy some time. A few minor explosions should add to the chaos.

She ran back to smiley corner and retraced her path to the sanctuary, checking every doorway she passed. Half way between, she found the room she wanted and entered. At the center, an unearthly, blue light descended in a column to illuminate the ancient, stone doorway and cast its skull niches in shadow where an array of World War II artefacts nestled. Army chests and other larger artefacts lay stacked in an area behind the stone formation.

What are you?

She opened the door, listening at the gap. This zone of the lair seemed quiet for now. She searched for clues, trying to discover how the doorway functioned but before she could do much Albert appeared, closely followed by Tahir and Zebedee.

"Wotcher, Missy."

"Albert! The contrap..."

Albert fished the contrap from his pocket and levered it back into its physical state. Tyler caught it as it fell from his grasp, hung it around her neck, and set it to the *Past Eye*.

"Keep watch."

Izabella appeared next to her.

"This is ancient magic, ancestor worship. They're using gallows iron to power the doorway. Place a skull in a niche and the correct ceremony will call forth the ghost. Apparently it also works with lesser artefacts." She glanced at the loaded table. "It is an evil and should be destroyed."

"You don't say." Tyler noticed small heaps of raw gallows iron in each of the niches: rusty nails and other scraps of decaying metal.

The stomp of army boots reached them from outside, and they froze, listening to Zebedee posing as an officer.

"This room is clear. Go and find the girl!"

Boots tramped on.

"It's supposed to find ghosts," said Izabella. "It's like the *Ghost Portal*."

"Does it work?"

"Who knows?"

Tyler scanned back in time, viewing the stones through the crystal lens as Albert and Tahir left to guard the entrance. Moments later she slowed to let the recorded images play at real speed and watched officers enter the room. Soldiers followed, bringing artefacts and depositing them on the table with the others. She didn't see who did it, but someone turned off the lights and switched on the column of blue light. An officer issued orders and the soldiers selected three helmets from the collection and placed them carefully in the niches of the stone doorway before retreating to the edge of the room. The commanding officer chanted and made signs with one hand in the air, following a prescribed pattern from an open book in his other. He stood back expectantly, eyes fixed upon the arch. Light shimmered between the stones, an iridescent, blue, otherworldly radiance.

No! Surely not.

Ghost German soldiers quickened from shards of bolting essence, translucent sinew and flesh coalescing into features. Uniforms and guns formed from amorphous radiance. Three phantoms stepped through the doorway ready to join the growing enemy army. The artefacts in the niches were replaced with new ones and the process was repeated.

Tyler had seen enough. She had to destroy the stone doorway before they brought more ghost soldiers back from the other side. Dumping her gun in the bag, she rummaged for a canister of nitro and strapped it to the closest upright stone. Using the niches as footholds, she climbed up to reach the lintel stone where she secured a second canister. Fixing a third canister to the last stone, she fetched more explosives and packed the niches.

"Try summoning Nazi ghosts when your magic doorway is nothing but rubble." She took detonation cords and linked the first few canisters. At her side, Izabella cleared her throat. Tyler turned to see her pointing to an enemy ghost officer crossing the room.

"My men are on their way. Step away from the explosives and surrender."

Tyler laughed. He had a ghost gun raised.

"Or what? You'll tickle me to death?"

He holstered the ghost gun as doubt flashed in his eyes. Tyler grasped the contrap.

"The chasm!" urged Izabella.

"There will be many others here soon who will be properly armed," the officer said, stepping back in fear.

Tyler switched to the flame symbol and drew the

lever to open the chasm.

"Vorago expositus. Phasmatis licentia."

The orange glow intensified and dragged the officer into the chasm with a rush as he tried to flee. Tyler closed the chasm, and the glow vanished, leaving its sulphurous stench.

"Compenso pondera. Albert! Tahir!"

She ran to the door and threw it open. Beyond the room, they fought hand to hand with enemy ghouls armed with gallows blades as more ghosts closed in on the room. Zebedee turned momentarily from his opponent.

"Miss May, the Führer and that wretched woman are heading this way!"

Ghost Finder

Scrambling to the bag, Tyler grabbed more cords and hurried to rig the remaining explosives. She clamped the last wire into place and snatched a detonator from the bag as the door flew open. Angel stepped into the room, the spearhead in one hand, a gun poised in the other. Tyler ducked behind the closest stone.

Beyond the door the battle raged as more of the Ghost Squad arrived. Distant animal cries mingled with screams and muffled gunfire.

Braun entered to join Angel, levelling a machinegun at Tyler's hiding place.

"Come out, Fräulein," said Angel. "You're trapped and completely outnumbered. I know you have the device. I sense it here. Surrender it to me now, or I will shoot you dead."

Tyler set the contrap to the chasm and muttered the

words.

"Vorago expositus." The chasm opened and she heard Angel and Braun back away to the door as the chasm's unearthly glow spilled into the room. Braun fired. Bullets zipped, ricocheting from the ancient stone shielding Tyler.

It's now or never!

"Phasmatis..." Tyler fell silent when Marcus appeared between her and Angel. Angel gazed as Marcus raised his bow and fiddle to play a long, high note that filled the room.

"Who are you, child?" asked Angel, momentarily perplexed. "What do you want?"

Marcus continued his sad melody.

He's buying me time, but for what? If I use the chasm now, I'll send Marcus in along with Angel!

Kylie coalesced before Angel, scowling at him.

Angel took a step back, pointing at her.

"I know you. Why do I know you? Guards! Get in here! Get rid of these ghosts!"

While Angel and Braun were distracted, Tyler raced for the gun in the bag and fled back into hiding.

Zebedee slipped in from the corridor behind Angel and Braun. He whistled to Kylie and slid a gallows blade across the floor to her. She stooped to claim it, brandishing it and closing on Angel.

"I know who you are," babbled Angel. "I know! You were the one!"

"Forget these fools. Get the girl!" yelled Braun, volleying bullets at the stone doorway.

"No." countered Angel, raising an arm to silence her. "You'll damage the Ghost Finder, or worse, blast us to pieces! Can't you see? She's rigged it to explode."

"Bet you wish you'd brought a gallows blade now, huh?" Tyler glanced out from the stone to see what was happening. Angel had lowered his gun and was holding Kylie at bay with the spear tip. Kylie eyed the spear with suspicion.

She thinks it's gallows iron. Perhaps it is!

"Ah! But I have something better, my dear. I have the Spear of Destiny. Its powers are limitless and, with it, I cannot be defeated."

"But the one he has is a fake," whispered Tyler to Izabella. "The real one is in a safe room."

She shouted to Angel. "Give me a break. If you believe that, you'll believe anything. It's not even the real spear. It's eight hundred years short of the mark." She peeked around the table to see Angel pale at her words.

"I'm through talking. The device, Tyler May, or you and all your friends here will suffer the consequences."

Tyler grabbed a battered gun magazine from a niche and hurled it at Angel and Braun before dashing out to dive at the table. Tipping it onto its side, she ducked as a spray of bullets embedded its surface. Izabella appeared next to her, crouching behind the table.

"What are you going to do, child?"

"Damned if I know. Any ideas?"

*

Grasping a mangrove, Klaus lowered himself down into the swampy river edge before helping Melissa in. She couldn't stop shaking.

"It's all right," whispered Klaus. "The ghosts will warn us if any caimans come too close. That's it."

"What about Piranha? They must be everywhere. I've seen the films."

"Are you bleeding?"

"No."

"Then you've nothing to worry about. Keep your gun above the water. Keep it dry. We're well clear of the lair so we don't need to worry about being spotted."

She stared at the shifting, brown water, wide-eyed, and nodded. Lucy, Weaver and Freddy were already halfway across, Freddy limping badly. Around them, the Korubu tribesmen searched for dangers.

"Come on. The quicker we move, the sooner you can get out."

Clambering ashore through mangroves on the other side, they regrouped while the Korubu scouted the forest ahead.

"This way." Pioka returned to wave them on, speaking softly. "Move like the jaguar. Keep low. No thrashing iron knife." They followed the tribesmen, ducking vegetation and scrambling over rotting trunks. Melissa glanced up to see a cluster of roosting fruit bats several feet above her head, and shivered.

"Wow. They're cool," said Lucy, pausing to admire them.

Melissa glared at her. "You won't think they're cool when they drop on your face and bite you on the neck."

"I wouldn't mind so much."

"Freak."

"Quiet, girls," whispered Weaver, dropping back to them. "We're nearing the lair. Pioka says it's just ahead. See, where the ground rises to the dome?"

They nodded, focusing on the armed guards set around the dome. Weaver signalled for Klaus, Melissa and Freddy to skirt left and Lucy joined him to follow the dome's edge around to the right, creeping low to the ground. A shout went up, sending a host of birds flapping into the air. Klaus opened fire at the guards as they raised their guns. Bullets rained, zipping through leaves and spraying bark.

"Retreat!" screamed Weaver, seeking cover but finding none.

Klaus hurled a smoke grenade as Weaver unclipped another and lobbed it across the lair. They returned fire and backed away, dropping more smoke grenades to hide their retreat.

*

Izabella peered intently at Tyler. "How many bullets do you have?"

Tyler disengaged her magazine to check. "A full clip and spares." She snapped the magazine back in. "Not enough to hold them off forever."

"The only leverage you have lies with the Ghost Finder. He does not want it damaged."

"I could make the contrap ghost again. At least then you could get it out of here."

Zebedee appeared on her other side.

"There are more coming. We can't hold them off! There aren't enough of us!" He vanished.

Tyler peered around the table edge briefly.

"I can't risk shooting at Braun. She's too close to Angel and if I hit him I will kill Steven Lewis."

"This is a stalemate, no?"

"Yes," said Tyler, eying the Ghost finder. "If only I'd had time to rig the detonator. Wait. I don't need the detonator!" She fixed her sights on the nearest nitro canister and called out as soldiers reached the door.

"Keep your men out of here or I'll blow your precious Ghost Finder to dust." She risked a look over the table. Angel gestured for his men to remain outside.

"You wouldn't do that. You would also be killed in the blast."

"Don't tempt me. I'm sure there're worse ways to go." She found an old German helmet and put it on, took a soldier's shaving mirror from the bric-a-brac and let it protrude from the table so that she could view Angel and Braun across the chamber. Looking as baffled by the situation as she felt, Angel was trying to edge closer to the stone arch.

"He wants to disarm it. Wait a minute," she whispered to Izabella, hunkering at her side against the table. "What would happen if Angel went into the Ghost Finder? There are two ghosts in him, right?"

Izabella nodded. "Three, if you count the spirit of Steven Lewis, the boy they used to create the glove."

"Right."

"One moment." Izabella searched herself for her old spell book and, pulling it from a pocket, flipped through its pages.

Tyler crept to the end of the table furthest from the Ghost Finder and launched a Lugar with a bent barrel at Braun, who returned fire. Still, they inched closer to the Ghost Finder.

"Not so fast!" Tyler fired into the gap between them and the trilithon to give Izabella time to search her book.

"Here it is!" hissed Izabella. "Ancestor worship." She scanned her notes quickly. "Do it, if you can! Put him into the Ghost Finder. If I'm correct, it should separate out the ghosts."

"What?"

"On the other side of that doorway, the spirits will not be able to coexist! The invading spirits will be forced out, and will display their true forms!"

"Go tell Albert and Zebedee. I'll let Angel get closer to the Ghost Finder."

With a nod, Izabella vanished. The battle outside spilled into the chamber. Yakubu the tall slave and Wulfric the Saxon fought empty handed against Nazi ghosts armed with blades. Kylie backed away from Angel, tossed her blade to Wulfric and he finished off his opponent and Yakubu's. Others came as NanoSects buzzed in the air.

Angel reached the Ghost Finder and dropped the spear to yank out detonation cords. Braun stood guard with her machinegun poised as he worked, preoccupied with the battle raging in from the entrance. Soldiers edged closer and bullets zipped about the room. Braun gestured for them to wait.

"Do not enter!" she shrieked. "No shooting! The Ghost Finder is rigged to blow!" Gunfire escalated as she shouted to Tyler. "You won't kill him, you know. The spirit of the oppressor will endure for all eternity. He cannot be destroyed!"

At the end of the table near the Ghost Finder, Tyler noticed an army chest sliding across the floor behind the stones.

Albert? Is that you?

She blinked at the shifting box and followed the line of the blue light up to the ceiling where a vast blue lamp blazed. She aimed her gun at the brightest spot and pulled the trigger as a troop of crazed baboons yowled into the room. The bulb shattered with an explosion of sparks.

Darkness and chaos. Screaming, yelping and shooting.

She ran out to Angel and skidded onto her side to

scoop up the spear. She glimpsed the box perfectly positioned in the gloom between the two stone uprights.

Thanks Albert!

Angel hadn't noticed. He was too busy precariously cradling volatile Nitro canisters amid pandemonium. He saw her and hurried to empty his hands of explosives as she rose behind Braun and thrust the spear into her left eye. Braun screamed, dropped her gun and fled. Tyler tucked the spearhead into her belt and turned her attention to Angel.

Come on Angel, just one step further into the middle of the doorway...

Angel closed on Tyler, a nitro canister in one hand, his gun in the other.

"You've made you're choice, Fräulein. Now die!" He raised his gun to shoot as Albert appeared, inching the chest closer. Tyler rushed at Angel, deflecting his aim and shoving his shoulders hard. He fired into the wall and toppled backwards into the doorway, releasing the nitro. Tyler shielded herself from the expected blast, but it never came. The canister hit the floor and rolled harmlessly away as a blinding light exploded from the Ghost Finder. She retreated, shielding her eyes and gasping at the strange spectacle. Amidst the shards of shimmering light between the stones, Angel bobbed, suspended by forces she did not understand. Peels of light ebbed and flowed around the body as the spirits of Hitler, Mengele and Steven Lewis vied for domination. Vast, blinding beams blazed around the chamber as their essences morphed, blended and wrestled. Hitler's features twisted and melded into Mengele's. Tyler glimpsed Steven Lewis' boyish face before it became lost, swamped by flowing essence, and the morphing continued. A static drone filled the air. A dominant spirit arose from the chaos, suppressing the others. Charred and spoiled, he formed, commanding a terrible beauty that Tyler somehow knew must once have been complete. His devilishly handsome face turned to her, and his piercing eyes locked onto hers.

She gasped and stepped back unable to look away, swooning at his severe gaze, feeling utterly naked, as though his eyes were looking into her soul. He unfurled powerful wings beyond the stones and momentarily seemed to fill the room with splayed, blackened feathers and the stench of burned hair.

Tyler shook herself from her trance. She grasped the contrap and switched it to the Brimstone Chasm, drawing the lever full-circle. The Ghost Squad gathered around her, forming a protective arc.

"Vorago Expositus." The chasm glowed hot through the crystal lens as Hell opened, and a hissing, roaring wind blasted from the contrap to sweep into the doorway. The reek of brimstone erupted into the room, sending enemy ghosts and soldiers into panicked flight. The baboons bolted, howling. Tyler squinted into the pulsing light of the Ghost Finder and bellowed over the rising maelstrom, battling to keep a hold as the contrap juddered and shook.

"No!" screamed Izabella, reaching out to stop Tyler.

What will become of Steven Lewis?

"I'm sorry, Steven!" cried Tyler. "Phasmatis licentia!"

Old Magic

The Ghost Finder exploded in a ball of brightness and a deafening blast. Tyler did not see what happened to Steven Lewis or the gloved ghosts in his body. She opened her eyes in another part of the room, blown from her feet by the blast and, peering through billowing smoke, coughed blood.

That's it. I'm dying. Only a matter of time, now.

She spat blood onto the rubble-strewn floor and tried to focus, feeling a pain in her chest and fearing a punctured lung. *Where's Angel? Steven Lewis? Anyone?*

Her ears felt strangely numb and barely registered a second alarm tone join the ongoing intruder alert, as an automated response system kicked in. Sprinklers in the ceiling released a fine drizzle of rain across the room.

"Fire detected on level six. Evacuate facility. Evacuate facility." The oddly-calm, automated voice repeated its message. Ghosts approached as the smoke swirled and, for a dazed moment, she thought she was in the contrap's *Ghost Portal*. She saw Albert in the gloom. She could not hear him but read his lips.

"Missy, you're alive."

Feeling as though she might fall, she realised she was still lying down, and despaired. Her world spun as the squad gathered around her. A pain throbbed in her left foot. *Has someone smashed it with a sledgehammer?* Blood trickled down the side of her face. A NanoSect hovered in her face.

"She has to get up," said Izabella. "She has to escape, now, or every one of them will die."

"Wulfric, check the passage."

"I will go."

"Yes! Now's our chance," Zebedee agreed. Tyler barely heard the words, as though from a great distance. "Make haste, Tyler. You *must* rise!"

"Hurry, Tyler!" urged Kylie.

"Up you get, Missy. You can do it. I knows ya' can."

Wulfric returned.

"The way is clear, but be quick! The warriors will return soon."

"Tyler, listen to me." Albert drew close to her face. "Mel and the others are trying to organise a rescue. They saw you set the timer in the munitions store. They're trying to get everyone out before the place blows up but you gotta get up and find a way to open them sky doors. See?"

Tyler visualized the Urubici castle with its open courtyard reaching up to the heavens, and understood the lair was the same except for its expansive sky doors, covered in false jungle.

"There are hundreds of innocent prisoners up there, men, women and children. And you are their only hope," said Izabella.

"Stand up, Tyler! Fight the pain."

She struggled to sit up and a flood of pain and nausea forced her back. Blood pounded through her head like the mighty Amazon and she coughed.

"I think I want to die now," she murmured, her voice sounding as distant as the others'. "Yes, I would like to die. Here. Now. I can't go on. I can't..."

Kylie's narrow face and round glasses filled her view, glowering.

"Get up, you selfish cow! Get up right now!"

Tyler tried again and succeeded in rolling over and crawling an inch towards the remnants of the Ghost Finder, buoyed by a desire to escape Kylie.

"This way!" hissed Kylie. "The exit is over here."

Tyler only wanted to know what had become of Angel and Steven. She squinted at debris and burning artefacts as she staggered to her feet, fighting the need to vomit. Dropping to her knees, she scanned the scene and found Angel's crumpled form beyond the wrecked stones.

"I have to know what happened."

In the corner, fire reached a canister of nitro causing a secondary explosion, though nothing like the first. She dreaded further detonations and searched for other rogue canisters.

"Tyler, leave it!" called Zebedee. "There's no time. Use the *Safeguarding Skull* this instant, or you will surely die."

"But I could take him out. Right now. He's just lying there."

"Your heart rate is slowing even as you speak. You

have internal injuries from the blast. Use the contrap to save yourself. If you don't, every one of those prisoners will die today."

Yakubu ran into the room to report.

"Twenty soldiers heading this way. They'll be here in less than a minute."

For an agonising moment, Tyler was torn. *Finally a chance to get Angel, but at what price? Without the correct artefacts, Steven Lewis would most likely be sucked into the chasm with him.*

"Tyler?"

"ALL RIGHT! I'M COMING!" she shouted, almost passing out from the effort it cost.

"Thank God," said Zebedee. "Follow us. We'll take you to safety.

"Vorago termino." She returned the contrap's lever to its original position and switched to the *Safeguarding Skull*, hoping to extend her ebbing life-force. An unnatural pulse radiated from the crystal and her breathing instantly eased. Grabbing the munitions bag, she shuffled round to face the door and, dragging her damaged foot, staggered after her ghosts.

"Still think I'm gonna die in this miserable hole."

*

Zebedee's head emerged from a closed door and nodded.

"In here. It's empty. Safe for now."

Tyler tried the handle.

"Locked. And I don't have my tools."

"Try this," said Zebedee, passing her one of the few gallows blades they had seized during the battle outside the Ghost Finder room.

Tyler peered blearily at the thin, tapering point of the blade and nodded. "Might work, I guess." She threaded it into the lock and tested the lock for trigger points, angling the blade with frequent, gentle twists. The lock clicked and she withdrew to try the handle and open the door. She dragged herself in and closed the door as shouts from searchers around the lair echoed. She dropped the spearhead copy into her bag as Albert came to her.

"They're looking for ya. They don't know what 'appened with that Ghost Finder, so they ain't sure if you survived."

"Right." A few minutes had passed since the blast and Tyler's hearing had recovered little. A high-pitched tone dominated all she heard and distracted her from thinking. It didn't matter. The Ghost Squad were bossing her around so much that thought was unnecessary. *This way. Go faster. Run! They're coming! In here.* She couldn't wait for it all to be over as she slouched to the floor against the wall of the empty chamber. She glanced around. *No. Not empty. A small filing room. Documents in grey metal cabinets along the opposite wall.* Trying to focus, she took hold of the contrap and switched it to the *Ghost Portal* as Zebedee jabbered on about what she should do next. *It isn't the same as suicide. Not really.* She reassured herself, and wondered if there would be pain as her spirit left her body and entered the portal. *Surely nothing more than I currently feel.* Gazing into the hypnotically swirling, grey mist, she whispered the command to end it all.

"Phasmatis licentia."

Nothing happened except the crystal turned smoky-black. She looked up to see Albert withdrawing his hand from the back of the contrap where he'd switched back to the *Safeguarding Skull.*

"Sorry, Missy. It ain't your time, yet. The skull will help you heal."

Zebedee leaned in. "You really must snap out of it, Miss May. You've work to do. Take a few moments to rest and order your thoughts."

She let the contrap hang on its chain, and stared at the cabinets for a long time, frustrated and aching. She examined her damaged foot. She had turned the ankle landing badly and a piece of twisted gallows iron from the explosion had lodged in the top of her foot through her boot. Plucking the iron free she tossed it aside and removed her boot and bloodied sock to inspect the bone-deep gash. *Oh well. Stitches will have to wait.* Tearing a strip from her shirt, she bandaged the entire foot, tightening the fabric over her ankle for extra support. She caught a nose full of her body odour. *Pretty funky. I need a shower, but that'll have to wait.* A trek through the jungle and numerous stresses had taken their toll.

"Where's Izabella? I want to know exactly what happened in there." She slipped her boot back on and stretched out her legs to rest, realising she had stopped coughing blood. *Perhaps my lungs aren't as damaged as I thought.* She ran her hands over her ribcage searching for damage, but found none. *Maybe I can still make it out of here alive. There's only one way to find out.*

Izabella came through the others to stand over her.

"What is it?"

"You told me to stop. Back there. Why?"

"I thought you were going to push him into the Ghost Finder. I didn't know you planned to use the contrap as well. I feared the two opposing portals would clash, and I was right. That is what caused the explosion. Why did you try to use the chasm?"

"I thought that while the spirits were separated they might be vulnerable to the contrap's draw, but it didn't work, did it?"

"No. You would have still needed artefacts from both the ghosts you wished to trap, which we don't have."

"So what happened to Angel? And what did I see in the doorway?"

"You saw the three spirits parting and fighting for control of the boy's body. You saw the spirit of the oppressor show his true nature. The old magic revealed him for what he really is. I had hoped the portal would expel the ghosts from the boy, but they are stronger than I thought."

"But I thought he was Hitler's ghost. What I saw looked more like a burned angel."

"There's nothing wrong with your eyes. He *is* an angel. A fallen angel with a purpose in mind. He's driven by it, and he will stop at nothing."

Tyler recalled a time when the twins had explained about the spirit of the oppressor.

"Throughout history he has plagued humanity," Danuta had said. *"He has influenced many nations. He dwelt amongst the Egyptians when they enslaved Israel, and the Babylonians when they took Jerusalem in ancient times. He coerced the Syrian king, Antiochus Epiphanes, into the sacking of Jerusalem and the murder of her people. He led the Romans in their campaigns to enslave the nations. He inhabited the murderous emperor, Nero. He brought about the crusades."*

"And he formed the Third Reich. We are at your service," Kinga had added.

"What purpose?" Tyler asked Izabella. "You mean he wishes to kill everyone who isn't blue-eyed and white."

"I fear his objective runs deeper than that."

"So what is it?"

"Child, I wish I knew."

"I don't understand."

"You understand as much as any."

"But what about the *full knowledge*? Don't you ghosts learn everything there is to know once you're dead?"

"Not everything. No. If we knew everything, we would know exactly what the enemy was doing at every moment, which would make defeating him considerably easier. We would have won the war by now."

"Won the war?" Tyler laughed cynically. "What war?"

"The war we are all fighting. Oh dear, you really have had a bang on the head, haven't you."

Zebedee stepped in. "Stop it! Stop it this instant! *We* are in this battle every bit as much as *you*. Do you think we cannot be hurt, just because we're ghosts? We have lost friends. We have suffered, struggled, been tortured and wounded. Now, pull yourself together. Find the old Tyler who is brave and courageous in the face of adversary; the Tyler I used to know, and get on with the job in hand. Find a way to open the sky doors."

Tyler rubbed at her head, smearing coagulating blood away from her eyes.

"Sorry." She thought, trying to formulate a plan, but nothing came. "I'm going to need all the help you can give me. I'm slow because I'm wounded and already exhausted. I'm also hungry and thirsty." She looked up at the squad. "I want to know what's going on out there."

"I'll take a look," said Albert as the fire alert ceased. "Wait here."

"Take a blade, just in case." Zebedee passed a blade. Albert poked his head through the wall to check it was safe before slipping the blade beneath the door, and leaving.

Tyler stared at the cabinets and decided to search them for any valuable information. *Who knows? We might never get a chance like this one again. And even if I don't make it, one of the squad can report to Chapman.* She opened the top drawer of the first cabinet and flipped through the file dividers within. Documents, letters and files. All in foreign languages.

Brilliant.

Not even sure what she hoped to find, she closed the drawer and checked the next one down. More of the same. The third contained thicker files bound in stiff card, but still she could not read a word. She moved on to the second cabinet and rummaged through papers, only stopping when she spotted a photocopied map among the white sheets. Plucking it out she unfolded and examined it. It was an enlarged geological chart of a section of the Amazon Basin. Useless, but Tyler now knew what she was seeking. Angel had let slip his spreading network of lairs throughout the rainforest; the perfect hiding place for subterfuge. If anyone stumbled upon one of the lairs, he or she would simply go missing, which was something that happened regularly in such a treacherous habitat, in any case. Who would wonder? Anyone missing would be considered a victim of the jungle and would most likely be someone from a local tribe, separated from the wider civilisation.

I need to find the map showing the locations of the

lairs. The information is invaluable for our cause.

She searched with a new intensity, skimming through wad after wad of paper and files. Minutes later she found the map and drew it out to unfold it, a full-colour map of a western portion of the Amazon, dotted with minuscule, black swastikas. She folded it and crammed it into a pocket of her combats as a blade scraped in beneath the door. Albert followed it, walking through the closed door. Tyler checked the detonator clock.

"Two hours and twenty minutes before the lair blows." *Plenty of time. Too much time!* She had time to kill, and wondered if she could even stay alive that long. "You learn anything?"

"Over 'eard soldiers talkin'. Some others was caught up in the blast. Must 'ave been some o'them soldiers, but they was so badly burned, they're not sure who they are. They even think one of the bodies could be you. The alert almost emptied the lair but some are coming back in now and they've put out the fires."

"Great. If they think I'm dead, maybe they'll stop searching for me for a while."

"They don't know you got in 'ere. Why don't you lay low for a while and rest."

Tyler nodded. "Did you hear anything else? Did Angel survive the blast?"

"Didn't hear no more, but I don't see how 'e could've. Everyfin' in that room was blown to bits."

"I survived."

Albert eyed her. "Only just."

She recalled her glimpse of Angel laying among rubble, scattered gallows iron and burning artefacts, and couldn't remember seeing any blood. He had not looked

damaged at all. The small voice in her head screamed.
He survived. Angel is still alive!

Night & Fog

Tyler sat against the wall, frustrated and tired.

"So, John, what's your story?" she asked the ghost of the British infantryman standing nearby. The Dickensian girl ghost stepped closer to listen in.

"I was there on D-Day, sixth of June, nineteen forty-four. The British Third Infantry Division, along with others, took *Sword* beach, Normandy."

"You died taking the beach?"

"Oh, no. I survived that, much to my surprise. With other survivors I marched inland, liberating the French as we went. It was hell. I saw many of my friends being blown to bits during the following three days. We arrived in Caen with my fellows, trying to clear the northern suburbs of the city. That's when a German sniper shot me dead. My body fell in a ditch. It's still there."

Tyler nodded and turned to the ghost girl. "And

you, Isla? What about you?"

"Who, me?" She sat down as Tyler nodded. "I was from a poor family. I never knew my Pa. Ma died when I was four and they sent me to the workhouse. There was six hundred and thirteen others in them cramped rooms. Most of 'em was sick or lame. I worked on them weavin' machines, you know, them steam-driven power looms, fetching the bobbins out whenever they dropped. But you 'ad to be quick, mind. They never stopped them machines. Near tore my 'and off, one time, I tell ya'."

"Did you get stuck in one of the machines? Is that how you died?"

"Naw. I got small pox when I was nine. There was a lot of the pox. Everyone was succumbin' 'cause we was livin' in such a small space. Died three weeks later in the infirmary. They chucked my corpse in a big pit with a bunch of others. No proper funeral, nor nothin'."

"I'm sorry," said Tyler.

"Oh, don't worry. Least the pox kept the body snatchers away. My best friend weren't so lucky. When she died they secretly sold 'er body to a surgeon for dissection."

Tyler nodded sympathetically and tried to rest, but doing nothing pushed her further into madness each passing minute. She could not keep still, despite her extreme fatigue, and paced the small room with increasing anxiety, wondering how long she should wait before exploring the lair in search of the control room that operated the sky doors. *I might find it in three minutes. Or two hours. How long is a piece of string? Perhaps I should go now. No. Wait. Let them get used to the idea that you're dead! Man, I'd kill for a drink of water.*

She wanted to return to the shattered Ghost Finder

and search for Angel, but knew that would be fruitless. Dead or alive, he would no longer be there, and she would only be risking her life and the existence of her accompanying ghosts.

She found a pen in one of the cabinets and scribbled out her list from memory on the back of a letter she could not read, adding ticks and crosses appropriately.

Extract Angel from Buenos Aires √
Locate and recover the Vice President of Brazil X
Find out how the NVF are recruiting their ghosts √
Find out what the ghost spies are doing √
Put Reinhard Heydrich and Adolf Eichmann into the chasm
Acquire the Spear of Destiny
Extract Angel (again)
Free the girls! √

The Vice President was dead but at least she had freed Melissa and Lucy. Her eye stopped at one item. Acquire the Spear of Destiny. *Why not? I have time, and sitting around here is driving me insane.* Tearing the list into shreds, she told the squad.

"I'm going after the spear."

"What? The spear is fake," said Izabella. "It's not the holy relic Angel thinks it is."

"But he doesn't know that and he's drawing confidence from it."

"You told him it's fake."

"Yes, but he might have decided I'm lying. It's still part of my mission. I'm just obeying orders. And anyway, even if it's not two thousand years old, it might still be gallows iron, which could make it powerful in Angel's hands."

"Don't do it. You don't need the risk. It's suicide," said Zebedee.

"And what part of this isn't suicide?" laughed Tyler, on the verge of hysterics.

They watched her as she searched for somewhere to deposit the shredded list, having no way of burning it. In the end she opened one of the filing cabinet drawers to shove in the shreds. A file name in bold capitals instantly caught her attention.

UNDER THE COVER OF NIGHT AND FOG

The phrase jolted a memory and she knew she'd read it before somewhere. She fought to recall where and when as she drew out the file and opened it finding, for once, pages of printed English.

Directives for the prosecution of offences committed against the furtherment and progress of the New Arian Validation of Territories, hereby and forthwith known as the NAVT act, as passed and approved by the office of the NVF.

I. **Within occupied territories (or regions hereby claimed as territorial grounds belonging to the NVF or desirable for conquest by the NVF), the adequate punishment for offences committed against the NVF which endanger their security or state of readiness is on principal the death penalty.**

II. **The offences detailed in paragraph I. as a**

rule are to be dealt with in the occupied territories or land only if it is probable that sentence of death be issued to the offender, and if trial and execution can be carried out swiftly. Otherwise the offenders are to be transported to secure locations known only to the NVF for containment until due trial and execution.

III. Offenders are to be detained and transported under cover of night and fog, or other clandestine means, in all cases to prevent the leaking of knowledge sensitive to the acquisition of territories.

Tyler stopped reading to squint at the signature at the bottom of the document, mouthing the name and the printed words beneath.

"Reinhard Heydrich, Minister for Reich Security." *So that's what Angel has you and your reveries doing. Man, you guys are so old-school.*

She remembered where she had previously read the phrase. It was in an article about Reinhard Heydrich's role in World War II. He was responsible for the secret removal and murder of anyone who stood in the way of the Nazi party's progress and Hitler's rule. He had also been tasked with the undercover killing of thousands of Jews, long before the Nazis' true nature became common knowledge. He had been responsible for an unfathomable quantity of furtive murders. She tore out the pages of the file, folded them and stuffed them into her pocket along with the map. *That should be enough proof to persuade the CIA of the NVF's true nature. I wonder what Eichmann's up to.* She turned to Albert.

"If I don't make it out of here, make sure these papers reach Chapman. They could shift the balance of the entire war."

"Right you are, Missy."

She used the *Present Eye*, hoping Angel was too incapacitated from the blast to sense the contrap. Empty tunnels and chambers confirmed Albert's report. The majority of the lair's operators could only be outside, in the jungle. She wondered what the rest of her team was doing out there.

"Now for the spear."

*

Weaver shook his head, swiping leaves aside to stomp back into the jungle clearing where the others were gathered, wet from the crossing. He tucked his satellite phone into his pack and checked to see what ammunition remained in his magazine. "Still nothing. It's like the satellite never existed."

"They could be controlling the signals," said Melissa. "Like they did in the Urubici mountains."

"Maybe. That would mean they have some pretty sophisticated gear."

"It's not the same as the dead zone of the mountain castle. Our phones have power and our gear still works." Lucy steered a NanoSect around the filing room in the lair. On a portable screen the size of a mobile phone, she watched Tyler use the *Present Eye*. "Is it possible they are only jamming the outward bound signal?"

"Who knows?" said Weaver.

"It's possible," said Melissa. "I wouldn't put it past them. Does anyone have any phone signal? Anything at all?" The others shook their heads.

*

Tyler focused in through the strongroom door and checked the drawer containing the spearhead. *All present and correct, just like before.* Shifting view she searched for a control room that might operate the sky doors but found nothing obvious.

She tightened the bandage around her ankle. "After you, Albert."

Albert checked the passage beyond the door and waved her on. She eased the door open and gingerly walked out, favouring her good foot.

Abandoned, clinically clean, white corridors.

She signalled for Albert and Zebedee to scout ahead, waving them on towards the strongroom. *If we're quick enough I might be able to take the spear and find somewhere else to hide out while I look for the control room. I could even return to the filing room.*

Reaching a junction, her scouts turned and Albert signalled for her to drop back.

Company!

She heard Zebedee sending a troop away and marvelled that some soldiers still accepted his Gestapo disguise. *Clearly not the brightest bunch.* Tyler followed her scouts, stopping at the secured door to the strongroom as the Ghost Squad entered ahead of her, all except Albert and Zebedee, who took up positions at either end of the tunnel to keep watch while she worked. She used the *Present Eye* again, to align the bolts of the locking mechanism and break into the room. Inside, she opened the drawer, took the Spear of Destiny and slid it into her bag. She took the bloodied copy and placed that into the drawer, pushing it shut. Again, she peered through the contrap's lens, seeking the control room.

271

With the *Present Eye*, she passed visually through familiar chambers, the sanctuary, the crypt, the filing room, the devastated Ghost Finder room and more. She tracked routes through the lair, found the arch, and overlooked the courtyard of miserable prisoners. Working her way upwards through the lair she checked rooms systematically on every level, finding a dining hall, private rooms and dormitories, laboratories, hospital wards, and offices with row after row of computers. She skipped back to the hospital zone and searched the beds for Angel. Minutes later she found him lying flat on his back, unmoving, his eyes closed. Monitors at his bedside beeped and flashed with small coloured lights.

But what's wrong with you? You don't look injured. At least you're out of the picture for now.

She continued her search and, at last, stopped in a room full of control panels and consoles. Lights blinked as men and women worked and security guards lounged before a bank of CCTV monitors. She backed up to double-check, counting. *Five operators in all. Shouldn't be too much trouble for one seasoned ghost haunter and a squad of determined phantoms.*

"How many blades do we have?"

"Three," said Kylie.

"We could use more."

"You think?"

Tyler reversed out of the control room to assess the approach. "Another problem. They have CCTV on that level. Camera's everywhere, and they all terminate at the control room. The room I need to enter."

"This is going to be tough without the blades."

"So we get some. Find some somewhere."

"Where?"

"I don't know. Maybe they have some stored in the munitions room."

"We can scout around. See if we can't bring down a few more enemy ghosts."

"Yes. Split the team. We'll try both. One team to the store. The other on the hunt."

Kylie formed the squad into two groups, deploying Zebedee, with a blade, as team leader of the munitions half, while she led the hunting party, carrying a blade herself. Zebedee came to the front of the others as Tyler reminded him of the quickest route to the munitions store.

"You'd better stay here, Tyler. Your injured foot..."

"You'll just slow us down," said Kylie.

"I'm staying with Missy," said Albert, tossing the third gallows blade in his nimble fingers as the two teams readied to head out through the strongroom walls.

"Wait!" hissed Tyler, sensing a presence approaching. "There are ghosts out there right now. Closing in. Can you feel it?"

Albert and the others froze as though listening.

"She's right."

Tyler turned the *Present Eye* onto the door and scanned through it. Flickering closer, the gallows blades showed easily against the white walls outside. "Two blades. I'm not sure how many ghosts."

"We'll take them out," said Kylie, stepping towards the door.

"No need to risk it." Tyler set the contrap to the *Ghost Portal* and hauled open the door. She limped out before the floating knives to brandish the contrap. "Phasmatis Licentia." She wasn't sure how many ghosts she trapped, even as they became visible as shimmering, blue essence to shriek into the contrap's crystal, but the two gallows blades clattered to the floor. Wulfric and Yakubu collected them. When it was all over, she balanced the contrap with the usual spell.

More Nazis in the portal. Not good.

"Five's better than three but let's get some more." Kylie led her group off, turning right, while Zebedee's team stole back towards the munitions store. Tyler hauled the munitions bag onto her shoulder and followed Kylie.

"Where d'ya fink you're goin'?" asked Albert.

"I'm hunting with you. You need me. I can sense ghosts better than any of you, and I have the contrap."

*

A gentle insect symphony hummed around them. Lucy sank blade after blade into the broad trunk of a tree, with uncanny precision. "We have to do *something*. We can't just sit here watching!" She paused to retrieve the knives, swatting at a pestering wasp.

Klaus, Weaver, Freddy and Melissa steered NanoSects around the lair, tracking the teams and watching Tyler leave the strongroom.

"You know as well as I do, it would be suicide to attempt entry again," said Weaver. "It's too heavily guarded and we can't sharp-shoot because the jungle's too dense. We're blinded by leaves that provide no cover. There's no way in without getting shot."

"There *has* to be something we can do," pressed Lucy.

Melissa looked at her. "I have an idea."

Hunting

Lucy stopped throwing blades and turned to Melissa.

"What idea?"

"We need to create a diversion. Something that will draw the guards away into the jungle, allowing us to slip into the lair. And we'll need some way to tackle the ghost guards carrying gallows blades."

"How do you know there're ghost guards? Did you see them?" A wasp landed on Lucy's arm and she flicked it away with the back of her hand.

"No, we didn't get that close but they'll be there, mark my words."

"Maybe the tribesmen can take care of them."

"Good idea. We can arm them with gallows blades."

Lucy nodded. "But what about the diversion?"

Melissa watched several more wasps buzz overhead, and tracked them back to their papery nest, suspended among the leaves. She glanced at the large, black kit bag at Weaver's feet.

*

Zebedee marched boldly while his team slipped through walls, invisible. He met a pair of soldiers without hesitation, waving them on as they paused to salute.

"Continue the search. Find the device!"

His team remained hidden until the soldiers passed and several minutes later he located smiley corner. He checked ahead.

"It's all clear. Quickly, now!"

His ghosts sped the rest of the way and Zebedee stood guard outside the munitions store as the others plunged through the walls to search. He checked his broken pocket watch nervously and peered left and right, listening to the ongoing, distant hunt.

Come, come. We don't have all day! What the blazes are you doing in there?

A metallic scraping answered his thoughts and, looking down, he saw narrow blades sliding out from under the door.

"Bravo!" He straightened to see the last of an armed ghost patrol gathering across the way, and instantly sensed they had not fallen for his disguise.

"Ah. What rotten luck."

*

Tyler paused to check the way through the *Present Eye*. Kylie and the others had left her behind with only Albert to accompany her. She located the team and visually skipped ahead of them to find an army of armed ghosts marching closer, ragged trench coats and domed helmets jostling in time with their stomp. Cursing, she hobbled faster before abandoning her efforts in favour of the contrap. She flicked the switch to *Flight* and levered herself into the air. Tilting the contrap forward, she sped to catch up, overtook the team, and set down between them and the oncoming army. Kylie saw the ghost soldiers rounding the corner and stopped as Tyler switched to the portal.

"Phasmatis licentia!" Enemy ghouls fled the crystal's draw. They rushed past her, hurling themselves against Kylie's team as the contrap swallowed a dozen of them with sizzling pulses of blue light. Tyler turned. The soldiers fought hand to hand with the team, rendering the portal useless. "Compenso pondera." She set it to the *Safeguarding Skull* and, slipping the bag from her shoulder, seized the spear.

Time to see if this really is gallows iron.

She limped into the fray and lunged at the back of a ghost soldier. To her amazement the ghost dissipated with a hiss. His abandoned blade fell and skittered on the floor.

Gallows iron, then! Perhaps it's the nail inlaid near the spear's tip.

She jabbed at another unsuspecting ghost's back and he, too, dissolved in the air. Longer than the gallows blades, the spearhead gave her a superior reach. She cried out in dismay as two of her team were pierced with blades and dispelled: a Jewish man and the British infantryman.

"NO!" She felt a tangible ache, a sudden pulse like a cry of pain from deep within her being.

Kylie fought with tenacity, and Wulfric finished off the last two enemy phantoms with one masterful stroke. The survivors stood, looking at one another, distressed by the loss of their comrades.

"Gather all the blades!" said Kylie. "More will come."

*

Zebedee closed his eyes as the ghost patrol tore at him screaming, a barrage of blade tips forging his way. His single, small blade was useless against so many. Yakubu rushed through the munitions door and, snatching two blades from the floor, charged at the patrol. Seeing the hulking slave running at them and brandishing the blades, the enemy patrol slowed. Zebedee's team streamed through the doorway, scooping up blades and meeting the attackers, head on. Zebedee mopped his brow with a ghost handkerchief and prepared to join the fight.

At the head of the volley ghost soldiers overran Yakubu stabbing him repeatedly as he dispelled. Zebedee stood back, helpless as his comrade in arms died again, then launched himself towards whatever afterlife fate awaited him.

*

Each of Kylie's ghosts collected a blade. Tyler gathered the rest, filling what little space was left in her pockets, and heaved the bag onto her back. She straightened, feeling that ache again, and knew another of the squad was gone. She glared back in the direction of the munitions store but knew she must press forward. Again, she checked ahead with the *Present Eye* and, setting the contrap to *Flight*, flew on, leading the way.

"To the control room. Follow me."

The team were quick, their translucent forms hampered only by the slight weight of the slim blades. Keeping pace easily with Tyler, they rushed up a level and threaded through the lair's complex. The noise of soldiers sent them skirting one area to avoid another conflict and they entered a long, stark, seemingly-abandoned tunnel. Turning a corner, they passed the corridor with the arched window overlooking the courtyard of prisoners, and climbed more levels until Tyler dropped to alight before a stairway and a viewing platform above the courtyard three levels below. She peered up from the balcony, eyeing the huge, white dome of the sky doors.

"We need to be careful from here in. They have security cameras everywhere." Unsure if she'd been spotted, she ducked back into the stairway as a search patrol massed onto a platform opposite, one level below. She climbed the stairs and led the team out into a hall circled with doors where she took another look at the CCTV cameras through the *Present Eye*. She turned to her companions.

"The control room's behind this door, further in. Slip in ahead of me and take out the cameras. You'll find a thin wire running from the base of each camera. The blades should be sharp enough to cut them. Use your invisibility. Locate the cameras and slice the wires. Let me know when it's all clear."

Kylie and the others vanished, leaving only a bunch of floating knives visible. Tyler inched the door open and the blades jostled through the gap. She waited, hoping the security crew in the control room were off-guard, preoccupied with other zones of the lair. She checked with the *Present Eye*. They were working manically, busy switching views on monitors and clicking buttons on panels to communicate with patrols as the search intensified.

Not good. Nothing left to do but hope for the best. A NanoSect buzzed near her head and a few minutes later Kylie appeared before her.

"Done. Go! Before they realise!"

Tyler burst through the doors and used *Flight* to speed down corridors to the door of the control room. It opened as she landed and she switched to the *Ghost Portal*, flattening herself against the wall by the door. A guard walked out and turned away from her, walking purposefully.

Can't risk you turning. Sorry. As the door closed behind the guard she raised the contrap and whispered.

"Phasmatis licentia."

The guard's spirit tore from his body to rush into the crystal and he collapsed, dead. "Compenso pondera." Blades glinted as Kylie and her team gathered to her. She used the *Present Eye* to scan through the wall. The operators on the other side seemed unaware of her presence.

"They got guns?" asked Albert.

She checked for weapons.

"Let me go first," she whispered. "I'll put as many as I can into the portal. There are two security guards with side-arms, one to the right, the other far left. Take them out before they shoot me. On three. One, two, three."

"Phasmatis licentia." She shouldered open the door and wielded the contrap into the room of surprised faces. Spirits howled into the crystal as workers shouted and fled from their posts. The guards grabbed their guns to shoot at her as she ducked back out, leaving the team to finish the job. A moment later it was all over and an eerie silence filled the room as bodies slumped. A wave of nausea hit her. Killing people did not feel good and she had to remind herself of her cause.

Beat yourself up later. Right now you have a mission to accomplish. Focus. Get on with it! Save the prisoners!

*

Zebedee slumped outside the munitions store.

"If only I'd been quicker. He saved me! And now he's gone."

"He would have been proud to go this way," said Izabella, straightening her tent-like dress and viewing the scattered enemy blades.

"Do you think so?"

She gave a curt nod. "Pull yourself together. We must find Tyler. She may need our help."

*

Lucy and Melissa watched as the guys drew straws. Freddy drew the shortest and the other two shook their heads.

"I'll do it," they said in unison.

"Let me," added Klaus. "I'm a little bigger than you. I bet I can throw it further." The black holdall a few metres away buzzed on the forest floor as a thousand trapped and shaken wasps droned their fury.

"You think the tape will work?" asked Melissa.

"Should do," said Weaver. "The bag hits the floor. The tape holding the bag closed breaks open. The wasps are released. They're going to attack the first living thing they find."

*

Tyler pulled the blind down on the control room door and turned the key, wondering how long it had taken her to get there. She noted the time on the countdown detonator.

Twenty minutes and counting.

*

Klaus gingerly lifted the bag by its straps. Weaver went ahead with the Korubu tribesmen, scouting for problems and seeking an easy path through the vegetation. Armed with grenades, assault rifles, side-arms and gallows blades, Freddy and the girls followed. As before, they stole close to the lair, dropping low and creeping nearer. Pioka raised a hand to stop the followers. His tribesmen gathered, blades at the ready.

"We are here. Get ready. Bring him through."

Drawing a finger to his lips, Weaver beckoned for Klaus to bring the bag. They parted leaves to peer out over the dome of the lair. Armed guards peppered the area. Weaver pointed out several positions where gallows blades glinted in the dappled shade of the jungle canopy to tell of ghost guards. Pioka nodded his understanding.

"You ready?"

"Ready as I'll ever be," said Klaus. Lucy, Melissa and Freddy joined them, exchanging nods.

"No grenades on the dome," hissed Weaver. "If we blow the opening mechanism, Tyler and the others could get trapped inside. Okay, Go!"

Klaus ploughed his way through the undergrowth and ran out into the open ground at the foot of the dome. Hurling the bag into the air, he fled for cover as guards turned. The bag smashed onto the fake forest floor of the dome's side.

Control

Wasps streamed from the bag in great swaths. The first guard to notice dropped almost where he stood, blood burning with toxins. Others ran, while the tribal ghosts fell upon the guarding phantoms, taking them by surprise, and stabbing swiftly. The ghost guards dissipated on the forest breeze, leaving the dome unattended except for a haze of wasps milling in the air over the shattered remnants of their nest.

Weaver and Freddy scattered smoke grenades across the area before forging out from the scrub with the rest of their team, checking for lingering enemies amid the drowsing insects and smoke.

*

Tyler stared at the screen depicting an overview of Angel's bed and surrounding medical machines. He looked asleep. A separate monitor below the image gave readouts of his pulse, respiration and cerebral activity. As she watched, men in white coats disconnected him and wheeled his bed out of view. Another monitor showed Braun laid out with a partially bandaged face. She, too, appeared to be sleeping and Tyler guessed the doctors had drugged her for her own good.

Tyler searched consoles for the sky door controls but found none. *It must be controlled via a computer.* She checked her clock again to find she had already been in the room for ten minutes. She gazed across the multiple desks and terminals, trying not to panic.

How could I let this happen? I thought I had loads of time!

She sat at the closest computer and searched through its programs only to find it was set in a language unknown to her. *That's all I need!* She ditched it and moved on to the next. The same. The third was in English. Sighing with relief, she sat down at the desk.

Mel, wish you were here.

*

Melissa swatted a bumbling wasp. On closer examination the domed roof was impressively camouflaged. The fake plants and forest litter were finished with a scatter of real debris and a creeping of true vegetation, denser at the lower edges. She searched for the doors' edges as the others studied the small, steel entrance that Tyler had used, now closed fast.

"We could blow it off its hinges," said Freddy. "But we'd be announcing our entry."

"No good," said Weaver. "We need a subtle way in."

Lucy turned. "You think they're not watching us right now? You think they don't know we're here?" She stepped close to the doorway and waved. "Hi folks. It's your friendly, neighbourhood spies. Let us in or we'll blow your house down."

*

Tyler glanced up at a movement in her peripheral vision. On a CCTV monitor previously showing a shot across the river, a blurred figure was close in and waving. Tyler squinted at the grainy image.

"Mojo?" She realised with a flood of euphoria that her friends were outside as Lucy stepped away, allowing a partial glimpse of Weaver's face. She stopped searching the computer to return to the consoles. *Where did I see the Riverside Door Release?* After a brief search, she hit the switch and it blinked green. A digital panel also turned green, illuminating the words *Riverside Door Opening.* Looking up she saw Lucy, Weaver and Freddy on the screen, drawing closer to peer suspiciously at the camera.

*

"Come on in, guys." Tyler noted their weapons and turned to Kylie and her team. "Looks like they've come prepared. I'm okay here. Go to them. Bring Mel and Lucy here if you can. I need their help." She returned to the computer as the ghosts slid their blades beneath the door and, one after the other, slipped away.

She resumed her search of programs but a single folder on the computer's desktop caught her attention. She clicked it open and a window popped up, asking for a password. *Bet your whole world is recorded in that folder, Angel.* She checked the countdown. *Five minutes and counting.* She rummaged in a desk drawer and pulled out a USB flash drive, planning to copy the folder and its contents, but the password protection prevented copying, each failed attempt causing the window to blink. She tried a few guesses at the password.

Gallows iron. No. Ring of gallows iron, the spear of destiny, Angel, angel of death, Joseph Mengele, Hitler... No, no, no. I'm wasting my time. All way too obvious.

She minimised the password window to search the computer again and found a program named Habitat Systems. Clicking it open, she was immediately lost in a multitude of virtual controls. None of it made any sense to her and most of it was labelled in unfamiliar languages and with strange symbols. She glanced at the detonator's descending digits. *Hurry, Mel!*

A scraping sound made her turn to the door.

*

Lucy saw movement deep inside the lair and raised her rifle, expecting an armed assault.

"Hey guys! Company!" She lowered her gun when Kylie glided out, followed by her depleted ghost team.

"About twenty-five soldiers heading this way," Kylie gabbled. "They know we've breached the door. Mel, Lucy: Tyler needs you. Follow me. Hurry!"

*

Zebedee passed through the door of the control room to collect his blade from the floor.

"By Jove, you made it!"

The rest of his team filed in, stooping to retrieve their blades. Tyler waited to see who was missing before murmuring his name.

"Yakubu."

"I'm sorry," said Zebedee. "It was my fault. Too slow off the mark. He took out a handful of opponents before they got him. Brave soul."

"Right." Tyler swallowed a throat-full of guilt and sorrow. "Don't suppose any of you can read this." She pointed to the screen with the mass of virtual controls. The ghosts peered blankly, shaking their heads. She checked the bank of CCTV monitors. Those her ghosts had ruined were full of static, but others still captured various segments of the lair's upper levels; soldiers marching, patrols searching, empty passages. She wondered where they were taking Angel, and if he was comatose, or dying. A ghost Lieutenant Colonel passed a camera, leading a troop of battle-hardened ghouls around a corner as she tried to gage the camera's location.

Brilliant.

Someone hammered on the door, jolting her nerves. Kylie entered.

"Mel and Lucy made it through."

Tyler scrambled to the door, unlocked it and threw it open, relieved to find the girls waiting. She dragged them over to the computer.

"We need to open the sky doors. I found a program I think does it, and there's this folder. I think it's important. We should copy it."

"Wait. Tyler, about the doors..." Melissa took a seat before the computer. "I'm afraid we couldn't get through to anyone."

"No evac," said Lucy. "Sorry. We're on our own."

"But..." Tyler gazed at each of them in turn as the news sank in.

"Sorry," said Melissa. "We tried everything. We think they've blocked the signals somehow." Distant gunfire reached the room, short blasts from automatics, punctuated by the sounds of explosions.

No airlifts. No help from the CIA, or London. No help from anyone.

"We're dead."

*

Weaver dropped and flattened himself to the ground. The guards, regrouped and well prepared, closed on the lair beyond the sprawling vegetation. There were fewer than before, the wasps having taken their toll. Klaus gasped as a bullet passed through the calf of his right leg. Buckling, he fell to the ground and groped in his pack for a tourniquet as a patch of warm blood sprouted over his combats. Freddy hobbled to his side, dropping to one knee to give covering fire.

"Where are they?" asked Klaus.

"Don't know." Freddy sprayed an arc of bullets into the jungle. "Can't see anyone."

Klaus finished setting the tourniquet and Freddy helped him crawl to the other side of the lair entrance. They sat, backs against the bank of the dome, trying to find the tell-tale signs of enemies in the mass of greenery. A grenade tumbled out of the air and rolled to a stop at their feet. Freddy launched himself forward, grabbed it and lobbed it back at the enemy. Klaus gave a nod of thanks, grimacing at the burning pain in his leg.

*

Lucy took one look at the screen and stalked away, murmuring, "I'll guard the door."

Mel tapped away on the computer keyboard and scanned the results of her efforts. She slipped a lipstick from her pocket and unscrewed the lid.

Tyler glared at her.

"Makeup. Really?"

Melissa slipped a false, pink tip free of the base, revealing a concealed USB flash drive. "Not makeup. We still need to open the doors. The guys have ropes and, with luck, they'll hold the surface of the lair. From what

288

we know of the layout, the doors will open up on the courtyard, several levels below. If we can use the corridors, all well and good, but the sky doors are going to be the quickest way of getting the prisoners out."

"But... Never mind. What's on that?" asked Tyler, nodding to the flash drive.

"The folder you found has been pretty well protected. Two hundred and fifty-six algorithms. That's a lot of possible combinations so I can't run any kind of system to test for the password. It's not like cracking a safe lock. This drive carries a decrypting utility tool, something I threw together." She plugged the flash drive into a USB port on the computer. "It may take a few minutes to run, but it will make a deep scan of the hard drive. Should get us into the folder." She set the decrypting utility working and maximised the Habitat Systems window. "In the meantime, let's take a look at this." She studied the virtual controls and nodded. "It's in German. Here, Türen Hubschrauber. Helicopter doors."

"That's it!" said Tyler.

Melissa clicked on a virtual switch. "Doors opening."

*

Weaver lay flat to the lair's dome, seeking enemies through the sights of his rifle as the ground beneath him shifted, groaning and vibrating. Gallows blades flickered into the jungle on the other side of the dome, and screams echoed from nearby as the Korubu ghosts knifed unsuspecting guards.

A few metres ahead of his rifle's muzzle a dark gap appeared as the jungle retreated. He glanced back at the lower slopes of the dome where the land seemed to be disappearing into the ground.

Time to move!

*

"There are other things here we can use." Melissa hovered the curser over various other virtual buttons, sliders and switches, mouthing their names. "Here. I can close and lock all the exits of the courtyard. Keep the Nazis out while we evacuate the prisoners."

"Do it. Isolate us as well, if possible."

Melissa worked the mouse. "Done." She maximised the decrypting utility window and dashed out commands on the keyboard. "Okay, we're in. I just need to check the scan results for the password."

Tyler glanced at the CCTV monitors while Melissa worked, and saw Nazi soldiers flooding the entrance tunnel.

"Hurry. We're cut off."

*

The deep, mechanical drone vibrated the air. Freddy curved his arm into the entrance and let bullets fly while keeping his body protected behind the lair's edge. The tunnel rang with a metallic clamour. Inside, soldiers retreated for cover.

"What's that?"

Klaus heard it, too.

"I don't know. Where's Weaver?"

"I think he got pinned down on the other side." Freddy ventured his head up to look over the dome, swiftly dropping back to Klaus' side.

"They've done it! The sky doors are open!"

The Inventory

A hit registered on the on-screen utility tool and Melissa typed it into the password submission box.

"Vault sixty-five. Odd password." She hit return and the folder opened. Without pausing to read its content files, she closed it; a little light reading for later. She dragged the folder into the flash drive and watched the empty progress bar slowly fill with green.

"Come on!" Tyler checked her timer. Checked Lucy. Checked the monitors.

After several painfully slow minutes, the progress bar completed. Melissa tugged the flash drive free of the port and tucked it into her pocket.

"Good to go."

Tyler turned from the CCTV bank.

"The troops are massing near the door. Our guys are holding them off. We might get through to a courtyard balcony while they're busy." She and Mel joined Lucy at the door.

"Okay? Can we go now?" asked Lucy, peering around the door, gun at the ready.

Tyler nodded, brushing past into the passage. "This way. The munitions store's gonna blow in four minutes! We need to get out and get the prisoners out, OR WE'RE ALL GOING TO DIE!" She ran, limping, from the control room and turned a corner to bolt through several doors and hobble down a flight of stairs. She led the way onto the balcony overlooking the courtyard where prisoners peered up at other levels, watching and wondering what was happening.

"We're taking you out of here," she shouted down to them. "Get ready to climb up!" She glanced upwards as a ripple of murmurs traversed the crowded yard. The sky doors were fully open and a circular hole in the jungle canopy overhead showed her a darkening, blue sky.

Boys, where are the..?

A black rope fell from the edge of the open sky doors to hang, reaching the crowd some thirty metres below, who fought and scrambled to climb. Weaver poked his head over the edge and, seeing the girls, gave an easy salute before leaving for more ropes. A second rope dangled, followed by a third and a fourth. Gunfire echoed across the courtyard and those who had started to climb descended and tumbled back to the ground. Across the void of the inner lair, soldiers gathered to shoot from another of the platforms. Tyler and Lucy dropped low to give covering fire while Melissa ran for the stairs, clamping her hands over her ears. More gunfire sounded distantly as fighting around the lair entrance and around the sky doors resumed. The sounds died and more ropes dropped from the upper edge. The patrol on the opposite platform scattered for cover as shots rained down from above.

"Climb!" bellowed Tyler. She released a burst of bullets across the void. "Climb for your lives!" The prisoners below clambered back up the ropes, climbing urgently. Tyler and Lucy took cover at the sides of their balcony, shooting at any man who dared venture near the opposing edge. A boom thundered from below. More followed as the patrols pounded on the locked courtyard doors.

"They're trying to break down the doors!" said Tyler, straining to see what was happening in the courtyard while bullets zipped past, inches from her borrowed helmet.

"Climb faster!" Lucy shouted to the prisoners. She fought alongside Tyler as the faster of the prisoners closed on the tops of the ropes. Below, doors splintered and soldiers forced their way in. An officer called an order and fire erupted from a flamethrower, drenching a multitude of prisoners in burning petrol. Screams filled the air as the weaker climbers fell and smoke billowed. Lucy turned her gun on the soldier wielding the flames and he fell, riddled. Unharmed prisoners continued to climb while others helped smother the flames to save those they could. A deep explosion rocked the lair, forcing a fire-ball through the broken doors of the courtyard and incinerating the soldiers within range.

The whir of mechanised blades reached the balcony as a Merlin invaded the patch of darkened blue sky overhead. Melissa joined Tyler near the edge.

"Is that one of ours, or theirs? Thought you said you couldn't get through to anyone."

"I did," said Melissa, as the helicopter lowered into the sky door space and dropped ropes.

"It's ours!" shouted Lucy. Between blasts she aimed at the persisting patrol opposite. Melissa and Tyler ducked back. "Chapman must have been watching all the time!"

"Thank God!"

Of course. The NanoSects. He must have received their relayed images.

Prisoners filed up and out, onto the banks of the lair where hundreds collected safely, as parts of the construction below collapsed. Fire raged at the edges of the courtyard and in entrances, licking from shattered windows. Opposite the girls, the level beneath the balcony dropped to shunt the patrol over the edge. They tumbled twenty metres to the courtyard where prisoners scurried clear. The first Merlin banked away, fully loaded, and a second took its place. A rope fell alongside the girls' platform. Tyler grabbed it and passed it to Melissa.

"After you."

Melissa climbed, labouring hard, as Lucy followed. Tyler set the contrap to *Flight* and flew, unsure if she had the strength left to climb.

The others heaved themselves up, hand over hand, to collapse on seats in the belly of the Merlin, and buckle themselves in. Burned and battered prisoners half-filled the craft and more clambered in each second. Other ropes fell further out beyond the sky doors as Merlins hovering above the jungle canopy stabilised. One of the crew shoved a bottle of water into Tyler's hands and she sucked greedily from the nozzle, sure that the only thing keeping her conscious was her searing headache. He said something to her in German and Tyler's heart froze. Her chest ached and she wondered if she had really damaged something vital. She had no more fight to give.

Tricked by the enemy!

"Who are you people?" she demanded. The German smiled and made calming gestures with his hands while he spoke words she did not know. He switched to English.

"Friends of Klaus."

"Okay." She set the contrap to the *Safeguarding Skull* and watched prisoners haul themselves up from the jungle floor to safety. She let her head rest back against the seat and passed out.

*

Soft, cool linen caressed her face. She rolled over, aware of the hot throbbing in her foot and the immense ringing in her ears. If anything, it seemed worse than before. Her body ached and felt like lead, but the hotel bed and room were clean and luxurious. Images of the burning lair flashed behind her eyes as she woke, recalling the torturous last few hours in the jungle. She could still smell smoke in her nostrils; something not even the hot shower could rinse away. She blinked her eyes open and rubbed them clean of encrusted sleep.

"Albert? You okay?"

"I'm all right, Missy. How're you?" he asked, perched on the edge of her bed.

"Fine. I think. How long have I been asleep?"

"Most of the night and all the mornin'."

She remembered dragging herself from the Merlin and falling asleep in a car, hobbling into a hotel lift, devouring a cheese and ham sandwich, being checked over by a medic, and stumbling from a shower into the heavenly bed.

'You'll live,' the doctor had told her, while packing away his stethoscope. "Though you might be a bit breathless over the next few days. If you were going to die from the blast you sustained, you would have done so by now. Perhaps the device saved you." Tyler had blinked at him. *I guess Chapman told you about it.*

She tried to focus on Albert.

Please be London. Please let me be home.

"Where am I?"

"San Antonio, Texas."

She nodded. Even that hurt her head.

"Why did they bring me here?"

"I shouldn't complain, Missy. It's nicer than where we came from."

"You got that right. I guess they just got us out of there and dropped us at the nearest airbase."

"Somefin' like that. Mel and Mojo are in separate rooms down the hall. The boys are stayin' somewhere else. I 'eard someone say you'll be flying home today."

"At last. How many... Did the..."

"Some o'them prisoners made it out. Some didn't. When them helicopters showed up, the Nazis started shooting 'em. Some got burned. But we did our best, and many now live who would 'ave been murdered."

*

An hour later, she hobbled cautiously down to the ostentatious ground floor to find Chapman and the other girls dining in one of the hotel's pristine restaurants. It was a scene so civilised it was surreal. She slapped the documents she'd taken from the filing room in the lair down on the table before Chapman and nonchalantly plonked the Spear of Destiny on top, like a paperweight.

"Evidence of their plans for genocide, and the

location of every other clandestine lair they have in the Amazon. It's like the Geneva Convention never happened. And the spear, of course. How are the boys?"

Chapman tugged a handkerchief from his pocket and swiftly wrapped the spearhead. He slipped it into his briefcase while glancing around and cleared his throat. "Thank you." He unfolded the pages to study them briefly, nodding his approval. "Good work. I'll get people onto this immediately. The boys are recovering in Lackland, courtesy of the CIA. Klaus was shot in the leg. Weaver has a suspected fractured skull, last I heard, and Freddy was hit in the ankle and is deaf from a mortar explosion, though they think his hearing will return with time. They're all stable, so you can relax. The bad news is this war is stretching us to the limit. All my agents are now already engaged or out of action. I'm afraid I can't spare a single man to help you."

Tyler nodded. The ringing in her ears was still louder than any of their voices and it sounded as if they were all talking in the next room.

"You should know Klaus was instrumental in your extraction. He's a member of the German secret service, a department of the BND set up shortly after World War Two, to prevent the German nation from ever being drawn into anything like that again. They've been watching you closely. When the team couldn't reach me and I lost all contact, they stepped up to implement the recue, calling the CIA. They also called me."

Tyler nodded. "What happened to Angel?"

"We still don't know. I have a team investigating the burn site in conjunction with ATF. There're bodies in the lower chambers of the lair but many areas collapsed in the explosion. It could be weeks before we've cleared the levels and identified the dead. The Americans want to know exactly what went on, blow by blow."

"Good luck to them. So you think he may've somehow escaped?"

"It's possible but it's early days. I don't have a single written report from an agent as yet. You were there. What do you think?"

"I saw his medics wheel his bed out of the recovery room. I don't know what was wrong with him. Something weird must have happened when the Ghost Finder blew up. And I don't know where they took him. Maybe they were trying to get him out of the lair."

"They must have had several exits," said Melissa. "We don't know where the other exits are. *Were*. It's possible they got him out. It's possible he's still alive."

"I hear we're going home today," said Tyler, taking a seat at the table between Chapman and Melissa. They exchanged looks.

"Yes, about that," said Chapman, at length. "I'm well aware you've been through quite a lot in the last few days, but..."

Tyler stared at him and then at the girls.

"Seriously?"

Melissa nodded. "Sorry. I took a quick look through the folder we copied and I have some troubling questions. I'm afraid we won't be heading home just yet."

"So where *are* we going?" Tyler perused the menu and stole Melissa's Coke while Chapman beckoned a waiter.

"How are you feeling, Ghost?"

"I hurt.

"I'll have a steak, medium rare, and a jacket potato, please. Oh, and two more Cokes."

The waiter nodded and left.

"It's about the ring and gallows iron, and vault sixty-five," said Lucy.

"The folder password?"

"Yes," said Melissa. "And we *have* to strike quickly. If the intel in that file's correct, there's a major shipment of gallows iron docking at Banjul, near Serrekunda, at precisely zero two hundred hours, tomorrow night. We don't know where it's headed after that. The rest of the docking itinerary is missing."

"We think it could be heading for America or Europe. Gambia is a relatively peaceful, little country. I guess they were hoping to slip under the radar."

"So there's some gallows iron. So what? Can't someone else deal with it? I can barely walk and I ache all over."

"If the stats are true, it's six tonnes of the stuff," said Melissa. "Probably dug up by low-life wrecking crews all over Africa."

"That's enough to arm an entire continent of ghosts with blades."

Chapman removed his spectacles to polish the lenses. "Sorry, Ghost. I need you on the case. The contents of the folder from the lair could keep my people busy for years, but this one issue has to take priority. We think there's a good chance Heydrich will be escorting the shipment."

"And that means reveries," added Lucy.

"So, you see? We need you and the contrap. It's too important. Unfortunately, the guys won't be joining you this time."

"Great." Tyler dropped her shoulders and willed her food to arrive. "So, what's this about the password?"

"Cog has a theory," said Lucy, as a waiter brought their food. Tyler stole onion rings from Chapman's plate, devouring them as she waited for her meal.

"I don't know for sure, but the password struck me as a little odd. Yes, people use random passwords and programs designed to generate random passwords but, somehow, I don't think this is the case. Don't forget, in some respects these guys are pretty old-school. They like to use passwords that mean something to them so they're easy to remember. So I made a search for vault sixty-five in the files."

"And?" Tyler ate chips from Melissa's plate. Melissa shoved the plate closer and handed her a fork.

"It's referenced only once, heading an inventory of objects. Among the list is..."

"A ring of gallows iron," guessed Tyler, through a mouthful.

"You got it. And some other pretty weird stuff. But if we could get hold of that ring we might be able to work out how it works. How to disarm the one Heydrich has. Assuming it isn't one and the same."

"Can I see the list?"

Melissa turned to Chapman, awaiting the go ahead.

"It's okay. This place is clean."

She took an iPad from her bag, opened a virtual document and passed it to Tyler, who scanned the inventory.

VAULT 65
1 x diamond and silver pendant, Western European origin.
1 x amulet, gold, Turkish origin.
2 x rings, gold, Egyptian origin.

1 x cauldron, gold, Germanic origin.
1 x ring, gallows iron, Eastern origin.
3 x hieroglyphic scrolls, papyrus, Egyptian origin.
6 x cuneiform tablets, clay, Mesopotamian origin.
3 x scarabs, jade, Egyptian origin.
1 x iron casket, origin unknown.

"That's quite a list. All stolen, I'm guessing. Looks like they're collecting other possible artefacts of power. Like the contrap and the gallows ring."

"Yes, and you can see why it's caught our attention. We don't know if this is Heydrich's ring of gallows iron or if they have found another."

"Surely they can just make as many as they want," said Tyler. "Like they do with the knives."

"I'm not so sure," said Melissa. "I think there is something special about the ring Heydrich has. Something they can't replicate. I don't know what, but we do know the gallows blades don't command the reveries. They just vaporise the ghosts they penetrate."

"The ring I read about in The Liar had some kind of seal that also gave it power. Should we be worried? I mean, all these artefacts can't really be magical, can they?"

"That's what we thought about the gallows ring, but now we're pretty sure that's how Heydrich is manipulating the reveries. We can't afford to ignore it. If they've found another gallows ring it could be bound for Angel or Eichmann. Either way, there'd be another army of reveries roaming the globe. And one's bad enough."

"Agreed," sighed Tyler. "Where *is* vault sixty-five?"

"We think it's on the Mariana, along with the gallows iron."

"If Heydrich might be there, we'll need to bring the Mordecai chains. When do we leave?"

Banjul

Hot, sticky air bathed their faces as they dragged wheeled suitcases from Banjul International Airport, the smallest, scruffiest airport Tyler had ever seen. Its modern, white-winged building, with inset curves of reflective glass, was an anomaly in the brown and green, humid landscape. Beyond their departure group, brightly garbed locals danced in greeting, hoping for a few pounds or dollars from wealthy westerners. The passing vacationers happily gave, yet the three girls remained unsmiling, their minds consumed with the terrors of the last few days. Lucy looked down at the orange and white Hawaiian blouse they had badgered her into wearing, and grimaced. She squinted at the joyful Gambians and accommodating visitors, shielding her eyes from the sun's glare that was *way* too strong, even through her shades.

"This place is so bright and happy. It's like a nightmare."

Melissa laughed. "Told you you'd like it." They

joined the other visitors, passing out pound coins and dalasi to glad hands. "Cheer up," she hissed. "We're supposed to be on holiday."

Ahead on the hot tarmac, tourists boarded a minibus while Gambian porters tussled baggage into the back. The girls climbed in to find seats and Tyler swallowed a red and yellow capsule with a glug of bottled water. Her foot was more swollen and painful today, despite the antibiotics. Black plastic seats burned their legs where their shorts and skirts failed to reach. They watched the tall palms and scrubland go by as the bus left the airport and, fifteen minutes later, they entered Banjul and arrived outside the cool, white rise of the Laico Atlantic Hotel. Collecting their baggage, they walked in, passing large, dark-wood busts of Gambians and creamy, stone pillars, and crossed matching floor tiles to book in at the long, curving reception desk.

The receptionist smiled. "That's all in order. Thank you. Some special baggage of yours arrived ahead of you. It's been sent up to your rooms. Please enjoy your stay."

Tyler returned the smile.

Black, armoured cases of guns, gear and blades. A lead box full of Mordecai chains. Good. We'll probably need it.

Melissa arranged a hire car for later and porters carried their bags to their rooms.

Tyler thanked her porter with a generous tip and flopped onto her bed still exhausted from her experience of the jungle lair, and nauseous from the eight hour flight. That and the rushed preparation for the trip had allowed little time for much else. She began to drift off but an urgent hammering on her door startled her and, concerned, she answered it. Melissa greeted her with an excited grin.

"Hey, you gotta come and see this! This place is amazing!" Melissa dragged her out by the arm as Tyler fought her off.

"Wait, Mel. My room key." She locked her room and took a lift with Melissa down to the ground floor, to exit out the back, onto the hotel's luxurious, azure pool. Beyond the enclosed pool area with its beach hut bar, palms and sun loungers, an entrance in the enclosing wall allowed a glimpse of the paradisiacal beach of pale, hot sand and cobalt sea beyond.

"Wanna swim?" asked Melissa.

Tyler checked her watch. *Seven hours before we need to prep for the operation.* "Why not?" She returned to her room to change and, stripping off, felt Albert's presence.

"Albert, do you mind?" she said, mildly amused. Feeling another's presence, she turned and lost her smile. Albert stood uncomfortably with another ghost's arm pinning his form and holding a gallows blade to his neck, ready to slice. Tyler took a step back, unnerved that she had somehow been followed despite the Ghost Squad's best efforts.

"Sorry, Missy."

"Don't hurt him. What do you want?"

The enemy ghost, the stubble-faced trench coated man, glowered back at her. She recognised him as the ghost who had locked them in the tomb in Chacarita. She glanced away, checking for others but finding none.

"The device, of course," Stubble growled.

"Are you alone? It's heavy. Too heavy for all but the strongest of ghosts. You won't be able to carry it." Tyler guessed no one else was coming, guessed he was acting alone for his own profit. *If that's true, you're a fool.*

"I'll take my chances. If I succeed, my rewards will be great. Where is it?"

Tyler let her eyes flick to the bag at the foot of her bed.

"Get it," he demanded.

Straightening her underwear, she walked to her bag and opened it to take out the lead box, which she offered on the palm of her hand.

"Don't be ridiculous. Take it from its box."

She removed the contrap, setting the box down on the bed. Stubble's eyes fired at the sight of the silver device. She pictured her life without Albert, recalled countless nights when he had stood watch, offering desperately needed words of comfort, and she did not know how she would be able to go on without him. *Not Albert. Take anything from me but him.*

"Take it if you can, but let him go first."

"Deal. Put it down and back away."

She did so and Stubble tentatively released Albert, swinging the blade between him and Tyler, unsure who constituted the biggest threat. He walked towards the contrap as Albert vanished.

"Even if you are strong enough to carry it, you're going to have a hard time getting it out of the hotel," she said. "I will have a squad of ghosts seeking you out and they'll each be armed with a knife like yours."

"That's not your problem." Stubble stooped to grasp the contrap.

"Do you really think you can lift it?"

Lucy kicked open the door and hurled a blade across the room with deadly accuracy. Stubble dispelled with a hiss and a wail.

"Guess we'll never know," said Lucy. "I was coming

to see you when I heard voices. Thought you might need a hand."

"Thanks."

"No problem. It's a..." Lucy's phone chimed and she pulled it from her pocket to read the screen. "Oh! It's here!" She ran, leaving Tyler bewildered.

"What?" Tyler glanced at Melissa.

"Beats me, but it must be important. She's not smiled like that for weeks."

A minute later, Tyler and Melissa caught up with Lucy on the hotel forecourt, where she clambered up onto the back of a battered, white truck that carried a large wooden crate. Dropping down from the cab, the driver handed her a crowbar and let down the tailgate to form a ramp. Lucy prised off the lid of the crate and let it clatter to the side before doing the same with the end panel. She climbed inside the crate and, a moment later, the roar of an engine engulfed the hotel's serenity. Not bothering with her motorcycle helmet, she throttled her black Aprilia out of the crate and down the ramp, grinning. Mel crossed her arms and jutted her chin.

"Are we happy now?"

*

The sea air stilled, leaving a clammy warmth as night deepened. Tyler watched the dark shapes of ships passing Banjul's peninsula from the deserted beach, dwelling on her part in the rising war. All around rolled an endless sea of foes, and she was a square inch of dry land, awaiting the inevitable tide.

Melissa put an arm around her shoulders, shaking her from her thoughts. They sipped iced drinks.

"Do you think one of those ships is the Mariana?" Melissa shifted her gaze to a mosquito that whined perilously close.

"Could be. Although there's over an hour before it's supposed to dock. Where's Lucy? She should be back for mission prep."

"Yeah. We'd better check the parking lot."

Finishing their drinks, they threaded through to the front of the hotel, arriving in time to see Lucy roar in from the road on her Aprilia. She parked up and dismounted. Melissa scowled, crossing her arms.

"You're late."

"Hey, I could die tonight. I might as well enjoy a last ride, don't you think?"

*

They gathered in Tyler's room, dressed in black and armed with an array of weaponry. Albert glanced from the window, standing guard as they prepared. Melissa eased her Taser into the shoulder holster beneath her jacket and, at Tyler's insistence, slipped a gallows blade into a jacket pocket.

"You know I'm no good with weapons. And I don't like hurting people."

"What about reveries?" asked Tyler. Melissa shivered uncomfortably.

"Can't I stay here? You two go. You guys are great at this stuff."

"No. You're coming. We might need you."

Lucy struggled to hide the sheer bulk of blades and guns secreted about her. Tyler stood back to take a look.

"You'll have to lose a couple. It's way too obvious. Looks like you're going into battle."

"There's a reason for that," Lucy mumbled, ditching several guns and a handful of knives. Several tell-tale lumps and bumps remained around her leather jacket, and the thigh pockets of her combats sagged heavily with the weight of numerous gallows blades. Beneath the leather, black straps, buckles, holsters and sheaths abounded.

"I really should stay behind," said Melissa. "I'm not cut out for this stuff. Not like Edward Scissorhands over there."

"Drop it. You're coming with us.

"Okay, Lucy, pull your jacket down a bit. That's a little better. Anything else you think you'll need will have to be concealed on your bike. We'll take the hire car and see you down at the docks. The Mordecai chains could give us away because they glimmer in the dark. If the ghosts carry them they wouldn't be able to hide from people because the chains are always visible, so we'll leave them in the boot until we've checked out the ship. We can go back for them if the gloves show up."

"Where's your Taser?" asked Melissa.

"Why would I need *that*?"

"You know why." Melissa grabbed Lucy's Taser from the bed and slapped it into her hands. "Keep it on you at all times. If you meet Heydrich or any of the other gloves, use it or you will be killing an innocent person."

"Okay." Lucy nodded, glancing at the sawn-off shotgun she'd requested from Chapman with its boxes of specialised shells containing fragmented gallows iron. She slung it with the ammunition into a shoulder bag and tossed in the Taser.

"Ready."

"Good. Now, no cock-ups this time. Maintain visual contact whenever possible and stay on comms at all times." Tyler set the contrap to the *Ghost Portal* and called for the Ghost Squad. They gathered amid the swirling mist of the crystal lens.

"Izabella, is what Braun told me in the Ghost Finder room true? Is it impossible for the spirit of the oppressor to be killed? I mean, even with gallows iron."

Melissa looked nervously at Tyler. "Do you think he's going to show up tonight?"

Izabella stepped closer to the lens and peered out, eyes clouded. "Regretfully, yes, it *is* true. Your only hope is to contain him. If he is ever to be destroyed it will be by a power far greater than any we possess."

Tyler nodded. "I'll take you to the docks and recon the place before releasing you. With any luck they won't be expecting us and they won't even be guarding the vault. Once you're out, find vault sixty-five and report back to me. If you see Heydrich or any reveries, report back to me. See *anything*, report back. Okay?"

The ghosts nodded.

"Izabella, what are the chances of anything on that list actually working? I mean, of actually being a real object of power."

"I wish I knew. Maybe one or two are genuine. I doubt they're all powerful but without studying them who knows? A short while ago ghosts were a rarity. Now the balance has shifted. One thing we do know; there's a ring of gallows iron on that list. Child, you do understand the contrap itself is fashioned entirely from metals taken from the grave. It undoubtedly has gallows iron beneath its silver casing." Tyler nodded. "You have the artefacts ready?" asked Izabella. "The finger bones of Heydrich, and the other objects?"

Tyler tapped her jacket pocket. "Yes, and Lucy and Mel have backups."

Izabella's veiled gaze bore into her.

"Be ready to use them. Secure the ring."

*

The rank stench of old fish wafted across the peninsula. Dark water glistened at the end of jetties and quays to lap eternally at the bows of boats. Mel tugged at Tyler's sleeve and pointed across the shadowed dockyard.

"Is that it?"

Tyler glanced sideways at her. "How can you be cold out here? We're way overdressed for this heat."

"I'm not cold." Melissa tried to stop shaking. "I'm sweltering."

"Give me a minute." Tyler swung her gaze from the silhouetted boat on the horizon to the hulking mass of a freighter near the quay, beyond the barrels and the hut where she and Melissa crouched. Through the *Present Eye* she focused in on the block letters of the name emblazoned on the towering, riveted flank riding proud of the dock.

"No." She searched several other ships, pausing on one with flaking, red paint and a huge, rusty streak ebbing from its hawse. She pointed it out to Melissa.

"That's the one."

"It's docking."

Dockworkers moored the ship and it came to rest against the quayside. A group of men left the ship, plodding down its gangway. Tyler searched for the blue glow of the gloves but found none among them. The men left the dock along with the dockworkers.

"Do you sense any ghosts?"

"Not yet, but we're probably too far away. Let's get closer."

Dropping low to the ground, they scurried from their hut to another and from there ran to hide behind a vast, blue shipping container. Nearby, more containers loomed in rough stacks.

"The place seems deserted," hissed Melissa. "Who are we hiding from?"

"I don't know." Tyler peered at the Mariana again. "Yet." On the deck, a single shipping container hulked towards the stern. She scanned through its metal sides and into crates of old nails, coffin handles and other iron bric-a-brac, before dipping below into its bowels, searching with the contrap. "The container's full of gallows iron. It's very dark below. Doesn't look like anyone's aboard. If they are, I'm guessing they're asleep. I think that was the crew leaving to get rooms."

"That's good. Isn't it?"

"Yes."

Before them, a long walkway bridged the water to a broad quay, forming a huge T shape around which the sea spilled out, expanding to the dark skyline. The Mariana sat alongside the quay, moored in quiet solitude. Tyler lowered the contrap to peer at the walkway.

"We're going to be pretty exposed while we approach."

The distant roar of Lucy's Aprilia reached them as she rode into view a short way further down the seafront.

"Delay," Tyler said into her comms mic. "Give me a minute. I want to check this out first." She turned to Melissa. "Stay here. I'll be right back."

Lucy's voice crackled through the comms. "Roger that." The noise of the bike dropped to a low rumble. Tyler stole out from the container to slink across the open walkway.

"Wish me luck."

The Mariana

Shadows swayed from the stern of the monstrous vessel and small waves kissed the hull as Tyler edged closer. Every few seconds its side gently nudged the dock's long, rubber bumpers that skirted the water-choked concrete as it buoyed. Halfway to the ship she slowed. A gangway joined an open gate in the gunwale at the top, sloping stiffly down to the quay.

Surely they wouldn't leave it unattended like that, would they?

She froze. *Someone must be on board. It* must *be guarded.* She checked her proximity to the ship. *A glove would have sensed the contrap by now. Are they watching me already?*

Ahead, the trappings of the industrial port offered a choice of refuges: a stack of five shipping containers, a clutch of plastic barrels, an old truck, a port office in darkness and an abandoned crane, looming like a petrified brontosaurus. The port office was closest. She ran to it and, hugging its wall, peered around for a closer look over several barrels that stood against the side with a rusting oil lamp perched on top. She used the *Present Eye* again, checking for movement in the ship's hold, the deck and the deckhouse. *Nothing.* Further down in the ship's belly she found several rooms with bunks, and tried to see if they were occupied. Frustrated by dim shapes that might only have been pillows and bedding, she moved on, seeking vault sixty-five. Other darkened chambers left her wondering about their contents and she abandoned the hunt.

"I can't sense no ghosts," whispered Albert, beside her.

"Me neither, but we could still be too far away."

Aware that Lucy and Melissa would be listening on comms, she switched the contrap to the *Ghost Portal* and whispered to the squad waiting patiently inside.

"I can't see anyone moving, but they could be asleep. I think there must be some men on board, so use your invisibility. I can't see or sense any ghosts. Go and find the vault. Report back. Be careful.

"Phasmatis licentia."

The Ghost Squad flashed from the contrap's lens in spinning tendrils of light to briefly form before vanishing into the side of the ship. Albert elected to stay with Tyler. She used the balancing spell and switched back to the *Present Eye*. Inside the hull, they drifted down the corridors of lower decks, passing into the galley, the engine room and more dark chambers. Tyler watched, marvelling at the *Present Eye's* ability to show ghosts even when they were invisible to the naked eye, and theorised that this might prove to be its most useful ability in the future. She tracked Zebedee, once more dressed in his top hat and tails, as he stepped spritely from room to room, tapping his cane and shaking his head at each vacant chamber. Remembering she had left Melissa behind, she turned to glance back across the walkway, and accidentally shouldered the closest barrel. As it rocked quietly, the old oil lamp toppled and fell to the ground, smashing loudly. Tyler skipped back behind the port office and closed her eyes. She edged to the corner and peeked around at the ship. On the bridge, a light blinked on.

Uh oh.

Melissa's voice hissed over the comms. "There's a light. Someone's on-board!"

Tyler rolled her eyes. "The Ghost Squad's in the ship. You don't think one of them triggered a motion sensor?"

"Do they have motion sensors on ships?" asked Lucy.

"How should I know?" Tyler fell silent as a silhouetted figure on the bridge rose above the gunwale, peering over the dock.

"I've a notion it's Heydrich," said Albert.

As the figure moved from the shadows of the deckhouse into the moonlight, his skin glowed with a soft blue iridescence.

"It's a glove," she whispered, nerves jangling. "It *must* be Heydrich." *A chance to put Heydrich into the chasm!* She fumbled with the zipper of her jacket pocket and, with trembling hands, took out the finger bone labelled Reinhard Heydrich. She opened the *Brimstone Chasm* and clamped the bone between her hand and the contrap's silver casing. Heydrich cursed as the contrap's pull tugged him closer to Tyler. *It's Heydrich all right!*

Men rushed to him at the edge of the deck, grabbing him and hauling against the unearthly draw as he grasped the gunwale.

Tyler counted the men and ducked below the barrels, knowing she wasn't close enough to achieve the powerful draw needed to tear Heydrich from the ship and the clutches of his men.

"Heydrich, plus four. Maybe more." She hushed, hearing footsteps descending the gangway. Between her hiding place and Melissa, a longhaired, pale, bedraggled ghost clambered up from the sea, hauling herself onto the walkway and, opposite Tyler, a ghostly hand reached up from below the quay to seek purchase.

"Reveries!" said Lucy. The roar of her Aprilia rumbled across the docks as she sought a better location. Melissa screamed and ran onto the walkway, tearing past the hag as she straightened. Tyler drew a gallows blade and waited for the inevitable head to pop up over the quay's edge across from her before launching it. The reverie dispelled with a hiss.

"Tyler! Look out!" warned Lucy, who had a better view of what was happening on the quay. Tyler glanced over the barrels. One of Heydrich's men was almost upon her. She fled to the sounds of distant gunshots, cries and more screams. The ghosts of long-drowned men and women emerged from the sea all around, drudging from the depths: ancient Gambians, slave traders and slaves, medieval merchants and sailors.

Melissa joined Tyler, running to the crane for cover. More ghosts appeared on the ship's deck to cluster around Heydrich and at his bidding they lumbered down the gangway towards the girls. A second man joined the chase. Judging they were beyond the contrap's range,

Tyler drew a gun and took a shot.

"Lucy, where are you?"

"Just dealing with a little problem." More distant shotgun blasts sounded in stereo with the comms as Lucy blew reveries to oblivion. "Ahhh! Take that, reverie scum!" Shots boomed.

"LUCY!"

"OKAY, I'M COMING!" Lucy roared the Aprilia closer and a moment later crossed the walkway, one hand steering the bike, the other wielding her shotgun. Boom! A gaggle of groping reveries received a hundred burning fragments of gallows iron. She sped through their mist as they dissolved on the air.

Reveries surrounded the quay, closing on the girls with vacant, gawping faces, seeking life-energy to devour. Tyler felt them all around, their sheer numbers overwhelming her sixth sense, rendering it useless. A shimmering in the air before her warned of an approaching phantom. She raised the contrap aiming the chasm's hot glow as one of the twins manifested.

"Danuta! Where are the others?" Lowering the contrap, Tyler tried to locate Lucy in the gloom. The Aprilia was silent, or idling so quietly that her damaged ears could not discern it.

"We've found the vaults, deep down in the ship, to the rear, but the reveries have the others trapped. Only I escaped. I'll lead you there."

Movement a matter of yards beyond Danuta drew Tyler's attention. *Lucy?* The dark shape slunk closer, low in the shadows of the port office. *No, not Lucy!*

"Danuta, lookout!" Tyler shouted, levelling her gun as Danuta turned. The man behind her darted from the shadows to thrust his gallows blade. Danuta felt the iron penetrate, and glanced back to Tyler, shock and anger in her widening eyes. She dissolved as Tyler fought to better her grip on the gun, and the bone slipped from her grasp and rolled under the crane.

"NO!" Tyler pulled the trigger and the man slumped to the ground with a bullet in his chest. She dropped the gun, at once sickened by what she had done. Steeling herself, she stooped to retrieve her weapon and search for the bone.

Melissa tapped her shoulder frantically. "Er, Tyler. The reveries..."

Tyler glanced up. Between the ship and her, a host of zombified ghosts advanced, blank eyes ogling. Other reveries ambled closer to her side, between the crane and the quay's edge. She closed the chasm and switched to the *Ghost Portal*, brandished the contrap at the nearest ghosts.

"Phasmatis licentia!" A handful of morbid ghost sailors crackled into blue light and sped into the crystal. She swung the contrap to gather those staggering up behind her and Melissa. Lucy raced her Aprilia out from behind the truck, heading for the gangway. She levelled her shotgun and blasted ghouls to vaporous dust. She cranked the gun, chambering another round, and blew another hole in the mustering ranks. Seeing her chance, Tyler grabbed Melissa's arm and ran for the ship. Lucy pounded up the gangway, using her last round to clear her way onto the deck, and launched from the ramp into the air as Tyler and Melissa raced after her. Behind them, reveries swarmed over the quay, their numbers growing as Heydrich called them forth from the depths. The Aprilia's tyres hit the deck with a screech as Lucy sped past Heydrich.

"Just how many dead people can there be in the ocean?" asked Tyler, sprinting for the ship's gate.

"Only a few hundred million, if you're counting from the beginning of time," said Melissa, between gasps.

"Great." Tyler willed the contrap to swallow ghosts faster. "Phasmatis licentia!"

Across the deck, Lucy spun the bike and ditched the shotgun, seeking cover. At the bow, Heydrich and one of his henchmen smashed out panes, aiming side-arms from the deckhouse windows. Lucy headed for the stern and steered the Aprilia behind the container. She swung from the bike to crouch at the edge, pulling her P99 and tracking Heydrich's blue glow. She peppered the deckhouse with bullets to give cover while Tyler and Melissa fled along the deck, ducking crossfire. Hearts pounding, they reached Lucy in the shelter of the container, breathless.

"I shot one of them. You?"

"Only reveries."

"That leaves three, unless I missed some when I first counted."

"Three against three. Not bad odds."

"They could be better," said Melissa. "One's a glove." She leant her back against the container and hunkered down, hugging her Taser.

"What do you think you're gonna do with that?" Lucy nodded.

"I don't know. This is your department."

"We have to reach the vault somehow," said Tyler.

"Good job I brought spares." Lucy slapped her gun into Melissa's arms. "Take this. Aim for the little glowing man. Point. Pull the trigger. You remember." Lucy pulled a compact semi-automatic pistol and sprayed the bow with bullets.

"Don't kill him," Tyler reminded them. "You'd be killing Susan Ellis."

"But right now Susan Ellis is trying to kill us!" countered Lucy, loosing more bullets around the side of the container.

"I lost the Heydrich bone."

"Like I said, good job I brought spares."

"I have mine, too," said Melissa, peering round. "But I don't think now's the time." Behind them, reveries seeped over the sides of the ship onto the deck, moaning and groping. Tyler spun around to collect them in the portal. Shotgun blasts from the quayside made her turn. Reveries shambling up the gangway scattered like ash. The girls looked at each other.

"So, if Mojo's here, who's that with the gallows iron shotgun?"

Vault 65

Further shots blew reveries to dust, clearing the gate. Chapman peered through at the girls, some fifty metres further down the deck. Slinging his shotgun onto his back, he raised a semi-automatic from his side to rain bullets through the upper windows of the deckhouse. His voice reached the girls via their comms.

"Sorry I'm late, ladies. Find the vault. I'll keep Heydrich and his friend busy."

Lucy pointed to an open hatch in the deck twenty metres from the container, between them and Heydrich. "We'll have to make a dash for it." She mounted her bike and kick-started. "Get on, Mel!" Melissa looked to Tyler but clambered onto the back of the Aprilia. "Sorry, Tyler. You'll have to fly. See you downstairs!" Lucy tore away from the container, taking Melissa out onto the open deck. Heydrich and his companion shot from the windows, ducking for cover when Chapman fired from the gate. Tyler set the contrap to *Flight* and took off, flying vertically into the night sky. Heydrich and his man did not see her go. She flew high enough to go unnoticed, plummeting when she was directly over the opening.

"Lean in and hold on!" shouted Lucy, turning the bike sideways and skidding to a halt by the hatch. She helped Melissa to scrabble off and together they dived into the cover of the lower deck as the overturned bike's wheels continued to spin. A moment later, Tyler dropped through the hatch to alight beside them.

"Any sign of the squad?"

"Nothing."

"Danuta said the vault was low down, near the back of the ship." Tyler took a moment to find her orientation, feeling her world spin. "It must be this way." She set off down a gloomy passage that ended in a staircase of grime-stained checker plate steel. Clambering down, they slowed, aware that a mechanical throbbing had erupted from the depths of the hull. "Do you hear that, or is it just me?"

"I can feel it. They've started the engines. We're moving."

"Heydrich is taking us out to sea."

Tyler swore and ran, desperate to find the vault and get off the ship. She opened the *Ghost Portal* and let its soft glow illuminate the dark way ahead.

"Albert, are you there?" With all the reveries on the deck above she could not be sure. Albert appeared beside her.

"Right here."

"Good. Stay close." They headed sternward, passing hatches and passages. "We need to get lower. Find more stairs."

Melissa and Lucy peeled off to investigate other tight corridors as Tyler pressed on. They returned to her, shaking heads.

"Nothing."

"Must be this way." The passage ended in a vertical drop, a fixed wall ladder the only way down. Hand over hand, she descended into the pitch below, fearing she was lowering herself into a mass of ravenous reveries. *A steak platter in a dumb waiter.* Reaching the bottom of the ladder she raised the contrap to illuminate the abandoned antechamber around her. She waved the others down, listening for the moans of the reveries but hearing only the distant rumble of the engines.

"Where are they? Danuta said the rest of the squad were surrounded by reveries."

"Maybe we're not deep enough yet." Melissa pointed into the gloom. "Over there. Stairs."

Tyler shuddered. "Something's not right."

"You think?" muttered Lucy, sweeping the muzzle of her gun before her and peering into the unknown.

"I wish I knew what was happening on deck. Damn it, where's the squad? Why isn't this place crawling with reveries? Hello?" Tyler swept the contrap around, checking for ghosts, and calling out. "Zebedee? Izabella? Kylie?"

"I'll go ahead, Missy. See what I can find."

"No, Albert. Stay with me. It's too dangerous. I don't want you getting reveried." Feeling out of options, Tyler walked on, but Albert overtook her and floated into the ship's unseen reaches. "Albert, no!"

"I'll be all right, Missy. Don't you worry."

She ran after him until he plunged through a wall.

"Well, that's that, then."

Lucy and Melissa caught up with her. Melissa waved the others over to a chart on the wall next to an alcove housing a fire hose and axe.

"It's a diagram of the ship. It shows the best fire escape route. We're here." She pointed to a place on the cross-section image midway between the upper deck and the keel.

"We're still not low enough," said Tyler, turning to go.

"Maybe we should wait for Albert."

"No. If he survives he'll find me." They traversed a long passage, passing dormitories and galleys. Another antechamber led to more metal steps and they descended, their clamour echoing loudly as the drone of the engines deepened. They stopped, aware of their din, listening to the sounds dissipate. Other clatter echoed.

"Someone else is down here."

"The fourth man," said Tyler, realising he was probably going for the vault. "Follow the sound!" They ran and halted to listen again. Distant footsteps echoed to them, and they sped to the end of another passage that terminated with another vertical decline. They descended and paused. Albert found them.

"This way, girls! There's a man in the vault room. He's dragging out one of the crates." Albert threaded through the ship ahead of the girls, stopping to hover at an open, iron door. "We're too late. 'E's gone!"

They gathered in the chamber to gaze at a row of iron vaults. The riveted door to number sixty-five lay open, swinging almost imperceptibly with the roll of the ship, the low chamber inside, empty. Tyler switched to the *Present Eye* and searched. In the near quiet, small scraping sounds resonated. She tracked visually through the labyrinth of the hull until she found the man as he struggled to heave a wooden crate up a flight of stairs. She read the stencilled text on the side of the crate.

VAULT 65

"Follow me." They clambered up stairs and back through the ship, in pursuit, Tyler pausing at each deck to pinpoint the crate and so alter their course. A pale, translucent glow greeted her as she ascended a vertical fixed ladder and she scrambled to aim the contrap while clinging to the rungs.

"Phasmatis licentia." Struggling from the ladder, she collected ghosts as Lucy climbed out behind her. Lucy hurled blades into the eerie crowd as ghosts pressed in to take the place of those squealing into the portal. They sallied in seemingly endless waves. Melissa reached the platform and drew her blade to stab at a reverie who ventured too close, while Lucy and Tyler were harried. When the last of the ghouls hissed through the air and crackled into the contrap, the girls steadied themselves, checking around, not quite believing it was over.

They climbed the last few levels to poke their heads out onto the upper deck through the hatch, generating a renewed plethora of crossfire. Across the deck, Crate Man dragged the crate towards the gunwale opposite the still open gate. Chapman returned fire from the stern where he sheltered.

"Back down!" screamed Tyler. They dropped back into the lower level. She scanned through the ship with the *Present Eye* to see where Crate Man was heading and found an inflatable speedboat roped to the gunwale, bobbing in the current. "There's a boat waiting below. They're trying to get themselves and the crate off the ship."

"Then what?" asked Melissa.

"They'll scuttle the ship, if they can," said Lucy. "Ditch the iron into the sea so no one can use it, and hope we drown. We have to stop them."

"Lucy, give me the bone. I'll get closer. Go for Heydrich with the contrap while you go for the crate." Tyler opened the chasm in readiness.

Lucy found the capsule bearing Heydrich's scratched name and unscrewed it from her necklace. She upended the open capsule, tapping it on her palm without reward. She glared into its small, empty void.

"Bloody ghosts! Must have stolen my artefacts when I was asleep."

"Here!" Melissa delved into a pocket of her jacket and produced a finger bone in a clear plastic forensics bag. Tyler tipped the bone into her hand and clamped it to the contrap, ditching the bag.

"Mel, we'll need covering fire. Sir, are you ready?"

"Ready."

Melissa nervously turned Lucy's gun in her hand. "Is the safety off?" She fumbled, dropping it at her feet.

Lucy glanced at Tyler. "We're doomed."

Tyler collected the gun and set it back in Melissa's grasp.

"Safety's off. Just point and shoot. You don't need to hit anyone. Just distract them."

Melissa nodded a little too vigorously as the others readied themselves on the ladder.

"On three. One, two, three!" Tyler raced out of the hatch and rolled across the deck beneath crossfire. Lucy followed, turning to sprint to the other side of the deck. Tyler dashed to an upturned lifeboat near the gate, ducking behind it as shots splintered into its outer side. Glancing around the edge she saw Heydrich clawing at the deckhouse walls as the contrap heaved him, and she relished the sound of his outraged cries.

Music to my ears.

On the other side of the deck, Lucy fought her way along the gunwale to a winch barely large enough to shelter her from the zipping bullets. Crate Man stopped dragging the crate, aware she was close enough to snipe him, and dropped behind it to return fire.

Tyler crawled to the end of the boat, edging closer to Heydrich, hoping to increase the contrap's draw. She braced herself between the gunwale and the lifeboat, feeling the tug grow. Heydrich dropped his gun, preferring to cling to the building. His companion returned fire at Chapman and Melissa while attempting to help Heydrich, but the draw was strong and the shots unsteady. Heydrich clawed at the window frames for a better grip, sliding closer still, through the building. Glass shattered as he hit the windows and part of the wall cracked with his impact. A moment later he ripped through the fissure, still clinging to a length of broken sill, and slipped across the deck towards Tyler, screaming in rage. Tyler readied herself to put him into the chasm.

Just a few more metres, Heydrich, and you're mine!

Pinned down by crossfire, Lucy yanked a smoke grenade from her belt and tossed it onto the middle of the deck where it rolled, spewing thick, grey smoke. She waited a few moments for it to spread and envelope her opponent crouching behind the crate, and sprinted down the deck. He didn't see her until she was leaping through the air a matter of feet from him. He wheeled his gun around only for her to kick it from his hand and knock him to the ground in one flowing movement.

Tyler felt the contrap's sudden power loss. The chasm's orange glow dimmed and vanished. The draw died.

"NO!" Tyler heard herself yell, knowing, at once, that the contrap had reached the end of its power. The ghosts inside were exhausted and there was nothing she could do.

I've overused it! No, no, NO! This is not happening!

She sprinted to Heydrich and pounced on him before he could rise, pinning his arms either side of his chest with her knees. She held the contrap an inch from his nose, desperate to squeeze out one last drop of energy as he struggled.

"PHASMATIS LICENTIA!"

Nothing. Not a glimmer of light from the crystal. Heydrich peered at her around the contrap's edge.

"Not this time, Fräulein." He cackled.

Chapman's voice reached her. "TYLER, RUN!"

She glanced up. Heydrich's companion edged out of the deckhouse door aiming for her. She leapt from Heydrich, scrabbling for cover as a bullet grazed her upper arm. Heydrich recovered and rose, seeking his fallen gun. He fled back to the deckhouse where it lay near the broken wall.

Lucy's opponent backed into the gunwale, his weapon beyond reach across the deck. Fear registered in his eyes.

"What's wrong, Nazi scum-bag?" she asked, stepping closer through the sprawling smoke that hid them from the bow. "Afraid of a girl, are we?" She took her time selecting an appropriate weapon, deciding upon a long knife that she slid slowly from her boot. Crate Man desperately clambered up the gunwale and toppled overboard.

Lucy smirked at the distant splash, stooped and used her knife to prise off the wooden lid of the crate.

"Wimp."

The Ring

Smoke rolled across the deck as bullets hailed from the stern. Heydrich's man dropped, a bullet in his head, leaving Heydrich to flee the wrecked deckhouse alone.

"Don't shoot him!" shouted Tyler, pulling her Taser and glancing at her wounded arm.

Heydrich approached Lucy's back as the smoke thinned, and knocked her to the ground. Her head smacked the deck with a dull thud, leaving her stunned and seeing double. She peered up. Two Heydrichs grasped two open crates and dragged them towards two gunwales. She tried to rise but staggered back to the floor, badly concussed. She reeled, glimpsing two Tylers heading her way from across the deck. Two Melissas approached from half way down the ship as two Chapmans ran to catch up from the stern. Each of them was too far away to stop Heydrich.

Lucy clambered to her feet as Heydrich reached the

edge and climbed over the side and, world spinning, she stumbled after him. At the gunwale, she took hold to steady herself and peer groggily over the edge. Heydrich was below on a ladder, making slow progress, hauling the bulky crate down after himself at each rung. Lucy clambered unsteadily onto the ladder in pursuit. Several rungs down she paused, clinging to the ship as a fresh wave of nausea washed over her.

Tyler reached the gunwale and aimed her Tazer down the ladder. *No good.* Lucy was directly between her and Heydrich. Below in the boat, Crate Man waited, dripping sea water. Tyler ran further along the ship to improve her aim, but stopped.

If I Taser him now he could fall in and drown. Susan Ellis would drown!

Lucy reached down to make a grab for the crate, missed and tried again, unsure which of the crates she was seeing was the real one. Heydrich hauled it down another rung and glanced at the boat waiting below. Lucy descended two rungs and stretched out to catch one of the crate's rope handles. The crate lurched, tugged upright between the two on the ladder. Packing straw and artefacts tumbled, some hitting the crate's inner end, others falling free and dropping into the foaming sea. Crate Man started the boat's motor.

"Nein! Lassen! Lassen!" Heydrich yanked at the crate, trying to wrench it from Lucy's grip. More objects plummeted; clay tablets, an iron casket the size of a shoebox, papyrus scrolls and a golden cauldron. Passing out, Lucy followed them, toppling from the ship's side and slapping into the water near the boat. Heydrich released the empty crate dangling from his arm, and hastened down the remaining rungs to leap into the boat.

At the top of the ladder, Tyler fired her Taser, but the figures below were beyond the weapon's limited reach. The wires of the dart dangled uselessly against the side of the ship as Heydrich cranked the boat's engine and sped away, while throwing her a mock salute and a wry smile. Lucy sank slowly from the surface, dragged down by the weight of her leather jacket and remaining weaponry.

"Lucy!" Tyler raced down the rungs, no longer able to see Lucy. She dived into the water as, above, Melissa and Chapman reached the gunwale. Tyler swam down, chasing Lucy's dark shape as she sank into the abyss. She caught her sleeve and heaved her back to the surface where Chapman grabbed her, at the foot of the ladder. Between them, they hauled her awkwardly back up the ladder to the deck, and arranged her in the recovery position to allow any water to drain from her lungs. With Heydrich gone, the reveries had lost all impetus. They returned to their various watery haunts as Chapman and the girls gathered around Lucy. Chapman carried out mouth to mouth, muttering "Come on," between breaths. He blew air into her lungs and compressed her chest until she came round, spluttering. She peered at them blearily before passing out again. Chapman released her, and sat back on the deck.

"She's breathing. She'll be all right."

Melissa glanced over at the bullet-riddled motorbike.

"Don't want to be here when *she* comes round."

They secured the ship, waiting for Lucy to recover. Chapman wrestled with the controls on the bridge, eventually figuring them out and killing the engine to give them time to work out exactly where they were. He dropped anchor. While Melissa watched Lucy, Tyler and

Albert searched the ship's lower depths hoping to find the rest of the squad. She returned empty handed a while later in time to see Lucy stir. Chapman brought bottled water from the bridge and passed it round. He dropped to a knee and offered Lucy an opened bottle as she sat up.

"How do you feel?"

"What happened?" She blinked and rubbed the bruise on her head where she had struck the deck. She coughed, took the bottle and swigged.

"You hit your head and went after Heydrich and the chest over the side. You must have blacked out because you fell in and nearly drowned. Tyler rescued you."

Lucy coughed again and downed more water.

"Geez. That's embarrassing." She handed back the water. "Does anyone have any coffee? Man, I have such a headache."

"I guess we were all worried about you for no reason," said Tyler. "Thanks, Tyler. I'm so grateful you risked your life to save mine."

"Can we have this fight some other time? I can't see straight right now. Wait. The crate! What happened to all the stuff?"

"It's at the bottom of the sea. It fell in while you and Heydrich fought on the ladder."

"Yeah. Yeah, that's right. I couldn't stop it. I remember." She dug into her jacket pocket with a sudden urgency. "All except this." She drew out a broad, iron finger ring and displayed it on the palm of her hand. "I snagged it from the crate before Heydrich reached me." They gathered to stare closely at it.

"May I?" Chapman plucked it from her hand to study it.

"I wonder how it works?" asked Melissa.

"It has a seal," said Chapman, showing the others. Rusty bands around the ring could be seen where iron nails had been crudely forged and hammered together. Chapman turned it to the side with the signet, where the surface had been hammered flat and inscribed with numerous curving strokes and dots. He passed it to Melissa. "You're the linguistics expert."

Tyler switched a Maglite on and they peered at the markings.

"Looks Arabic, which I can't read, but if it is we can translate it." She looked out at the dark sea surrounding them. "If we ever get back to civilization."

"Don't worry," said Chapman. "It takes a ship this size a while to pick up speed. We can't have gone far and the anchor has stopped us drifting. We should be able to track our passage and estimate where the artefacts went in."

"We'll know when we're in the right spot. The *Past Eye* will tell us."

"Why bother?" asked Melissa, passing the ring back to Chapman. "We have the ring. That's what we came for."

"But we don't know what other objects down there are powerful," said Tyler, recalling the Ghost Finder. "Heydrich knows where they went in. If the gloves value the lost artefacts, they'll organise a recovery team. That's what we'd do."

Tyler wanted to call up Izabella and Zebedee but they were no longer in the contrap. Nor were they anywhere on the ship.

*

Clinging to the gunwale, Tyler called their names into the night but no one came to her except Melissa.

"Chapman says we're in for a bit of a wait. He's scrambled a crew to help us out, but they'll be a while getting here. Wants an expert in the bridge to help track our voyage. Come with me."

Chapman led them over to the container doors where a crew member with bolt cutters stood waiting. At a nod from Chapman, he chomped off the padlock and swung the doors open. They entered and shone torches around at the packing crates inside. Chapman found a crowbar and levered off a crate lid to reveal an ocean of rusty nails.

"Good work, girls. We'll have this lot forged into ghost blades. Then we just need to gather some troops. Are you up for the task, Agent Ghost?"

"Yes, Sir."

"Still no sign of the Ghost Squad?" he asked.

"No. What if they were all stabbed? I need them. *We* need them."

"Yeah. I bet Izabella would know what to do with the ring if she saw it. Though I doubt she could read the writing. Maybe they'll turn up, Tyler. They could have fled. You know, if they were forced to. They could be waiting for us back on dry land."

Tyler nodded, swallowing a sense that Melissa was wrong and the ghosts were gone for good. She glanced up at the top of the bridge where Albert's translucent figure stood guard, shimmering, and searching the depths of the night.

Where are you?

*

It took more than an hour for the crews to gather. A small helicopter found them in its searchlights and settled precariously on the open deck between the winches and the deckhouse. Chapman ushered the captain to the bridge where they set about tracking the ship's trajectory and speed since leaving Banjul. A dive team assembled, climbing up from their boat to unload their gear and extra gear for the girls. Medics examined and assessed the girls in the deckhouse. Tyler sat impatiently in a fixed plastic chair while they cleaned and dressed her bleeding arm, listening to them tell her what she already knew.

"It's little more than a deep scratch. It'll heal without any real lasting damage." When they were done with her she left them to try the contrap. Switching to the *Ghost Portal*, she found it unresponsive, the crystal dark. *Still out of action.* It didn't matter. *What would I do with it anyway?* She joined Albert outside on the upper deck.

"What do you think's happened to them, Zebedee and the others?"

"Wish I knew, Missy."

"Any sign of Heydrich?"

"Naw, 'e's long gone. I'm pretty sure we're alone out here."

"Just as well." She told him about the contrap dying. Chapman found them and she remembered him shouting her name across the ship.

"You broke protocol," she said.

"Yes. A moment of panic. Still, they know your name anyway."

She nodded. "Thanks for coming to the rescue. You're a regular knight in shining armour. Well, knight with a shotgun. We'd be dead without you."

"Just protecting my own."

"So, what now?"

"We've a little more work to do on the tracking. Some calculations to allow for currents and wind drift, etcetera, but we'll get there. How are you feeling? You don't have to dive. They others can take care of it."

"No. I'll be all right. Might as well see this thing through to the end."

Melissa joined them, waving a printout.

"Guys, I've been checking over this itinerary, and I'm wondering what this is. It's listed as an iron casket but it doesn't say anything else. I'm thinking it could be gallows iron."

"Can you make a box out of gallows iron?" asked Tyler. "Surely it's one thing to hammer a few nails together into a simple ring or blade, but a box?"

"It doesn't have to be made out of nails. If it was retrieved from a grave it would naturally be gallows iron."

"Of course."

"If it is, it may have some kind of power all of its own. Or it could just be an iron box containing something else."

"I wish Izabella was here. I should've asked her more about the list when I had the chance. I'm an idiot."

"No, you're not. You weren't to know what was going to happen."

"All the same..."

"Just relax for now," said Chapman. Ahead, an orange glow shot the dark horizon with glimmers of light. "I'm having an agent at HQ work on the translation but he might be a while. There're some basics downstairs. Go and eat something. Maybe get some sleep. Won't be long before dawn."

*

Tyler awoke to the rumble of the engines and the

nauseating motion of the ship.

"We're moving. How long did I sleep?"

Melissa glanced across from her borrowed bunk. "Four hours or so. We've only been moving for the last half hour. Won't be long now. Wanna go see where we are?"

They walked out onto the upper deck, bathed in warm sunshine, and took in the view. Port side, blue sea rolled out to the edge of the world. They turned to see Banjul Port, a distant shape at the end of the headland and a stretch of coast dominated by beaches, hotels and local fishing boats. A few small outriggers rocked in the water between.

Chapman and Lucy met them at the gunwale.

"The captain and I have been working on this for hours, but we're pretty sure the goods went in here. How do you feel about a dive?"

"I'll need the contrap." Tyler checked the crystal lens and nodded. "It's back. Let's do it. Wait. There's something I want to check first."

"Take your time. The artefacts aren't going anywhere."

"Is it possible to have the ship rerun the exact same course? I mean track the exact same passage we took when Heydrich set us moving?"

Chapman frowned. "Yes. To within a few metres, probably. We have the coordinates and the speed. The satellites tracked our passage. Why?"

"Have the captain do it. I want to know what happened to the Ghost Squad. The only way for it to work is if we start from the last place they were seen: the docks. From there I can watch things unfold through the *Past Eye* as the ship follows its previous movements."

"Tyler..."

"I know it'll cost us some time and effort but it will also confirm the exact location of the artefacts. Think about it. If we're in exactly the right place I'll be able to watch them fall in the sea again. Then we dive."

"Couldn't you do that now, without all the backtracking?"

"No. For one thing the ship's facing the wrong way. If we rerun I can help track the precise route. If we're going off course I'll tell you."

Chapman looked to the girls in turn.

"She can do it," said Melissa. Lucy nodded.

"All right. We'll try." Chapman turned to cross to the bridge and called out to the captain.

"Change of plan."

The Casket

Chapman's crew finished the cordon around the quay as Tyler, sweating in a body-hugging wetsuit, searched for herself in the *Past Eye*. She watched the Ghost Squad pour from the contrap's lens and vanish as they headed into the side of the ship, and realised her mistake instantly. The *Present Eye* showed ghosts as visible, whether they were visible or invisible, but not so with the *Past Eye*. The *Past Eye* showed what had happened, just like a CCTV recording but with sound. She swore. This complicated things to the extreme. *I can't track them if I can't see them.* She was about to call Chapman over to call the whole thing off when she reconsidered. *I can still track us. I can still track the ship's progress and watch what happens. Who knows? Maybe I'll learn something.*

She followed her other self and glimpsed Melissa crossing the walkway, saw Danuta disperse on the end of a gallows blade for the second time, and herself shooting the man. His body was gone now but police tape remained, marking out his body by the crane. She called Melissa over and had her rummage around beneath the crane for the lost bone while she tracked the *Past Eye* Lucy up the reverie infested gangway and witnessed the battle all over again, as more reveries clambered aboard to swamp the ship. She signalled to the captain when she saw herself, Melissa and Lucy drop through the deck hatch in search of vault sixty-five and, a moment later felt the ship ease away from the dock. From then on, things became extremely hard to follow. The ship, never quite in perfect sync with its previous voyage, left her fighting to find anyone in the lens and, at best, the rising and falling ocean caused a disconcerting disparity. Regardless, she followed, muttering voyage corrections to the captain through a headset as she traversed the lower decks and from time to time waited for the ship to lurch slowly back into line with the replay.

She knew the ship better now and was able to run ahead of her other self. She wanted to know what had happened at the vault before they had reached it the night before, but it was not like other times when she had used the *Past Eye* at her leisure. This time, when she missed a chance to see an event, the ship would move on and she was left to search frustratingly, hoping to pick up the trail again at some point further in time than she wished to be. She turned a corner and stumbled through a host of *Past Eye* reveries.

She reached the vault room and knew at once that something had gone wrong there. The door was already open and in the corridor an iron casket lay open. The iron casket from the list, she presumed. She heard talking, and turned to train the *Past Eye* on figures in the room. Several enemy ghosts gathered around Crate Man and the open crate.

"They come," said a ghost officer in German uniform at Crate Man's side. "It is time!"

Tyler backed out of the room, wondering what they were planning, and stopped a few steps down the passage, turning the *Past Eye* on the open casket and the surrounding area. Crate Man walked to it and stooped to place a candle in the box. He struck a match and lit the candle before retreating back into the vault room. She heard the moans of reveries as they neared from the other end of the corridor and turning, glimpsed more coming from behind. Looking back to the box and the approaching reveries, she watched shapes forming out of thin air: the Ghost Squad, hemmed-in by reveries. The squad peered at one another in alarm, glowing in the candle light. They muttered desperately to one another as they were forced into visibility by an unseen power.

"There's more coming!" said Izabella. Kylie gawped at her own hands.

"Why do I feel like I'm not invisible anymore?"

"It's because you're not, my dear."

"We need to do something." Zebedee peered back and forth at the reverie masses. "They have us trapped! Izabella, what should we do?"

With widening eyes, Izabella noticed the burning candle in the casket.

"Oh dear. Oh dear me. We're done for!"

Crate Man uttered a command and the candle flickered out. In the dimness of the corridor, the squad morphed into blue essence and crackled through the air. Their substance streamed into the casket and as the last of them vanished inside, Crate Man stepped out to snap the lid shut. He closed the casket's three clasps and snapped padlocks on each one, laughing to himself. The reveries drifted away down the corridors. Crate Man tossed the locked casket into the open crate and replaced the wooden lid before hammering its prised nails back into place. He dragged the crate out of the chamber and she watched as her other self and Melissa and Lucy rounded the corner into the passage. She tracked Crate Man back up to the deck and watched the rest of the drama play out, grimacing as she lost her chance to put Heydrich into the chasm. When artefacts started falling from the open crate on the ladder she took the contrap's chain from her neck.

"Captain, mark our exact coordinates and orientation. This is the place." She passed the contrap to Melissa and threaded her arms through the straps of her air tank, clicking its clasps shut over her chest. "The Ghost Squad was cornered and put into the iron casket. It's some kind of ghost trap. I watched it happen. Zebedee, Izabella, Kylie... They're all at the bottom of the ocean." She donned diving fins, pulled her mask onto her forehead, and stepped up onto the gunwale ladder to descend the other side. Melissa called down to her as she climbed.

"Tyler, don't get your hopes too high. With drift and the ocean currents, the artefacts could have dispersed half a mile or more."

Tyler nodded. "It doesn't matter. I have to try."

"Good luck."

Other divers waited, perched on the tubular edges of a black, military inflatable. She dropped feet first, plunging into the water and searched for thirty minutes.

When she returned empty handed, Melissa was

waiting with her laptop. She read from the screen.

"Ghosts in Tibetan culture. Ghosts may be slain with the aid of a ritual dagger or captured in a spirit trap." She clicked to a different browser window and summed up. "There're plenty of stories about ghosts trapped in boxes. There's one here that talks about a wine box being used but I guess a box of gallows iron would work better. I think the NVF found the casket amongst gallows iron looted from random graveyards and found a way to turn it into a spirit trap."

"Sounds about right," said Tyler. "I'm going to find it and bring them back."

*

A month and a half of diving ensued with nothing recovered from the lost inventory, and with only a week's reprieve back home for debrief and convalescence. The ring's tiny but complex inscription was translated, only to reveal a list of ancient Arabic names, which left the girls frustrated and no wiser as to the workings of the ring. Tyler surfaced one afternoon from yet another fruitless dive to be greeted by Chapman in shorts and flip-flops.

"Thought you and the girls would want to know. A stray missile landed in the Urubici mountains this morning. By chance it levelled a castle out there."

"American military?" She spat salty sea water from her mouth.

"Uh huh. Seems an air force training exercise went disastrously wrong. It'll hit the news later today. It proves we still have some friends in high places, though I can't say for how much longer. The NVF are spreading their web."

"Any casualties? The gloves?"

"No."

"Then it was leaked. They've a spy in the CIA."

"Like I said, their web is far-reaching. It was a good test. It's good to know who to trust. The fact there is one less Nazi facility in use is just a bonus."

"Yes." *I'm glad I trusted you, Mr Chapman.*

"Unfortunately it may be a while before much is done about the numerous other facilities your map flagged up. So much red tape.

"Listen, Agent Ghost. You've given it your best shot." He helped her into the dive boat and passed her a can of carbonated mango juice. She cracked the ring-pull and drank. "No one could ask any more. It's time you called it a day."

She glared at him and stripped off her wetsuit.

"Isn't that for me to decide?"

"I'm ordering you home for your own good. You've been at this for far too long. You might never find the casket and, meanwhile, the war rages. It's not even safe out here anymore. Mali is a warzone, just a few miles away. You're a specialist, Ghost. There're no others out there with a device that can do what the contrap does. Or who can sense the approach of enemy ghosts. Like it or not, you're a seasoned specialist and an expert cat burglar, to boot. I could well use you in Libya, or back in Argentina, maybe Syria. Basically anywhere but here. I can't afford to squander you."

"It's nice to know I'm valued, but I'm all right here, thanks. You can leave me to get on with it. I know what I'm doing. My dive scooter arrives tomorrow. That should help, and you've seen the quadrant of the mapped area we've already searched. The artefacts have to be there somewhere. I'll stop when I have the casket."

"You're not listening, Ghost. I'm not asking."

"I need my squad back."

"You can find another squad."

"Not like that one. I can't replace Zebedee. I can't replace Izabella, or Kylie. They're experienced spies who know all about the contrap. They are to me what I am to you. Would you leave me down there on the ocean bed and find someone to replace me so easily?"

"There *is* no one else like you."

"Point proved. I stay."

Chapman peered out to sea, unable to hold her gaze. "I'll give you one day with the scooter."

"Five."

"Okay, two days, but that's it."

"I'll take two days, if that's all I'm allowed."

"Good luck. Don't forget, we're on the same side, you and me."

"Yes, Sir." She grabbed her towel and stalked away to find Lucy and Melissa in the cabin where she broke the news.

"Wow, you got two days out of him," said Lucy. "That's good going."

"The scooter will work. You'll see." Melissa scanned the horizon through field glasses. "One day will be enough." She settled on a yacht a mile or so out to sea. "You think that's kosher?" She pointed it out and passed the binoculars for Lucy to take a look. Checking for suspect, enemy dive parties had become a pastime since the casket sank. "Just do what you did in the Thames. Find the moment when the stuff went in and follow it as it sinks with the *Past Eye*. It'll lead you right to the casket."

"Very suspect." Lucy nodded.

Tyler squinted at the yacht. "It's not as easy as it

sounds and, anyway, I only had to follow Angel then, not a small box. We're a lot deeper out here than the Thames. I can't get down far enough and operate the contrap at the same time with any degree of mobility, but the scooter should change that. It's going to be very dark down there. The stuff went overboard in the middle of the night. Do you know how dark it gets under the sea at night?"

"Pretty dark, I guess. That's settled then. Do you think we should check that out?"

"Definitely. Call it in and learn what you can. I'm going for a closer look. I'll see you back at the hotel." Lucy passed the glasses back to Melissa and left the cabin. She mounted the Jet Ski tethered at the boat's side, freed its ropes and fired it up. Turning it about with a spray of foaming, salty wake, she headed out to investigate the unfamiliar yacht.

*

Tyler sat on a white, plastic chair between Melissa and Lucy, seeking more space, the scent of wet neoprene still fresh in her nose.

"Budge up. What you got?"

"They're a rich, Swedish-American family, travelling on European passports. Name's Bergman. The father, Devan, and his wife, Brooke. They're on holiday and seem pretty harmless. They've come up from Sierra Leone on a tour of the northern-west coast." Melissa sipped hot chocolate in the cool of the evening, feeling the last of the day's heat radiate from the sand against her bare feet. Across the beach, hotel workers stacked white, plastic chairs as the complex rhythms of Gambian djembe drummers drifted from the neighbouring hotel. Lucy watched the suspect yacht through binoculars.

"I still don't like it. They have a heap of dive gear and they're hanging around *way* too close to our search grid."

"Nothing we can do right now. Not unless they show an unusual interest in what we're doing. Did they seem interested in us?"

"Not really, but who knows. I'm just saying we should keep an eye on them." Lucy voiced what they were all thinking. "Heydrich could have sent them to recover the artefacts. They were clearly important to him if he chose to guard them himself."

"And the ring is obviously a different ring from the one he's using. With any luck we'll find the casket tomorrow and be out of here." Tyler sipped chilled mango juice.

"What about the other artefacts. Are we staying to find them if you get the casket?" asked Melissa.

"If we find one thing from vault sixty-five we should be able to find the rest. We just track a line from that spot parallel to the Mariana's documented passage, and search along it. The artefacts can't be anywhere else."

*

Tyler unpacked the dive scooter in a hurry, not pausing to admire its sleek, hydrodynamic design and integral control computer. She ditched the instruction manual and stepped into her wetsuit to pull it on, along with the rest of her dive gear. She perched on the edge of the dive boat, rotating the contrap's lever, speeding back time within the *Past Eye* to the night, over a month before, when the Mariana had passed by. When the ship neared her, looming from the darkness within the crystal, she slipped into the water, watching Heydrich and Lucy struggle on the ladder. The crate tipped, ditching its contents into the water.

She dragged her mask into place and submerged, allowing the dive scooter to drag her closer. Packing straw floated in the wake near Heydrich's getaway boat. Small boxes drifted beneath the surface, waterlogged and sinking slowly. The clay tablets entered and sank like stones. With the contrap's lens pressed against the glass of her mask, she waited for the casket, and tilted the scooter to dive as the box dropped into the darkness below. The current took it. She could see that now. The casket, sealed well and maintaining some buoyancy, drifted for what seemed an age. When the sea bed smouldered into view from obscurity, Tyler watched the iron box settle, dispelling a cloud of silt.

"Lucy, Mel? You there?"

"Roger that," Lucy's voice crackled over the dive comms. "You okay?"

"I have the casket!" Taking the contrap from her eye, she searched, expecting to find the casket right there, but the seabed was barren.

A small fish darted past.

"Wait." She scoured around for the box, thinking the current may have dragged it a few metres but it was not there. "Scratch that. It's gone. It should be right here. Give me a minute."

She looked again through the *Past Eye* and turned back through time from the present to learn what had happened to the casket. For a minute she studied the seabed as it flashed with the passing of days and nights until the casket appeared again. She allowed time to roll from that point and a glow to her side caught her attention. *Dive lights! Someone's been here ahead of me. Were they watching me? Tracking me?*

She watched a diver with a scooter drive in, take the box and leave. Tilting her scooter, she throttled after the dwindling light.

Sheol

The diver ahead rose slowly from the gloom to the shallows. Tyler followed, keeping a distance and backing off as visibility improved closer to the surface. The scooting diver hauled along a net containing a box that dragged low.

The underbelly of the Bergman's yacht drifted into view and Tyler hung back as the diver surfaced and climbed out, onto the boat.

"It's the Bergmans. They have the casket." She let the contrap fall on it chain around her neck.

"What? The Bergmans' yacht is pulling out of the bay right now."

"We have to stop them. Lucy, get down here now. Bring a crowbar."

Tyler surfaced and checked her air gauge. *Fifteen minutes. Should be enough.* Frustrated, she peered across the sea at the yacht tacking away from the harbour. Five minutes later, Lucy surfaced alongside her in the water.

"We have to cripple that yacht before they get away."

"We can disable the rudder." Lucy waved the crowbar. "They'll stop to investigate when they see they're going in circles. Let's go."

They dived again to chase the yacht, each with one hand on the scooter to speed them closer. Reaching the hull, they worked around to the rudder and Lucy slipped the bar between the hull and the rudder. Between them, Lucy and Tyler heaved at the bar until the rudder splintered away from the boat to hang uselessly in the water. They returned to their dive boat.

"We'll stake-out the yacht," said Tyler, having explained to Melissa what they had done. "Any sign of them running and we'll be all over them."

"What, an armed assault?" asked Lucy. "In broad daylight?"

"If necessary. I want that casket."

*

Black neoprene glistened in the night. Tyler clipped on a mini oxygen tank, one far less cumbersome than the usual large dive tanks, and slid into the water. She needed to be agile and fast. Lucy secured a Glock 19 in her thigh holster and slipped into the sea alongside her as Albert materialised above them on the dive boat.

"All clear. No ghosts, an' everyone's sleepin'. The mother an' father are in the master cabin. The three kids are in the starboard cabins."

"Great. Come with us anyway, just in case. I don't like that there're kids on board."

Albert nodded.

"Would you rather I stay behind?" asked Lucy.

Tyler hesitated. "No."

"I'll only shoot in defence," said Lucy. "Promise. Tonight, consider me your bodyguard. Let's go."

Melissa peered into the black water over the side. "Keep a lookout for sharks. They feed at night."

Lucy turned to Tyler. "Forget about sharks. If they want to eat us we're not going to see them coming."

Tyler glared at the girls and at the water lapping around her shoulders.

"Gee, thanks, girls. I feel so much better about this."

Lucy grinned. "Just spreading the cheer."

Beneath the surface, limited visibility allowed her to see little more than two metres and she tried not to think about the sharks. She stayed near the surface where moonlight penetrated. Albert shimmered softly close by like a strange neon fish. Tyler checked the large Suunto dive compass strapped to her wrist and navigated the gloom until the keel of the yacht loomed into view. Lucy swam beneath it and fixed a tracer to the hull. They surfaced at the boat's side, swam round to the ladder and quietly pulled themselves up onto the boat ladder and out of the water. Tyler drew the contrap from the neck of her wetsuit and surveyed the cabins through the *Present Eye*. Her senses confirmed Albert's report. *No ghosts. Good.* She searched for the casket, frustrated by darkened rooms and the uncertain shapes of baggage, dive gear, and an array of boat tackle. At last she found the box.

"It's in the worst place."

"The master cabin?"

"You got it." Beckoning Lucy to follow, she crept around the ship to descend stairs into the lower deck to test the cabin door. *Locked.* She took tools from a pouch at her belt and worked on the lock. It clicked open and she gave Lucy a nod. *We're in!*

Tyler waited. The click was not loud but anyone awake on the other side of the door would have heard. The *Present Eye* reassured her that the occupants slept. It also showed her a handgun resting on the bedside table. Nerves jolted her and she paused, willing herself to calm, waiting for the sensation to pass.

Be slick. Be silent. Retrieve the casket. Get out.

She turned the handle and eased open the door. The box lay on a fitted dresser near the couple sleeping in the bed. Gesturing for Lucy to wait in the doorway, she dropped to her knees and crawled around to the dresser, reached up with one hand and grasped the casket. It was heavy. Too heavy for one hand. She rose to her feet and took it as a voice behind her made her spin.

"Hey!"

Mr Bergman was awake, his wife stirring. Tyler tore around the bed and out of the room. With Lucy in tow, she bolted back up the stairs and fled to the edge of the yacht as the man pursued, shouting. Tyler didn't care. Where they were going he couldn't follow.

And she had the box.

Albert appeared on deck before the man to delay him as he surfaced from the hatch.

"Unlucky."

The girls dived into the water and descended as the man loosed half a dozen shots. Albert grinned and doffed his sooty cap, before vanishing.

*

Back on the dive boat, the girls motored to shore. They moored up and gathered in Tyler's hotel room where she placed the casket on a coffee table and they all stared at it.

"What now?" asked Melissa.

"We open it, of course," said Lucy.

"What, just like that?"

"I guess." Tyler finished towel-drying her hair and studied the box: a rectilinear iron container with scalloped mouldings along its domed lid. Three heavy, padlocked clasps held it firmly closed. It looked old, its surfaces worn and pitted with rust and a thousand scratches, the once-gleaming iron dulled to a taupe lustre.

"Lucy, bolt cutters."

Lucy passed the tool and Tyler prepared to snip off the first of the locks, clamping the croppers over its curved bar.

Albert appeared from nowhere. "Wait!"

Tyler relaxed the cutters.

"Why? Our friends are in here."

"No. They ain't, beggin' your pardon, Missy."

"Albert, what are you talking about?"

"That there box ain't magic. It's just been used for magic."

"What do you know about it?" asked Melissa.

"Quite a lot, as it 'appens. Ya' see, Izabella told me about such boxes. Warned me about them, in the event of this very occurrence. The box 'as been used as a gateway."

"To where?"

"Shoel."

They gawped at him.

"The abode of the dead," Melissa interpreted. "A Hebrew term for the grave."

"Great." Tyler threw the bolt croppers onto her bed. "So what do we do?"

"Don't open it here or the magic will be broken and you'll never see Zebedee and the others again. The box must be returned to the grave whence it came, and opened there. That'll realign the doorway to shoel and give the others a chance to return."

"*A chance?*"

"Yeah, well. You know what this magic stuff's like. It's never a cut and dried kind of a fing."

"You could have said before."

Albert met her gaze. "Just doing what Izabella said. I didn't know if you'd actually get the casket and she said not to mention it unless I really 'ad to. She don't like you usin' all this magic, see."

"I have to now if I want to get them back."

"So, we have to find the grave this casket came from?" asked Melissa. "How the heck are we supposed to do that?"

"We're screwed," said Lucy.

"Well, ordinarily that would be a problem," said Albert. "But you got the contrap. See? You got the contrap an' you also got an artefact from the person buried with the casket. A real, good artefact. One that's even associated with the person's grave." He nodded at the iron box.

*

They waited expectantly as a gentle glow in the air thickened to form features. An entity coalesced before them, sullen and glowering, the ghost of a Victorian lady in a dull-blue bustle dress. Around her neck, a string of pearls glowed softly, and matching earrings accentuated her glamour, on a backdrop of dark curls that cascaded from a pinned bun towards the back of her head. Her sharp gaze fell on the girls each in turn as they shuffled uncomfortably, and at last settled upon the casket in Tyler's hands.

"You have my box," said the strikingly beautiful ghost, frowning. "Why have you disturbed my rest? Why did you bring me here? And where am I?"

"You're in Gambia. We're sorry," said Tyler, setting the casket on the table. "But we need your help. Our friends were trapped with your casket. The only way we can get them back is to return the casket to your grave, and release them there."

"You wish to disturb sanctified ground to commit sacrilege?"

Lucy stepped forward.

"Yes. Kind of."

"We wouldn't do it if it wasn't the only way to bring our friends back," said Tyler. The lady glanced at the casket.

"The idea is abhorrent."

"Yes. No one's arguing, but you would get your casket back. It was stolen from your grave. Not by us. In a way, we'd be returning it, but we'd need to know where your grave is."

The lady considered this with a pensive nod.

"Very well, I shall help you, but first you should know my name. I am Edwina Newton. You will find my grave in the grounds of All Saints Church, in Clevedon, England."

*

A heavy fog shrouded the graveyard. Crooked crosses and gravestones jutted from hallowed ground in the shadows of the old, gothic church. At one o'clock in the morning, the girls left the car parked on the road outside, not another soul to be seen, as Clevedon slept. Edwina appeared at the gates, gowns billowing in a breeze the living did not feel.

"It's this way." She beckoned them.

"At least the mist will hide us as we work," whispered Melissa, glancing around. She shuddered and gripped her spade tightly. "All the same, I hate this. Why do we always end up grave digging in the dark?"

"Man up," muttered Lucy. "Consider it your war effort."

"No one will see you," said Edwina. "My grave lies on the other side, between the church and the trees. It is far from the road."

They followed, entering the graveyard to walk between the disturbed, repacked soil of desecrated graves.

"Angel's wrecking crews were here."

"Makes sense. Guess that's how they got Edwina's casket in the first place."

When they were inside and treading grass, Tyler turned to Albert. "Stay here and keep watch." He nodded and stood guard, looking out beyond the ornate lych gate.

Edwina led them between graves to a worn gravestone so old it had sunk into the ground to leave little more than a foot protruding. Tyler checked for an epitaph but the stone was worn smooth and blotched with lichen.

"This one?" she asked.

Edwina nodded. They dug, the scraping of spades in soil the only sounds in the night. The ground was easy to dig and less than an hour later they stood back, hot and tired, to view their work. Parish workers had done their best to reinter the coffin remains and Edwina's bones, and the girls dug no deeper than needed. Tyler knelt in the hole on top of the old, splintered wood, damp dirt and stained bones. She placed the casket down and cropped open its three locks. She paused for a deep breath.

"Here goes nothing." She opened the iron box and peered inside at an overturned candle that lay on a layer of dry, dusty soil. The others looked over her shoulder expectantly.

"Hello? Is there anybody there?"

The Tyler May series so far

The Haunting of Tyler May
(book one)

The Thieves of Antiquity
(book two)

The Brimstone Chasm
(book three)

Gallows Iron
(book four)

Follow the Tyler May series

www.tylermay.co.uk

Acknowledgements

Gallows Iron was edited by Edward Field.

10039704R00219

Printed in Great Britain
by Amazon.co.uk, Ltd.,
Marston Gate.